The
LADY IS TEMPTED

*Also by Cathy Maxwell
in Large Print:*

The Wedding Wager

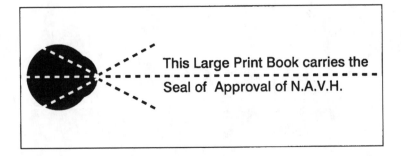

This Large Print Book carries the
Seal of Approval of N.A.V.H.

The LADY IS TEMPTED

CATHY MAXWELL

WHEELER
PUBLISHING

Published in 2002 by arrangement with Avon Books, an imprint of HarperCollins Publishers.

Wheeler Large Print Hardcover Series.

The text of this Large Print edition is unabridged. Other aspects of the book may vary from the original edition.

Set in 16 pt. Plantin by Myrna S. Raven.

Printed in the United States on permanent paper.

Library of Congress Cataloging-in-Publication Data

Maxwell, Cathy.
    The lady is tempted / Cathy Maxwell.
      p. cm.
    ISBN 1-58724-346-6 (lg. print : hc : alk. paper)
    1. London (England) — Fiction.   2. Large type books.
  I. Title.
  PS3563.A8996 L33 2002
    813′.6—dc21   2002028241

For Mary Taylor Burton

If I was stuck in the wilds of Virginia,
even if it was the middle of a cold and rainy night,
and I had to call one person
who would come to my side without
asking questions
and without fail . . . it'd be you.

I am wealthy in my friends.

Chapter One

The Peak District
England, 1818

Deborah Percival should have been on her guard from the moment she had first received an invitation to Dame Alodia's Spring Afternoon Soiree.

After all, although her sister was married to the dame's favorite nephew, it had been years since she'd been included in their social circle. However, Deborah had been so pleased to be out of mourning and reinvolved in society, she'd forgotten how Dame Alodia adored using her soirees as an opportunity to arrange the world to her liking.

That is, she forgot until the dame singled her out.

"Your mourning has passed, hasn't it, Mrs. Percival?" The dame's gravelly voice resounded in an unexpected lull in the conversation. She was a tall, rawboned woman with a ruddy complexion, gunmetal gray hair, and a love of the color purple. Her pug, Milton, sat on her lap licking his nose.

The magpie chattering of gossip came to a halt. The twenty or so other women guests, the "acceptable" members of Peak District's cloistered society, sat perched in ornate chairs set up in a circle in the center of the dame's cavernous drawing room. They turned as one toward Deborah, their eyes bright with surprise . . . and interest.

Deborah shifted her cup and saucer from one hand to another. "Well, yes, Dame Alodia, I am three months out of mourning."

"Then isn't it time you should be thinking about a new husband?" the formidable dowager said.

For a second, Deborah couldn't breathe, let alone answer. Eleven years ago, shortly after her father's untimely death and at exactly such a Spring Afternoon Soiree, Dame Alodia and the others had decided a too-young, too-naïve Deborah should marry Mr. Richard Percival, a man almost thirty-seven years her senior. He had been feuding with his adult children. He had asked for Deborah's hand with the intention of starting a new family and putting their noses out of joint.

Like any sensible young woman, Deborah had shuddered at the thought of being wed to a man so much older, but the women of the Valley, *these* women, had insisted her duty was to marry in order to support her widowed stepmother and two half sisters.

Her duty. Deborah always did what was expected of her. Her overdeveloped sense of responsibility had been honed to a keen edge over the years, sharpened by the knowledge that, even all these years after her death, her mother was still considered an interloper. Some even considered her immoral. First, because she'd been French, and second, because she'd upset the village's plans for their favored bachelor.

In turn, Deborah had learned early on she must walk the straight and narrow lest she be accused of her mother's perceived sins.

Now, she glanced around the room. Every one of them waited, eager to hear her reply — all, that is, save for her sister Rachel. Seated next to Deborah, she had acquired a sudden fascination in the curve of her teacup.

Since Mr. Percival's death, Deborah had been forced to live with Rachel and her husband Henry. Her widow's portion had been a pittance, which Henry found humiliating and a blow to the family pride. The fact Deborah worked harder than his wife and servants held no sway in the face of his resentment, and she couldn't help wonder if Henry now played a part in his aunt Alodia's questioning.

"Have you naught to say for yourself?" Dame Alodia demanded, with a haughty lift of her brows. She sniffed to the others. "I ask a question and don't receive an answer. Do young women not use their ears anymore?"

Oh, Deborah had an answer: *Ambushed by the Dowagers of Ilam. Again!*

As her late husband would have said, *Double damn.*

9

But she couldn't speak in such a manner in front of the cream of Ilam society.

Instead, she cleared her throat self-consciously, and admitted, "I had not thought on the matter, ma'am."

"No thought on *marriage?*" Dame Alodia emphasized the last word to show her astonishment. "Every woman should be married."

Deborah could have pointed out that Dame Alodia was a widow and happy for it, but she bit her tongue. "It is still too soon —"

"Nonsense!" Dame Alodia interrupted. The purple ribbons and lace of her cap bobbed with her enthusiasm for her topic. "You've done your mourning. How old are you? Eight-and-twenty? Almost thirty? No longer in your prime breeding years and no children."

"No, no children," Mrs. Hemmings reiterated. She was Dame Alodia's constant companion, a colorless, nondescript woman and a warning to Deborah of what might become of her. Life was not pleasant for a genteel woman forced to depend on the mercy of relatives.

"Actually, I'm seven-and-twenty," Deborah corrected, feeling hot color stain her cheeks. She did not like confrontation.

"Twenty-eight, seven-and-twenty, what difference?" Dame Alodia said with a dismissive wave. She picked Milton off her lap and unceremoniously handed him to Mrs. Hemmings. The dog growled at being moved from his comfortable position. "Take him out of the room

10

for his walkie-walk, Hemmy," Dame Alodia ordered, "while the rest of us talk sense into Mrs. Percival."

"Yes, sense," Mrs. Hemmings echoed, and left the room.

As soon as the door shut, Dame Alodia came directly to the point. "Every woman needs a husband and children unless she is barren, and then she is not fit for a thing. Whatever your age, Mrs. Percival, you are not growing younger. Furthermore, those dark looks of yours are not in fashion. Blond hair and blue eyes, like your sisters have, is the style. Black hair and black eyes are too foreign-looking. Too Continental, and no one likes the Continent anymore. Not after the war."

Deborah felt the heat of scrutiny as the others judged the truth of Dame Alodia's assessment. Even Rachel stopped her teacup examination and stared. Deborah frowned her sister into submission.

Dame Alodia capped off her damning assessment by saying, "Nor does a straight nose age well."

It took all Deborah's willpower to not raise her hand to hide her nose. Her looks came from her mother, a Lyonnaise noblewoman whose family fortune had been wiped out when the Revolution swept her country. She and Deborah's father had met while he pursued his law studies in London. Their marriage had created a bit of a scandal, since everyone in the

Dove Valley had expected him to marry his childhood friend Pamela Elwood. And, when Deborah's mother had died in childbirth, he'd done exactly that.

Pamela had been a good stepmother, God rest her soul, but Deborah had always been aware that others felt she was the child who should never have been. She'd heard the whispers. She knew there were those who felt her father should never have strayed from the local girls. Her sisters were the daughters he had been meant to have, not Deborah.

"I am aware I am not the family beauty," she replied quietly.

"Then you are fortunate I have found a husband for you," Dame Alodia said.

Uh-oh. A sense of foreboding drummed in Deborah's veins. "You have?"

"Yes! Parson Ames," the dowager announced with triumph.

The circle of woman exclaimed over her cleverness. "Of course!" several agreed.

Mrs. Hightower from Dovedale leaned forward, patted Deborah's hand, and said, "Absolutely, absolutely. You'd make a lovely pair."

Deborah choked on a response. The good cleric was a foot shorter than she, bald, and officious. Worse, he had six children who were the scourge of the village. Even his late wife had been unable to exert control over them, and the parson himself was one of the most ineffectual men Deborah had ever met. He was mealymouthed, bumbling, and boring. Why, she could barely listen to the first words of his sermons without wishing to nod off!

What would it be like to have him at her table every night? She couldn't bear considering the thought. A parson's cottage and six unmanageable brats would be worse than living in a lunatic asylum.

As if from a distance, she heard herself murmuring something about pining for her late husband.

Dame Alodia cheerfully dismissed the notion, "What rot! Get out from under your sister's roof. You need your own household. Besides, he's the only eligible man in the village for a woman with your family background and lack of fortune."

And she was right. *Double, double damn.*

The others jumped into the conversation, excitedly planning Deborah and Parson Ames's future. They even offered advice on how to cage his incorrigible children.

Deborah held her tongue. But only until the party had ended, and she and Rachel were walking home.

Then the words burst out of her with anger.

"You knew what was going to happen, didn't you?"

Rachel pretended innocence. "I don't know what you are talking about." She climbed the steps leading over the drystone wall that marked the boundary between Henry's green pastures and his neighbor's. The day was a pleasant one for a walk, with snowy clouds the shape of fat sheep dotting a blue sky.

Deborah followed right at her sister's heels, but at the top, jumped to the ground, placing herself in Rachel's path. "I can't marry Parson Ames. I don't like him."

"You didn't like Mr. Percival that much either," Rachel said, and attempted to step around her. Deborah blocked her way.

"Oh, no you don't. We need to have this out between us — without Henry's presence. You put Dame Alodia up to finding me a husband."

For a second, she expected Rachel to deny the charge . . . but she didn't. Instead, her sister's shoulders sagged. She sat on the drystone step, taking Deborah's hand, and pulling her down next to her. "Darling, you must make a life for yourself. I love you, and I know what you have sacrificed for Mama and Lizbet and me, but Henry is, can be, an impatient man." She gave Deborah's hand a squeeze. "And I'm going to have a baby."

Elation crowded out anger. "Rachel, that's wonderful. I know you and Henry have wanted a family."

"We have." A frown of worry marred her brow. "But Henry worries about too many mouths to feed and if we will have enough space."

There it was. Henry wanted her to leave. "It is a good thing Mr. Percival never felt that way."

Tears rose in Rachel's eyes. "I know." She threw her arms around her sister's shoulders, knocking her bonnet back, and sobbed.

Deborah let her cry. The habit of caring for her sisters, even when she was disappointed in them, had been ingrained in her at an early age. She even unbent enough to murmur, "It will be all right, Rachel. I understand, I understand."

Rachel lifted her head. "Do you?"

"Of course," Deborah managed past the lump in her own throat. She'd known this day would come. Henry's impatience had been clear for all to see. Still, disappointment was a bitter pill. "I can make arrangements. There is Lizbet —"

"Lizbet is too full of her own self-importance to worry about us!" Rachel straightened the brim of her bonnet and dried her eyes. "Ever since she and Edmond left for London, we've rarely heard a word from them even though you told her to never mind the postage, that you would pay it."

"Edmond's position is very important and, I'm certain, Lizbet is busy serving as his hostess. Don't forget, she has a new baby."

"Yes, and she has a nurse and a cook and an army of household servants. That's what Henry says."

"She needs them," Deborah said loyally. "Appearances are important in London, and we want Edmond to advance in his career." Her brother-in-law was a secretary to the duke of Etheridge. He hoped someday to have an important position in government.

"Yes, well, Lizbet has left everything on my shoulders," Rachel said, pitying herself. Deborah finally felt her temper snap.

She stood, straightening her own bonnet. "Life has not been hard for you. Mr. Percival gave you everything you wished and, when you wed, you received a good marriage portion. Why, you didn't even have to take care of Mother when she became ill." Pamela had died a year before Mr. Percival's death. "Now *I'm* the stone around your neck, and although I agree having two women under one roof can lead to difficulties, I am not that big of a trial!" She started down the path through the sheep pasture.

Rachel had to rush to catch up with her. She hooked her arm in Deborah's and made her turn to face her. "No, you aren't, but, darling, don't you yearn for children of your own?"

Deborah stopped short. She did. There were moments when she ached for them.

As if reading her mind, Rachel pressed her case. "I know Parson Ames is no pearl. But he's not as ugly as Mr. Percival was, and you made a good life with him."

"A good life?" Deborah stared at Rachel, uncertain whether to laugh or cry. "He was over thirty years older than I."

Curiosity colored Rachel's blue eyes. "You never complained."

For a second, her sister's insensitive acceptance robbed her of speech. Then, "What good would it have done if I had?" She turned and started walking away, needing to put distance between the two of them.

Rachel hurried behind her. "You could have said something. Mama, Lizbet, and I thought you were happy."

"I did what I had to do." She took an angry swipe at a tall weed.

"You can't expect us to know what you didn't say."

Deborah kept walking. Rachel had been too young to understand when Deborah had married Mr. Percival, but now she should know. Now, she should grasp what Deborah's life had been like without having the details spelled out.

"It wasn't my fault!" Rachel said with a wail.

Deborah stopped. She turned. Her sister stood ten feet behind her, all grown-up. And yet, when she was around her older sister, she still acted like a child. They had roles they played, the two of them. Deborah was the upstanding, reliable one who forwent her own feelings for the sake of her family. How could she explain, even to a married Rachel, what her wedding bed had been like? Of the weekly visits from her husband? Of the emptiness she'd felt, even though he was a good man?

The only time Deborah had defied her husband was in her insistence her sisters be allowed to marry for love. And they had. She just hadn't expected their husbands to be so selfish.

Or her sisters to believe that at only seven-and-twenty Deborah had no desire for more out of her life.

More. The word haunted her. There had to be something more to living, to *being* than obligations.

"You wouldn't understand how I feel," Deborah said simply.

Rachel came to her. "But I want you to be happy."

"Then don't help marry me off to Parson Ames."

"There is no other man suitable for you. Not in the Valley."

"Oh, may heaven help me," Deborah said fervently, and linked her arm in her sister's. They continued across the green stretch of pasture, the stone roof and chimneys of Rachel's house appearing in the near distance.

"The parson is not the best," Rachel admitted, "but he isn't a bad man either. He is good-hearted and will treat you well. After all, he doesn't raise a hand to those terrible children of his."

Rachel's logic startled a laugh out of Deborah and eased the tension. But there was nothing more she could or would say.

How could she explain to her socially conscious sister that she had had longings lately . . . but not the sort Rachel would approve?

She didn't want an old man or even a "suitable" one.

No, the *un*suitable ones had caught her eye. Kevin the cooper, with his laughing eyes and brawny arms, and David, Dame Alodia's head groom, with his muscled chest and horseman's legs. Strong, lusty, vital young men whose rumored sexual exploits fueled Deborah's spirited imagination and made her restless at night.

Of course, she couldn't let them know of her admiration. It was strictly her secret. Deborah Percival was far too sensible for lust. Even if it meant selling a piece of soul. And she wasn't about to let the gossips confirm all their suspicions about her "lamentable French blood" by acting on her fantasies.

Still, a woman could dream . . .

Arm in arm, the sisters walked up the drive to the farmhouse. Henry stood on the steps waiting for them. He was a handsome man, powerfully built, who, in spite of his tightfistedness, was actually a successful farmer.

"Promise me you will think on the parson?" Rachel asked as they approached the house. "He's really not a bad sort, and his children do need a mother."

Deborah didn't speak. She couldn't. She was praying too hard that something would happen to save her from another arranged marriage.

"Please?" Rachel pressed.

"I'll think on it."

Her sister gave her a quick hug. "I knew you would come round." Before Deborah could respond she raised her voice to tell her husband, "Deborah doesn't think Parson Ames is a bad sort."

"She'll marry him then?" he asked bluntly.

"Of course," Rachel said, and quickly turned so she wouldn't have to meet Deborah's eye. The coward!

Henry abruptly changed the subject. "There's a letter from your sister in London. Things are not well."

Immediately, he had both women's attention. He held out a heavy envelope, which Deborah reached first. "It's been opened."

Her brother-in-law shrugged. "It's addressed to my house." He looked to his wife. "The duke has discharged Edmond. They are living hand-to-mouth now and are probably begging to come live under my roof." He turned and marched in the front door, his action making his feelings on the matter very clear.

Deborah scanned the writing on the pages. Lizbet's handwriting had never been good, but now the words were smudged by tear stains. Worse, she'd been so agitated when she'd written, very little of what she shared made sense. But from what Deborah could make out, Henry had summed up the matter neatly.

All save for the last desperate paragraph.

"What is happening?" Rachel asked with concern.

"Edmond is searching for a new position, but they've had to let the servants go." Deborah folded the letter in half. "She's having trouble managing the baby. She wants me to come to help her."

"You? Go all the way to London?" There was a pause and Rachel added, "Alone?"

"Yes." The idea at first was beyond Deborah's comprehension, too. She'd never been as far as Derby. But people went to London. Sometimes every day . . . if they lived close enough.

"And I suppose you'll want me to put out the coin to pay for the trip?" Henry's voice interrupted the beginnings of a plan. He'd come back out on the step, obviously unable to keep his opinions to himself.

"I've never asked you for money," Deborah replied, doing a quick mental calculation. Her funds were limited, but certainly she could afford a trip to London to help her sister? "I have enough." Barely, but enough. And pride helped her reach her decision. "I *shall* go. And I won't need *anything* from you."

"Deborah," Rachel pleaded.

"Is that right?" Henry challenged. He always hated to be proved wrong, even when he set himself up for it. "Well, I don't want you to return with Edmond, Lizbet, and their brat in tow."

"Henry!" his wife demanded.

"I won't," Deborah promised serenely.

Her brother-in-law harrumphed his opinion. "But what about Parson Ames?" he asked. "I'm certain my aunt Alodia will insist he call on you. What shall I tell him?"

Deborah smiled. "Tell him I'm not at home."

London

Anthony Aldercy, Earl of Burnell, was not a gambling man. He'd worked too hard for his now considerable fortune to fritter it away. And he was a loner, not always by choice, but certainly by fate.

Therefore, when Colonel Phillip Bord and Captain Allen Christopherson invited him to join them for a game of cards, Tony was flattered. Bord was an old schoolmate, one he'd not seen in years. They'd been acquaintances in their youth, at least they *had been* until Tony's father, a notorious bankrupt, had blown his brains out reputedly over his wife's many infidelities.

After the ensuing scandal, many aristocratic families had discouraged their sons from befriending the young earl. His mother's affairs did not bother them as much as his father's messy way of handling the situation. Furthermore, the suicide was coupled with rumors of some sort of mental derangement that could possibly run in the family. And did they really want their sons and heirs associating with that sort of person — especially one with no money?

The Aldercys were branded "bad *ton*," a verdict that had ostracized Tony and still dogged his heels.

Consequently, he'd learned to keep his own counsel. He'd worked hard over the years, with spectacular success, to rebuild his family's fortune and to restore his good name. Of course, his true goal was to prove he was not his father.

So he was surprised, and yes, a bit excited, when he discovered Lord Longest, one of Society's most notorious sticklers, had consented to be the fourth card partner. In fact, Lord Longest went to pains to make it clear he had been the one to suggest Tony's name for their card game.

Tony knew when he was being courted and was anxious to learn what the elegant Longest wanted.

He didn't have to wait long to find out.

About an hour into the low-stakes play, Longest asked, "Burnell, are you aware of my daughter Amelia?"

Tony raised his gaze from his cards. He glanced at his companions, who appeared equally bewildered by this question.

Since an answer was obviously expected, he admitted, "Who hasn't heard of the Divine Lady Amelia? Poems are published in her honor daily, suitors line up outside your house, and everything from perfumes to puppies are named after her."

Longest smiled, pleased. "Yes, she's created

quite a sensation her first season out, if I do say so myself." Ignoring his cards, he leaned forward. "Would you be interested in marrying her?"

For a second, Tony didn't believe his ears. Bord and Christopherson appeared equally stunned. "Are you offering her to me, my lord?"

"Yes."

"Why?" His question was blunt, but honest.

Longest did not take offense. He lazed back in his chair. "I've been watching you, Burnell. We're in a new age now that the nonsense on the Continent has been settled. There are changes in the air. You are the sort of man I want on my side, a man who knows money and how to create it. An alliance between us would be advantageous."

"Have you gone mad, my lord?" Bord said, the words practically exploding from him. "You can't marry Lady Amelia off to the son of a suicide! His father was said to have been unsteady in life . . . and who knows of the son. If I had known this was your purpose, I would not have honored your request to seek Burnell out and deliver him to you!"

Tony's temper sizzled. But he was more hurt by those words than he cared to admit even to himself. The extension of friendship had been a sham.

Before he could speak, Longest said coldly, "Whom I choose to marry my daughter off to is none of your concern, Colonel. Besides, you are the one who volunteered to set up this meeting when I said I wished to speak to Burnell."

"I did so because —" Bord broke off abruptly, apparently questioning the wisdom of speaking his thoughts.

He looked across the table to Christopherson, who bowed his head as if wishing he were someplace else. Stiffly, Bord stood. He gave Tony his back, addressing himself to Longest. "I'd heard you were into the duns —"

"Careful now," Longest warned. "You may be forgetting yourself."

"I forget nothing," Bord shot back. "If you are going to sell your daughter for money, why not choose some fat cit. Certainly he'd be better than a madman's get of dubious lineage —"

Tony had had enough. "I'd be honored to marry your daughter," he said to Longest, cutting Bord off. He stood, using his superior height to lord it over the bantam-sized military man.

And why not marry? After all, he was one-and-thirty and had to marry sooner or later. Why not wed the woman considered the most beautiful in London? Her fame could enhance his reputation while her father's connections would open doors he'd assumed long closed.

Bord reacted as if Tony had physically struck

him, his jaw tightening, his eyes blazing with anger.

Christopherson rose from the table. "Come along, Colonel. Perhaps we'd best leave."

"I can't leave," Bord ground out.

"But you must," Longest said, steel in his voice, "because our business is done. Burnell and I need to discuss the marriage settlement."

The idea he'd been used did not set well with Bord. "This is all about money, isn't it?" he accused.

Longest's voice turned silky with threat. "This is the second time you've forgotten yourself, Colonel. If I were you, I'd choose wiser words." He had the social connections to make military life difficult for Bord.

Immediately, Christopherson came around the table to soothe his friend's ruffled feathers while Longest dismissed them both. He addressed Tony.

"I'd like to see the marriage take place as soon as possible. You will present yourself to Amelia on the morrow."

Ignoring Bord's angry glare, Tony replied, "Of course. However, I'm going out of town. I have business in the North." He referred to his family seat in Yorkshire.

"We'll do everything with special license," Longest said lazily. "What say we hold the wedding upon your return?"

Tony nodded. "I'll be back the middle of next month."

"Excellent. A few weeks after your return . . . perhaps the fifteenth?" He did a quick calculation. "That should be a Wednesday, a good day for a wedding." Longest motioned to a servant for more wine. "We must drink to seal our bargain —"

Bord flipped over the gaming table. Cards, glasses, and coins flew everywhere. He glowered at Tony. "You are not worthy of her. I'll die before I see her married to you."

Tony hardened his jaw. "You are stepping out of bounds," he warned.

"You can't step out of bounds with a dog," Bord snapped back.

The challenge could not be ignored. "You will meet me."

"Gladly," Bord replied evenly. "And I'll solve the problem by slicing you in half."

Tony didn't answer. He was an expert swordsman and an excellent shot. When one was the butt of jokes, one quickly learned to defend himself. His skill would speak for himself better than words. And he'd had to prove himself more than once.

Longest said nothing, but seemed satisfied.

Bord straightened. "We shall meet at dawn since you are so anxious to be on your way for Yorkshire. After all, why let something like a betrothal and an affair of honor interfere with your *business* interests." He said the last words as if they left a bad taste in his mouth. Tony was not surprised. Many of his contemporaries treated him with disdain because he actually liked to work.

"Until the morrow," Tony agreed pleasantly.

There was nothing left for Bord to do then but leave, his back rigid, his pride affronted. Christopherson followed.

"Rash young fellow," Longest said. "The battlefield makes them believe they can bully their way." He directed his servants to clean up the mess and ordered a fresh bottle of brandy. "Now, Burnell, let us discuss the financial arrangements like the gentlemen we are."

Gentlemen we are.

Longest smiled. "I'll warn you, my Amelia will not come cheap."

"I did not assume she would," Tony answered. After all, everything had its price — even respectability.

The next morning, under heavy skies, Tony met Bord under a chestnut tree in the Park and quickly, ruthlessly, drew first blood. Allendale, Tony's man of business, served as his second. Bord wanted to fight to mortal wound, but his seconds physically pulled him away.

Honor satisfied, Tony and Bord parted — enemies.

The outcome did not give Tony pleasure. Wiping the blood from his blade, he felt more alone than ever.

Allendale came up behind Tony and offered him his hat. Sheathing his sword, Tony said,

"I'm to be married, Allendale. In two months' time."

"Very good, my lord," came the taciturn reply. He was Tony's age, sandy-haired, with weak blue eyes behind spectacles.

Tony looked in the direction of the coach containing Bord and his friends as it pulled away. They would take him back to his lodgings, bind his wounds, and commiserate on what a complete bastard Tony was. Meanwhile, he would return to his empty home.

He swung his gaze back toward the efficient steward. "Have you no words of advice for me? No insight? You've been married for —" He paused, suddenly realizing how little he knew of this man's personal affairs, and Allendale had been in his employ for over five years. He'd hired him away from the duke of Kenmore, and a wise move it had been. Allendale's counsel and experience had skillfully guided Tony up the social ladder of the *ton*.

"Eight years, my lord."

And Tony had never met his wife. When he was in town, he and Allendale spent hours working together and yet never spoke of anything personal.

"Is marriage worth the price?" Tony asked cynically.

"I have found great pleasure."

The unexpected note of warmth in the usually reserved man's voice caught Tony's attention. "I pray I do, too," he admitted candidly.

Allendale nodded, but made no response. No clapping of a hand on Tony's back with warm wishes. No teasing. No good-spirited bonhomie. But then, the man wasn't a friend but paid for his services.

"Well, come," Tony said. "We've work to do if I'm to leave at first light on the morrow." He started toward his waiting horses, Allendale falling in step beside him.

They'd walked several yards before Allendale said, "If I may be permitted an observation, my lord?"

"Yes, what is it?" Tony replied, his mind already turning to business. He reached for the reins of his horse.

"You've never struck me as the type of man who would like a cold bed."

The unanticipated familiarity of his comment opened a door between them. "What are you saying, Allendale?"

The steward looked as if he'd already said too much. He pushed his glasses up his nose. "I don't wish to be presumptuous —"

"Out with it."

Allendale cleared his throat, then admitted, "I'd always imagined, given your history, that you'd be one to marry for love."

"My history?" Tony questioned. "Or my parents'?"

The man knew he trod on dangerous ground. "Yes, right, my lord. I believe their —" He paused before continuing uncomfortably, "*Un-*

fortunate marriage had been arranged?"

Tony admired his tact. "It is the way things are done, Allendale. How alliances are forged. And has been since the beginning of England's history."

"Yes, my lord, very well." Allendale's took up the reins of his own horse, the subject apparently closed between them.

"You don't approve?" Tony prodded.

"I'd assumed you would be more modern, my lord." He started to climb on his horse.

Tony mounted. "And what is modern? What are the fashionable morals?"

Allendale blushed furiously even as he confessed, "Affection. Couples marry out of respect and, yes, desire." He pinned Tony with his spectacled gaze, and admitted, "They marry for love."

Love. Love was the reason his mother had flagrantly cuckolded his father. Love had driven him to suicide and destroyed Tony's life.

"Not in my class," he said dismissively. "Love is the common man's dream."

The moment the words left his lips, he regretted them. The fragile camaraderie between them was broken. They returned to their roles of employer and employee.

Several hours later, Tony presented himself in Longest's sitting room. Lady Amelia was waiting for him, as beautiful as ever in spite of the puffiness of her eyes and the redness of her

31

nose. She appeared to have been crying for hours.

Formally, Tony asked her for her hand. She agreed, her voice barely audible.

Longest immediately stepped between the couple and proposed a toast. Lady Amelia took a sip of her sherry, pleaded a headache, and escaped from the room.

"You know women," Longest said confidingly. "They are emotional creatures. She's so excited over the thought of your marriage, she's gotten herself all worked up. She'll be calm by the time you return from Yorkshire."

Tony had his doubts.

That night, he ate dinner alone in his big house, furnished with the best money could buy, and wondered why he wasn't more satisfied. Allendale had advised him to postpone his trip — especially with something as important as a marriage contract to negotiate. Tony would not. He already had been too long in London. He had important responsibilities outside the city demanding his attention and he needed to see Marmy, to tell her of his upcoming nuptials. Allendale could pen in the details.

One thing he did *not* do was pen a note to his mother about his impending betrothal. One of their assorted relatives in town would certainly write and tell her.

Instead, the next morning, he left London the way he liked it — alone. No valet, no personal servants, just he and his horse. Allendale had long been urging him to hire a secretary, but Tony had not reached a decision on the matter yet. The circle of those he trusted was very tight. He'd learned the hard way that the closer people were to you, the easier they could betray you.

Outside the city, he paused and smelled the air. A storm was brewing in the south. He'd try to outride it.

And try not to think about a future spent in a cold bed.

Chapter Two

Relentless rain did not provide an auspicious beginning for a great adventure. However, in the face of Henry's disapproval at Deborah's refusal to marry Parson Ames, she wasn't about to delay her journey. Despite the weather old Mr. Stanley was still making his twice-weekly run to Derby to collect the Valley's mail. Deborah could accompany him and, from Derby, she would embark on the London stage.

However, a little more than a mile into the trip, she was questioning her decision. The River Dove rushed through the Valley more rapidly than she'd ever seen before. Mr. Stanley's lumbering cart bumped and jarred over the road. It was pulled by a shuffling, swaybacked nag that seemed oblivious to the dangers on the muddy, winding path. At any second, Deborah feared, the horse would lose its foothold and send them all tumbling into the coursing water.

Mr. Stanley had rigged a canvas cover over the wagon, but it offered a pitiful barrier against the forces of Nature. The wool cloak Deborah wore soon grew heavy, itchy, and uncomfortable in the spring's cold rain. Worse, she didn't like the smell of wet wool and sneezed several times, huge body-shaking sneezes that pushed her brimmed bonnet forward with their force.

"Perhaps we should turn back?" she suggested when the river threatened to overflow its banks.

"I can't do that," Mr. Stanley assured her, his broad accent breaking the words into many different syllables. "I be having this route for ten years and more and never missed a day."

"Perhaps tradition should be broken in extraordinary circumstances?" she asked, one worried eye on the rising water. If they were swamped and she did drown, she had only her own stubborn pride to blame. Henry would tell one and all he had suggested she delay the trip — but once again she wouldn't listen.

Mr. Stanley made a guttural objection. "Howie and me," he said, referring to the horse, "have made our way through waters higher than this." He proceeded to tell her one alarming tale after another as the water rose higher and higher.

Deborah held on to her seat, her grip so tight, her fingers hurt. She imagined tragic scenes of her death. She knew her sisters would miss her but doubted her brothers-in-law would feel the slightest sorrow for her demise.

When the spire of the church marking Derby came into view against the gray haze of the day, she wanted to shout a heartfelt "hosanna."

"See there now, Mrs. Percival?" Mr. Stanley leaned close. "We made it safe, although I can tell thou now, I was a tad concerned."

Deborah could only nod. She was soaked to the skin, shivering with cold, and her bonnet brim was so wet, it had wilted. What would her appearance be by the time she reached London?

Mr. Stanley took her silence for fear and chastised her. "Thou should not have worried so much! Howie and I'd not let anything happen to Parson Ames's next wife."

His words sent the heat of indignation through her. She swiveled in her seat to confront him. "Who told such a thing? Where did you hear that?"

Mr. Stanley pulled his wet pipe from his mouth, obviously surprised by her questions. "The word is all over the Valley . . . and a fine match we think it will be, too. Those youngsters of his need a firm hand. Meaner group of sprites I've yet to see."

"Then why would you want me settled with them?" She didn't bother to keep the exasperation from her tone.

"A woman needs a husband, Mrs. Percival. Especially a young one like thou."

"But why Parson Ames?"

He drove them into the posting inn yard, which, of course, in the downpour, was deserted. "Because Dame Alodia is arranging the match." He reined the horse to a stop, but Deborah didn't hurry inside.

Instead, raindrops pounding on the canvas

covering, she confronted him. "I've *been* in an arranged marriage. This time, shouldn't the gentleman be one of *my* choice?"

Mr. Stanley stared at her as if horns were growing out of her head. "Thou are gentry," he replied. "Quality must marry Quality. You are no milkmaid to dally where you will."

Oh, but sometimes she wished she was! She wished he understood. She wished *someone* understood. She'd let her sisters marry for love — although, in truth, if they had set their caps for someone truly unrespectable, she would have protested. Still, it was *her* turn now. "If I follow your view, Mr. Stanley, then marriage is little different than sorting wool by color."

"Aye, 'tis almost the same. Of course, thou's problem is there aren't many men of thou's age in the Valley so thou's choices are slim."

Deborah didn't like the unpalatable truth. "Perhaps I would prefer someone younger," she said stiffly.

"Nah, thou wouldn't be happy. The young ones, they be brawny but not many brains." He tapped his own forehead for emphasis.

Deborah gave a little shake of her head, coming to her senses and embarrassed to be complaining to him. There was no arguing the matter. The Valley had decided she should marry Parson Ames and take his unruly children in hand and, once she helped Lizbet through her problems, Deborah probably would.

Resigned to her dreary fate, she said, "You are right, Mr. Stanley. Parson Ames is a good man."

She was rewarded with a relieved smile. He changed the subject. "Here now, the innkeeper has opened the door twice, peeking to see what we are up to. Let me help thou down." He jumped to the ground, ran around the horse in the rain, and offered his hand. She climbed down from the wagon and dashed to the inn's door while he reached for her portmanteau, then quickly followed.

"What about the horse?" she shouted as she reached the door.

"Howie doesn't mind the rain if I'm quick about my business."

He held the door for her to hurry inside to a cramped, narrow hall filled with travelers avoiding the rain. Deborah and Mr. Stanley were greeted by the innkeeper's bustling wife, who was handing out tankards of ale until her tray was empty. "Lor', Mr. Stanley, we weren't expecting thou in this weather!"

"Always got to pick up the mail, Mrs. Tupper. Haven't missed a day in over ten years."

"Well, thou can't have it today," she informed him. "The bridge is washed out, and no one is going north or south, east or west."

"Howie and I will," Mr. Stanley assured her.

"And be washed away for thou's efforts," she shot back.

As Mr. Stanley said, "Naaah," Deborah peered with growing concern around a corner into a taproom.

People were everywhere. Men and women sat on benches or stood in groups. Children entertained themselves by chasing each other around the adults, until a sharp word would make them think of another game. The air smelled of ale, smoke from the hearth, wet wool, and too many human beings packed into too small a space.

Deborah took a step back and stepped on the boot of a burly gent. "Excuse me," she murmured, shifting her weight.

He didn't even acknowledge her but continued talking politics to the man on his left. Two people over, another man attempted to catch her eye and give her a leer and a wink, and he wasn't the only one ogling. People forgot their manners in such a crush.

The innkeeper's wife was saying to one of her customers, ". . . good weather for business but not for traveling."

Deborah interjected herself into their conversation, "But the mail coaches are running, aren't they?"

"Nothing is going through until the bridge is repaired," Mrs. Tupper replied. "Which they can't do until the rain lets up. Mr. Tupper believes this could go on for a day or two."

"A day or two? If the mail can't run, then there won't even be stagecoaches!"

"Nor would Mr. Tupper be willing to hire out a private team," Mrs. Tupper agreed. "It's a bad time for travel."

"But I must go to London," Deborah insisted.

"Here now, Mrs. Percival," Mr. Stanley said. "This is an act of God. Thou can not fuss at God." He looked to Mrs. Tupper and explained, "Her sister needs her. Her husband's having a spot of trouble, and they are a very close family."

Deborah opened her mouth to protest his gossiping, but then resignedly, closed it. *Was there nothing people in the Valley didn't know about her affairs?*

Worse, he decided to take the decision about her fate into his own hands. "Thou'd best return to the Valley with me, Mrs. Percival," he advised.

Here was a place where she could take a stand: Deborah wasn't about to return to Ilam. Even if the rain was an excellent reason to delay her trip, Henry would smirk. She had too much pride to accept his attitude gracefully.

"I'm staying here." The words sounded right. "Then I can catch the first available mail with a berth for London."

Mr. Stanley reacted as if she'd volunteered to throw her skirts over her head and do a jig. "Thou cannot stay here! Why, look at this crowd." He lowered his voice. "A group of ruffians, they are."

Deborah had to admit that a few of the men looked as if they could rob coaches for a living, and some of the women were colorful. But there were also three older women working their knitting together and another twosome trying to herd children into quieting down. All in all, everyone appeared more weary than villainous.

"I'll be fine," she told him before saying to Mrs. Tupper, "I'll need a room for the night."

"I can offer thou a bench or a spot on the floor, ma'am, but thou'll be with the rest of these folks. All my rooms are let."

Deborah rocked back on her heels, taking in the push of humanity around her.

Mr. Stanley came to her rescue. "Here now, she can't be doing that! Mrs. Percival is Quality. Her father was Niall Somerset, the solicitor. You know the family name. She can't be sleeping on the floor."

"Look around thee, Mr. Stanley. It's all I can offer," Mrs. Tupper answered.

Frowning, he turned to Deborah. "Well, thou best be coming back with me."

"If thou can make it with the river rising!" Mrs. Tupper noted.

"I'll make it," Mr. Stanley promised. "No one knows the Valley passes better than my Howie. Come along, Mrs. Percival, and I'll see thou safely home."

Considering the matter settled, Mrs. Tupper started to tend her other customers, but

Deborah wasn't going to give up so easily. "Please, wait," she begged the innkeeper's wife. "Certainly there is some establishment in Derby where I can find a room?"

"Thou expects me to give away business?" Mrs. Tupper asked, incredulous.

"You know I don't want to spend the night on the floor, and if I must, I must," Deborah said. "However, there's hardly any space left even for that."

As if to lend credence to her words, the front door opened and another party of travelers barged into the hallway, bringing wind and rain with them. Everyone in the hall had to shift to make room, and several of the gentlemen bunched together in a corner started grumbling complaints. Then someone elbowed another's side and there followed a bit of a scuffle, for which Deborah would be eternally grateful. The growing dissatisfaction of her patrons spurred Mrs. Tupper into revealing there was a house not far from the inn that occasionally let rooms — but only to people of Quality.

"Owned by Miss Chalmers, a lovely woman, and I don't mind giving her a bit of business. The house is called Morning Glory Place. Thou should be pleased . . . if she has a room to let. In this weather —" She shrugged her guess.

"Thank you, Mrs. Tupper," Deborah said fervently. She prodded Mr. Stanley. "Let's be on our way so she can see to her other guests."

"I'm not certain, Mrs. Percival —" he started, but Deborah had made up her mind. She was *not* going back to Henry. So she practically commandeered Howie and the wagon and forced him by sheer will alone to concede to her wishes.

He would hear no talk of his spending the night. "I like my bed," he confided.

Deborah didn't reply. She was mentally counting her meager funds. How much did a room in Derby cost? Whatever the price, she had no choice but to pay it, then pray the rain stopped soon and the bridge was rebuilt quickly.

Although their drive was short, the rain made it difficult. Still poor swaybacked Howie trod on. The horse splashed his way through puddles the mile or so to Morning Glory Place, which turned out to be a comfortable-looking brick farmhouse. From its windows, there was a welcoming light that dispersed the gray gloom of the day. Deborah's spirits began to lift. It was quite nice.

Mr. Stanley insisted on going in with her. Their knock was answered by a petite, stoop-shouldered lady in an oversize mobcap and one of the friendliest smiles Deborah had ever seen.

"I'm here asking for a room," Deborah said.

Without an introduction, the lady motioned them in. "Please, come out of the rain with you," she said in a soft, lilting voice.

They hurried into a generous hallway with a

set of stairs leading up to the first floor. The scent of roasting meat for the evening's dinner filled the air. To Deborah's immediate right was a formal dining room. To her left, she assumed a sitting room. Still, the door was half-closed, and she couldn't be certain.

"I'm Miss Chalmers."

Deborah held out her hand. "I'm Mrs. Percival. Do you have a room available for the night?"

"You're lucky. I have one, but only one." She looked to Mr. Stanley expectantly. "You are Mr. Percival?"

Mr. Stanley blushed at the suggestion. He pulled off his soggy hat. "No, no, Mrs. Percival is a fine lady and a widow."

"A widow, and one so young," Miss Chalmers cooed sympathetically. She spoke like a grandmother always ready to tell a bedtime tale, and Deborah felt tension ebb from her. Miss Chalmers continued, "Well, sir, you can sleep on the couch or in the stable."

While Mr. Stanley recited again his vow to return home, Deborah took off her heavy cloak, embarrassed by the rainwater dripping off her hem. Her bonnet was hopelessly ruined. "Mr. Stanley, please set down my portmanteau. And you must stay. It can't be safe to return to Ilam in this weather."

"No, no, no," he protested. "However, thou will be fine here for the night. I can leave you in good conscience."

"Yes, I believe so," Deborah agreed. She reached into her reticule to offer a coin to him. She'd already paid him for the trip, but felt he deserved something extra. Her cold fingers trembled as she struggled with the wet drawstring.

But Mr. Stanley would have none of it. "Please, Mrs. Percival, I'd not take payment for a neighborly deed. Here now, I've seen thou safe. Godspeed on the rest of thou's journey. Come home to us soon."

His simple blessing touched her heart. "Thank you, Mr. Stanley."

With an embarrassed nod as if he'd said too much, he left, hurrying out into the rainy gloom where the ever-faithful Howie waited.

And Deborah was on her own.

For the first time in her life.

She stood a moment, startled by the realization . . . and found she was excited by the prospect. Of course, her feelings might have been different if she'd been forced to sleep on a taproom bench.

"Here, let me help you with your wet cloak," Miss Chalmers offered.

"I can manage," Deborah said. "Do you wish me to hang it in my room or someplace else?" She pulled loose the ribbons of her bonnet. The brim sagged down into a limp point, but she didn't take it off. Her hair had to be a dreadful mess. She would remove the hat in her room.

"There's a hook down this hall. Let me show you." Miss Chalmers led the way toward the darkness in the back half of the house. From there, Deborah could swear she could smell baking bread.

Her stomach growled rudely. She made a soft sound of embarrassment, but her hostess laughed. "Dinner will be served in another hour. I'm certain you will want a moment to freshen up."

"I would appreciate it greatly. I fear my bonnet has seen better days." To emphasize her words, she pulled down the topmost of the brim. She hoped she could mend the damage since it was her best bonnet. What had possessed her to wear it for the trip was beyond her comprehension. She'd been so intent in putting on a good face in front of Henry, she hadn't been thinking wisely.

Miss Chalmers patted Deborah's hand. "We'll see if we can reblock it. I have a touch with mending."

"I'd appreciate any magic you can work," Deborah answered, following the older woman back up the hall.

"Let me show you your room." She raised her voice, "Roald!" A tow-haired lad of about fourteen came out of the dining room.

"Yes, ma'am?"

"Please take Mrs. Percival's luggage to the room at the top of the stairs."

The lad nodded a shy bow to Deborah,

picked up her bag, and started up the stairs. Miss Chalmers followed. Deborah started up the stairs after her, but then caught a glimpse of the sitting room through the partially open door.

She stopped, charmed. Colorful rugs covered the floor. The furniture was cozy and plush, with two chairs facing a cheery fire and a matching set of settees creating an area for conversation. But what had captured her eye were the books, shelf after shelf of precious books.

With a soft exclamation of delight, she pressed the door open farther, unable to stop herself from entering the room.

Miss Chalmers followed. "You're a reader," she said with satisfaction.

"A good book is my favorite thing in the world —" Deborah pulled up short as she realized the room was occupied. Booted feet had been stretched toward the fire. Their owner, upon the sound of her voice, closed the book he'd been reading and gracefully rose from his chair, one of those facing the hearth. Or perhaps a better phrase would be that he unfolded himself, for he was tall, very tall.

He turned — and for a second, Deborah couldn't think, let alone speak.

Here was a Corinthian. Even in Ilam they'd heard of these dashing men about Town. Every young man in the Valley with a pretense to fashion aped their casual dress. But the gentleman standing in Miss Chalmers's sitting room was the real thing.

His coat was of the finest stuff, and the cut fit his form to perfection . . . as did the doeskin riding breeches. His boots were so well polished that they reflected the flames in the fire and the nonchalantly careless knot in his tie could only have been achieved by a man who knew what he was doing.

More incredibly, his shoulders beneath the fine marine blue cloth of his jacket appeared broader and stronger than Kevin the cooper's. And his thighs were more muscular than David's, Dame Alodia's groom's. Horseman's thighs. The kind of thighs with the strength and grace from years of riding.

He was also better-looking than both Kevin and David combined.

He wasn't handsome in a classic way. But no one — no *woman* — would not notice him. Dark lashes framed eyes so blue they appeared to be almost black. Slashing brows gave his face character, as did the long, lean line of his jaw. His lips were thin but not unattractive, no, not unattractive at all.

Then, he smiled.

A humming started in her ears. Her heart pounded against her chest . . . and she felt an *unseen* pull toward him, a *connection* the likes of which she'd never experienced before from another human being.

And he sensed the same thing.

She *knew* — without words — that he was as

struck by her as she was by him. The signs were there in the arrested interest in his eyes, the sly crookedness of his smile.

Miss Chalmers was speaking, making introductions, but the sound of her voice seemed a long distance away. ". . . Mrs. Percival, a widow from Ilam. This is our other guest, a great favorite of mine, Lor—"

The gentleman interrupted her, "Aldercy. Tony Aldercy."

Aldercy. His name had a musical ring.

"Mrs. Percival," he said, making a small bow. His voice struck something deep within her. Her heartbeat kicked up another notch. She couldn't speak. She could barely think —

And then, Deborah realized how shabby her appearance was. She looked like a drowned cat. *What was she thinking, standing in front of him like this?* The brim of her bonnet still sagged, her hem dripped water, and her hands were clammy and cold.

The spell between them broke.

What sort of silly woman was she to drool openly over a man? She stepped back — stumbling for a plausible reason to excuse herself and escape her own folly — and practically fell over petite Miss Chalmers. "I'm so sorry!" she blurted out, reaching for the fragile woman before she toppled over.

" 'Tis nothing, dear," Miss Chalmers assured her, but Deborah was horrified.

"I shouldn't be so clumsy. Please excuse me

—" This she said to Mr. Aldercy and, mustering what little dignity she had, she turned and walked right into a side table.

A charming porcelain shepherd leaning on his crooked staff went flying off the table. With an alarmed cry, Deborah dived to save it from toppling to the floor, just as Mr. Aldercy did.

They caught the piece at the same time. Their hands touched. Time halted.

If lightning had rent the air right there inside the room, Deborah would not have been more affected.

Long, masculine fingers curved around hers. His nails were short, groomed, his skin blazing warm to the touch. Slowly, Deborah lifted her face toward him and found him so close she could make out the line of his whiskers.

Their gazes met, and held. Emotions rolled through her. Erotic, dark, hungry ones. The sort no respectable widow should ever think.

In his midnight eyes, she saw he was thinking them, too.

And the most amazing thing was — he was just her age.

Chapter Three

Tony's hands covered Mrs. Percival's, and he had the conscious, very direct desire never to let her go. Ever.

He'd been dozing in front of the fire when he'd first overheard her low, well-bred voice with its delightful hint of a country accent. Now, looking in her warm, amber brown eyes with their feminine tilt, he welcomed the rain that had forced a delay in his journey.

Here was no milk-and-honey English miss. The tilt of her eye was too exotic, the curve of her lower lip too full. The dark slash of her eyebrows hinted at a strong-willed character while her high cheekbones spoke of breeding. He wanted her to remove her rain-soaked bonnet, to see her hair. He imagined it as a blue-black shining curtain of silk.

Tony's attraction to her was instantaneous and overwhelming in a way he'd never felt before.

He wanted to bed her. Now. On the rug if need be —

Marmy, the name he used for Miss Chalmers, his childhood nanny, cleared her throat, bringing him back to reality. He and Mrs. Percival had been staring at each other like moonstruck puppies.

As much as he hated breaking contact, he released her hands.

She blinked, looking down at the porcelain as if not certain how it had appeared in her hands.

He knew how she felt.

"It is a pleasure to make your acquaintance, Mrs. Percival," he said.

A becoming shade of color stained her cheeks. She lowered her gaze. "And I yours, sir." Awkwardly, she turned to Marmy. "I'm so sorry. I shouldn't have been so clumsy."

"You weren't clumsy," Marmy corrected, taking the porcelain from her. "I've been meaning to move the table. More than one person has tripped over it. Come, let me take you to your room so you can remove your wet things and relax."

Tony wanted to volunteer to follow and help remove her wet things from her. As if sensing the direction of his thoughts, Mrs. Percival slid a wide-eyed glance in his direction.

Never before had he ever seemed so attuned to a woman. For a second, he couldn't breathe. Outside the rain fell harder, pelting the windows in its fury.

Inside, Marmy broke the spell. She took Mrs. Percival's arm and led her to the door, where Roald waited for further instructions. Tony watched the feminine sway of Mrs. Percival's hips and knew which room Marmy would give to her. The one at the top of the stairs . . . next to his own.

He always visited Derby on his way North and often on his return. Marmy had been more than a nurse to him. She'd been his governess, his mentor, and later his conscience. His parents he dismissed as shadowy figures in his childhood, coming and going as they would, but Marmy had always been there. She alone understood him. She'd earned his devotion.

However, Mrs. Percival's unexpected arrival interjected a note of excitement into his customary visit.

Sexual tension tightened him.

It had been a long time since he'd been with a woman. He was not like his contemporaries, who kept mistresses or prowled at night for willing prey. No, he was judicious in whom he chose to bed.

And he wanted to bed Mrs. Percival. Very much. Even now, minutes after she'd left, he could still sense her presence in the room, the scent of her, the heat —

"You'd best behave yourself, Lord Tony." Marmy's soft voice cut through his thoughts. He turned to find her entering the room. She shut the door behind her, a sign her temper was up. She appeared nothing less than a diminutive rooster.

"I always behave," he assured her, crossing the room to help himself to the whiskey decanter on the liquor table.

Marmy put an arthritic hand on the decanter, forcing him to look at her. "Why didn't you tell her your title?"

"I thought it simpler."

She waited, a signal she would accept nothing less than his full reasoning.

He capitulated. "My title's a burden. After the scandals my parents created, my name is infamous even in remote sections of the country. I found Mrs. Percival quite remarkable. Is it wrong of me to wish to meet her as a man and not as the focus of lurid gossip?"

She was not appeased. "Listen to me well; I could tell at a glance that Mrs. Percival is not sophisticated. Or jaded. She has already told me she's never left the Valley, and she won't understand the rules to the sort of game you have in mind. She doesn't even know there *are* rules."

"And what makes you think there is a game to play?"

Marmy removed her hand from the decanter and poured Tony's drink herself. "I changed your nappies, my lord. I bounced you on my knee, picked you up after scrapes, and did my best to make a man out of you." She leaned closer to confide, "Sometimes, I know what is going through your mind before you do. Do you truly believe I do not recognize desire? Or lust? You could have heated the room with it."

Tony took a thoughtful sip of the whiskey, letting the smoky taste of it linger on his tongue. "What if Mrs. Percival is not —" He paused for the right word, one Marmy would accept. "What if she is not *unreceptive* to me?"

"She's receptive, my lord. She is such a country mouse, she doesn't even know it herself, but she is more willing than she'd be ready to admit."

Tony was pleased. The drive to taste her pounded in his blood.

"However, you are soon to be a married man," she brutally reminded him. She was not pleased with Tony's decision to marry Lady Amelia, and she accurately predicted, "You are not pleased with my reminder, are you, my lord?"

The whiskey lost its pleasure. He set the glass down, unfinished. "The marriage is an excellent match. Lady Amelia is the most beautiful girl of the Season and Longest is a powerful man. I'd be a fool to refuse the offer."

She leveled her rheumy gaze on him. "I thought you weren't going to be like your parents?"

The barb hit home.

He backed away. "I am bound to this marriage," he said quietly.

"Not yet. In London, they may be announcing the banns, but no clergy has made it fact."

"I've given my word. A gentleman does not cry off."

With an impatient sound, she turned away, obviously so angry she needed distance between them.

He hated disappointing her. "Marmy, the last time I visited, you even chastised me yourself for not marrying."

She nodded, her back to him still rigid. Then, her gaze fell on the shepherd porcelain. She lightly tapped the crooked staff the figurine held. "What color are Lady Amelia's eyes?"

Tony said nothing. He thought they were blue . . . but he wasn't sure.

Marmy interpreted his silence correctly. She faced him. "Does she love to laugh? What pleases her? Music? Art? Can she speak French?"

"I'm certain she manages many of those talents. She has been bred to be a nobleman's wife."

"What color are Mrs. Percival's eyes?"

He did not answer. *Golden brown with centers as black as coal.*

Her smile was tight. "And what about those qualities most important to a marriage, my lord? You and your intended barely know each other. You worry about the impact of your scandalous title on Mrs. Percival's sensibilities and yet have you given any concern to your future bride's feelings on the matter?"

"Her *father* approached me. It is not my responsibility to coax her into the match."

Marmy waved a dismissive hand. "I encouraged you to rise above your parents' disgraceful behavior because I knew the great man you could become. I knew the road would be diffi-

56

cult, but you have succeeded, my lord. You have made me proud. However," she continued without sentimentality, "I did not expect you to shut out love. Indeed, I prayed that someday you would fall truly, deeply, *desperately* in love."

Tony pulled away from the idea. He'd gone whole years without hearing the word — then first there was Allendale and now Marmy. "Love is a myth."

She shook her head sadly. "Love is all there is."

"Like friendship?" he asked derisively, thinking of Bord and all the others who would use him while destroying him behind his back. "Those are two emotions I can live without. Give me respect, and I'll be happy."

"And you'll gain it by marrying a chit you barely know?"

"No, by marrying a 'chit' whose father is one of the most powerful men in England."

A sound of frustration escaped her. "You forget, I know you. I know the passion in your soul you hide from the world. I know your greatest fear is people will compare you to your father. And yet, my lord, you cannot escape being the man you are. You may try, but you will fail."

He didn't like the prophetic touch of her words. "You are wrong, Marmy. I never fail. I will not allow myself to."

Her answer was a frustrated sound of distress

as if she feared something only she could see.

A knock at the door interrupted them. Anxious for a reason to end the disturbing conversation, he crossed the room and opened the door. Roald stood there with a huge pitcher of water. "Excuse, ma'am, I'm to take this up to our new guest?"

"Yes, yes, yes," she replied impatiently, then as an afterthought asked, "It's warmed right? You didn't make it too hot?"

"No, Miss Chalmers."

"Then hurry it up," she urged the lad. "Remind her dinner will be within the hour."

"Yes, Miss Chalmers." He started up the stairs.

Marmy raised a distracted hand to her head as if she suddenly felt unwell. Tony was by her side immediately.

"I hate growing old," she answered.

"I shouldn't have upset you."

She patted his arm. "Then don't make a mistake you will pay for every day of your life."

He took her frail hand in his. "I've given my word."

"And you would sell your soul rather than admit to making a mistake."

"This marriage is not a mistake."

She leaned her head against his shoulder with a heavy sigh, relaxing into his strength. "I pray you are right. I just want what is best for you."

"Wait until you hear of me dining in all the best circles."

She smiled. "Or having the Lord Chancellor ask your opinion."

The phrase had been part of a game they'd played when he was a boy. Now, he said proudly, "He already does, although he doesn't want the fact to be known."

"But this alliance with Lord Longest . . . ?"

"Will change all that," he finished.

"So you say." She attempted to rise from her chair. "Come, I believe I shall lie down. I'm afraid I'm having one of my spells."

Instantly concerned, he demanded, "Is it bad?"

"No worse than the others. I shall be fine in the morning. Come, walk with me."

"Let me carry you." He would have been willing to give her his health, his well-being had it been possible.

"No. Absolutely not. I'm not that far gone." As they walked toward the door, she said, "My hope is that you marry a woman who cares for you as deeply as I do."

"Then I shall never marry," he said. "There is only one person I've ever trusted completely, and that is you."

She smiled, pleased with the compliment, and they were once again in perfect accord.

Tony saw her to her room, and after Mrs. Franklin, whom he'd hired along with her son Roald to look after Marmy, fussed over her, he returned to tuck her in.

"She's growing weaker," he said when they left the room.

"It's nothing more than old age," Mrs. Franklin assured him. "She has her good days and her bad ones. Rest is the best medicine. Here, now, I'd best finish seeing dinner on the table."

Tony returned to the book-lined sitting room. He picked up the drink he'd set aside earlier. He didn't know if he could navigate the world without Marmy's sensible counsel and unvarnished honesty to guide him. He took a sip of his drink. The whiskey's color reminded him of Mrs. Percival's eyes. *Golden brown.*

But on the matter of marriage, Marmy was wrong. A man of his class had to marry for prestige.

At the same time, the night ahead was full of possibilities.

And Mrs. Percival was not as naïve as Marmy wished her to be.

Deborah was so nervous her fingers fumbled with the lacings of her dress.

When she'd been introduced to Mr. Aldercy her appearance had been a fright. Now she was determined to make up for it.

He was everything she'd ever dreamed a man could be, a hero of her imagination come to life.

For a second, she could barely breathe from the anticipation of seeing him again — only this time, she would not make such a fool of herself.

She hadn't forgotten her responsibilities or her obligations . . . however, lust burned deep within her. Bright, vivid lust. Furthermore, not a soul in the house had met her before this evening. They didn't know her family history, her sisters, her status and connections.

Freedom was a heady thing.

A fire glowed in the grate, warding off the gathering darkness of the stormy evening. The room was simply, but elegantly, furnished. The accommodations were far better, she was certain, than anything Mrs. Tupper ever could have offered at the inn.

Roald had generously lit three beeswax candles. Deborah had assured him she could manage with one. His answer was Miss Chalmers liked her guests well tended. She was only charging two shilling four for such a comfortable room, including dinner and breakfast, so money was obviously not an issue for her hostess.

Deborah caught sight of her reflection in the rectangle of mirror over the washstand. Spidery wrinkles from laughter and life made her look older than she should. Crossing to the glass, she attempted to press those wrinkles out. She wasn't ready to age, not before she'd even started living . . . and her thoughts returned to the handsome man downstairs.

His intentions toward her were very clear in his eyes. A prudent woman would avoid him. And yet she could not have avoided going downstairs even if she'd wanted to. He was something usually beyond her, and yet, for to-night, tantalizingly in reach. She had no doubt he was wealthy, but there was something else about him — an air of mystery.

Deborah hung up her wet things, then brushed her hair until it was dry and alive with shine. From the recesses of her bag, she pulled out her one good dress, a corn-silk yellow she wore to church. It had also been her wedding dress when she'd married Mr. Percival.

Carefully, she slipped the dress over her head and tied the laces. Her hair was hopeless. She'd like to put it up in a topknot, but it was too heavy for the style. Instead, she wound it into her usual chignon at the base of her neck and secured the heavy mass in place with several silver pins. They had been a gift from her father when she'd turned sixteen . . . only a few months before his death.

Leaning over the washstand, she pinched her cheeks and bit her lips to bring a bit of color. There was nothing she could do about the wrinkles.

A bell from downstairs signified dinner was ready to be served. Her heart hammering in her chest, Deborah opened her door and started down the thickly carpeted steps.

To her disappointment, Mr. Aldercy was not waiting in the hall. A curious glance around the corner into the sitting room told her he was not there either. Perhaps he and the other guests were already in the dining room?

The sound of silverware clinking against china drew her to the dining room. Roald was there, placing a dish on the side table. The smell of roast beef made her stomach rumble. The sound of the rain against the house, the glow of candlelight, and the fire in the hearth created the impression of a safe haven away from the angry night.

The table was set for two.

"There are no other guests than me and Mr. Aldercy?" she asked Roald.

"No, just us," came a deep voice behind her.

Deborah turned quickly. Mr. Aldercy followed her in, his masculine presence seeming to stretch into every corner of the room. He'd changed to a coat of midnight blue that matched the color of his eyes. He sent an appreciative glance over her figure, and the temperature in the room rose ten degrees. She bit back a whimper.

Roald shifted from one foot to the other, making them both aware of his unwelcome presence. "Mum wanted to know if you wished wine, my —"

"I do," Mr. Aldercy said confidently. Deborah admired confidence in a man. Then he added "gallantry" to his list of admirable qualities by pulling her chair out for her. "Mrs. Percival, do you care for wine with dinner?"

"Yes, please," she managed. It was hard to breathe when he was so close to her. He smelled of sandalwood soap.

Never in her life, save for the day she'd married, had a man shaved solely for her.

He sat in the chair opposite hers and stretched out his legs. Their toes touched. Even that small contact set her pulse racing.

Deborah studied her plate, too shy to confront him, and, yet, she did not move her foot.

Nor did he.

What should one do?

With a boldness that surprised herself, she tapped the toe of his boot with her shoe and pulled back.

He laughed, the sound deep and rich. Dinner, food, rain, sisters, all vanished from her mind. Mr. Aldercy was even more dashingly handsome when he laughed. She could sit and stare at him forever.

Only Roald's presence kept her grounded. He looked at the two of them as if he thought they were growing goose feathers. "I'll fetch the wine."

As he left, a jovial woman with two chins and a huge aproned belly entered. "Here now, son, is Lord —"

Mr. Aldercy came to his feet and stretched out his hand. "Aldercy," he said clearly. "*Mr.* Aldercy, and this is Mrs. Percival."

The woman blinked. A funny expression crossed her face, and Deborah frowned. Something was up. But she didn't understand what.

The woman introduced herself. "I'm Mrs.

Franklin. A pleasure to meet you Mrs. Percival and Mr., um, Aldercy. Wine. I was thinking about the wine."

"Roald has gone for it," Mr. Aldercy supplied helpfully.

"Ummmhmmm." The woman frowned, then seemed to remember her purpose. She addressed herself to Deborah. "I help Miss Chalmers and cook the meals. If you wish anything, you have only to ask. Miss Chalmers wants you both to enjoy a good dinner."

"Where is she?" Deborah asked.

"She's gone to bed already," Mrs. Franklin said. "She usually turns in early, but with this rainy weather, well, she has a touch of the rheumatism. Roald and I take good care of her." She glanced at Mr. Aldercy. "Here now, should I serve?"

"No. We can help ourselves."

"Very well . . . sir." She stood awkwardly a moment. Roald entered with the wine. She stepped aside and watched him uncork the bottle.

Deborah rarely drank. On occasion she would have a mug of home-brewed ale, but usually preferred tea with her dinner. This wine was full-bodied and finer than any she'd ever tasted.

"You can leave the bottle on the table, Roald," Mr. Aldercy said, then, smiling, added, "Thank you, both, for your service, but we can manage from here."

"Yes, my-Mr. Aldercy," Mrs. Franklin said, and bowed out of the room. Her son pulled a forelock and followed her.

Something was amiss. Deborah sensed it . . .

"Will you let me serve you?" he asked smoothly. Before she could answer, he picked up her plate, rose, and turned to the sideboard. She took the moment to study him. He moved with languid grace, completely at ease. In spite of his height, he moved like a natural athlete. He was also considerate. First asking her if she preferred peas — yes, if they were creamed — and what slice of the capon she favored — no, she fancied the beef.

He set her plate in front of her and turned to help himself. She looked down at the succulent beef, the creamed peas, stuffing, and a boiled potato. It was simple fare. This was a simple meal. Yet the man she was with was obviously wealthy and most likely accustomed to traveling in fine circles.

He sat in his place and reached for his glass, but then paused. "What are you thinking?"

She made a pretense of arranging her fork and knife on the table. How could she admit she sensed all was not as it should be, especially in the face of his graciousness. "I'm surprised, what with all the inns overflowing, there aren't more guests to join us. Or have there been those who were turned away."

"Not to my knowledge. However, Miss Chalmers's is a private residence. Not everyone knows she occasionally lets out rooms. You were fortunate."

"And what of you, Mr. Aldercy? How did you come here?"

He cut a bite of beef. "Miss Chalmers and I are old friends." Almost as an afterthought, he explained, "She was my nurse and later my governess. She's always been present in my life."

His response soothed her apprehension. The rain outside was coming down harder than ever and creating a cocooned sense of well-being. She smiled and took another sip of wine. Its taste was really very pleasant.

He set his fork down, watching her.

She took another nervous sip. When he didn't speak, she prodded, "What?"

"I think you are a beautiful woman."

Deborah almost dropped her wineglass at his directness. No one had ever called her beautiful. She set the glass on the table, her face hot with embarrassment and made a fluttery movement with her hand. "I fear you flatter me, sir." She picked up her fork and knife, focusing on what was safe. "My family would laugh to hear you say so."

"Are they blind?" He continued with his own dinner as if this sort of conversation was commonplace.

"No, honest."

He looked up and laughed. "I never listen to my family. If I did, I'd be ready for Bedlam."

"You are wise," she agreed fervently, and had to laugh with him — but then stopped. He was watching her again. "What is it?"

"You are even more lovely when you laugh."

Her appetite for food vanished. In the depth of his eyes, she could see the reflection of the candle flames and her own face. Creamed peas could not compete with lust.

He set aside his own fork. "From the first moment I laid eyes on you, I've felt this attraction that I've not experienced for any other. Ever."

Oh dear. Deborah swallowed, her mouth suddenly dry.

"You feel it, too," he continued. "I know you do."

She did not deny it.

"I want to kiss you," he said.

Common sense warned this was too sudden — and yet her body yearned. "I beg your pardon?"

"Oh, you heard me," he chided softly. "What's more, you *want* me to kiss you. You have from the first moment we've met."

She couldn't answer. She should be outraged, incensed. Instead, she longed to feel his lips upon hers.

"Mrs. Percival, what is your given name?"

"Deborah."

"Deb-or-ah." He let the syllables roll on his tongue. "A biblical name."

She nodded dumbly.

Obviously, no words were necessary. He pushed back his chair and stood. She watched, eyes wide, as he came around the table to her. He held out his hand.

"I'm not certain we should," she whispered truthfully.

"We shouldn't." His expression grave, he added, "But I don't believe we can help ourselves."

She stared at his outstretched hand . . . and realized he was right. She wanted him to ravish her, to take her up to her bed and introduce her to what she suspected had always been beyond her grasp.

However, she was a lady. Ladies did not throw themselves at gentlemen. "We haven't finished eating," she protested weakly.

"I'm only asking for a kiss," he said. "One kiss."

One kiss. Could that be so terrible? Especially here, where no one knew her? Especially since she wanted one so much?

She placed her hand in his. Moving as if in a dream, she came to her feet. They stood facing each other, toe-to-toe, the scent of sandalwood making her senses swim.

Staring at the knot in his neckcloth, she said, "This isn't wise."

"I only want a kiss," he answered. "One little kiss." Before she could object, his lips covered hers right there in the dining room.

Chapter Four

Deborah's mind went blank. She should protest, proclaim her innocence.

But then, another part of her, a part born from curiosity and unfulfilled lust, wanted to mew like a hungry kitten for more. Mr. Aldercy's kiss was a far cry from her husband Richard's perfunctory pecks. This was a full-lipped, on-the-mouth, real-man-behind-it kiss.

Lust won out.

What harm could a little taste do? After a marriage to a man who'd been more of a father figure than a lover, she was more than a touch curious about what she had been missing.

With a soft sigh, she let down her guard.

Mr. Aldercy's hand went to her waist and pulled her closer.

The kiss changed. His lips became more searching, insistent. She hesitated, uncertain . . . and then decided that if she was going to experience kissing properly, she must throw caution to the wind. She kissed him back for all she was worth.

But —

Something was wrong.

He broke contact. She would have pulled away, but he held her near, his arm still around her waist. The light of a thousand devils danced in his eyes. "Mrs. Percival, what are you doing?"

Hot embarrassment flooded her cheeks. She wasn't sure how to answer. "I thought you knew what we were doing," she replied stiffly.

A low hum in the back of his throat was his answer. "If that is all you know of kissing, then, with all due respect to your late husband, you have been sorely neglected." He took her hand and pulled her toward the door. "Come."

Apprehensive, she asked, "Where are we going?"

"To a place where I can teach you to kiss properly."

Deborah hung back. "I don't see why you can't show me here."

He turned. He was so tall, so strong, so overpowering, and yet his reassuring squeeze on her hand was gentle. "I don't want Roald or Mrs. Franklin to walk in. Not if we are going to be after a proper kiss."

That would not do.

As if to lend credence to his words, a footfall sounded behind the pantry door. It started to open.

"Come." This time she didn't hesitate but hurried behind him. She couldn't help herself. Her hand felt safe in his . . . and she did want her kiss — if for nothing more than to satisfy her curiosity.

After all, she couldn't very well ask anyone in Ilam to teach her. Mr. Aldercy was providing an excellent opportunity.

However, she did have second thoughts when he started for the staircase. She balked. "Why not the sitting room?"

He paused, one foot leading up the stairs. "Too public. At least for the kiss I have in mind."

She shouldn't.

Upstairs were the bedrooms. She wasn't so naïve that she didn't suspect his intentions —

Roald's low voice came from the dining room. "They've left the table. I'll clear it now."

Deborah panicked. What if he looked out in the hall and saw the two of them standing there in this ridiculous pose like she was a reluctant mule Mr. Aldercy had to coax forward?

They could dash into the sitting room — but then, she wouldn't get her kiss. And she wanted one very much.

With a glance over her shoulder to ensure no one saw them, she charged up the stairs. Mr. Aldercy fell into step behind her, and they hurried like schoolchildren afraid of being caught in a prank.

However, at the top of the stairs, games stopped. He whisked her up the last step, twirled her around until her back was against the wall, and kissed her.

She was caught by surprise, her lips parting in a small gasp — and he didn't wait for her to press them together before settling his mouth over hers. Startled, she attempted to close her lips together, but he'd have none of it. His body pressed against hers, further pressing her to the wall. He slanted his head and urged her to open even more to him.

This kiss was much different.

For a second, she was awkward, inflexible . . . and then, ever so slowly, she realized it was quite pleasant. *Very* pleasant. So much better than a hard buss with tight lips.

She'd always sensed there was something *more,* now she knew she'd been right! This was what she'd been searching for.

More importantly, kissing him was as natural as breathing.

The sounds, smells, and morality of the world faded, and there was only him and their kiss.

His tongue stroked her bottom lip. It tickled, but before she could laugh, his tongue stroked *hers.*

It was something altogether different, something beyond kissing. Something intimate.

But instead of shying away, of ending it all right there, thanking him very much and going to her room like the good, well-bred woman she was — she accepted him.

She even kissed him back.

Their legs were entwined. He leaned against her. The hard length and breadth of him was molded against his breeches, and he fitted himself to her. She was so aware of him, even through the layers of her skirts. Dear Joseph, he was huge . . . and strong . . . and so very vital.

His hand slid down to her waist and along the curve of her hip. She could even feel the racing of his heart, a beat that matched her own.

Who knew something as simple as a kiss could open the soul?

With a trust born of instinct, she turned herself over to him. All she wanted were kisses, more and more kisses.

It wasn't until she first felt his touch *intimately* that she realized *he* was thinking *very* clearly. His roving hand had lifted her skirts and followed the line of her leg, without her truly being the wiser for its passage.

She struggled for sanity. Well-bred women didn't let men touch their more intimate parts in public. She started to push away.

The kiss broke.

But he didn't release her. Instead, his voice in her ear, he whispered, "Steady. Relax . . . just enjoy this. I won't do anything you don't wish."

His finger stroked. Deep muscles clenched. Demanding need spiked through her. Of its own volition, her body curved to meet his caress.

"You're a jewel," he murmured against her neck. "So hot. So ready."

She couldn't answer. He was robbing her of speech, of sense, of judgment. In a moment, she'd get her senses back and tell him to stop . . . in a moment . . . or two. Raw with yearning, she turned her head toward his, sought out his lips, and began kissing him.

His breathing was heavy, as if he were running a long race and she was panting. He was taking outrageous liberties and, yet, she thought she'd die if he didn't complete what had started between them.

He knew what she wanted even if she wasn't certain herself. Blindly, she trusted him. His tongue stroked hers, then began mimicking the movement of his hands. Her legs no longer supported her. He held her up against the wall, strong enough to hold her easily and take his pleasure.

His finger slid inside her. Deborah gasped, interrupting their kiss. She looked heavenward as he again pressed toward the core of her.

She shouldn't be letting him do this.

And yet, she could not stop him.

Her husband had *never* touched her like this. Wave after wave of longing for something she'd always sensed existed and had never found vibrated through her.

She moaned, unable to hold herself back —

"Yes, Roald, what did you say? My hearing's not so good lately."

Mrs. Franklin's voice cut through the heady haze of lust. The woman had to be as near as the foot of the stairs!

Panic sobered Deborah. She crouched, afraid to be discovered, even as Mr. Aldercy removed his hand and protectively cradled her to him.

"Shh," he whispered in her ear.

"No, Mum," her son said. He'd been in the sitting room.

"Funny, I could have sworn I heard you say something. Never mind, have you put the fire out in the grate?"

"Yes, Mum."

"Good. I'm done in the kitchen and ready for my bed. Come along."

A foot stepped on the first tread.

Mr. Aldercy grabbed Deborah's hand at the wrist and ran with her. They made it safely to the nearest bedroom and closed the door before Mrs. Franklin and her son could climb high enough up the stairs to catch a glimpse of them.

For a heartbeat, Deborah could feel nothing but relief as did he. They collapsed in each other's arms. And then, he started laughing quietly. His laugh was infectious, and she couldn't help but join him — then he was kissing her again.

And somehow, he'd maneuvered her to the bed she'd been only peripherally aware of. She bumped into it with the backs of her legs. His deft fingers started loosening her lacings.

It wasn't her room.

Well-appointed hangings framed the bed. A fire burned in the grate and candles in shining brass sticks burned on the bedside tables. The realization shocked her. She'd run into his room. She struggled for sanity. "Please —" she started, but his kiss cut short her protest. Why couldn't she think clearly whenever he kissed her? The taste of him was as intoxicating as the wine from dinner that still flowed through her veins.

Then, he placed his hands on her breasts.

He pressed them together, weighing them. His tongue entwined with hers. His hot, hot mouth tasted of wine and promise. His thumbs circled the hard buds of her nipples. What he was doing felt good. Very good.

His leg pressed between hers and he was leaning her back, toward the bed. "Just one more little kiss," he murmured against her lips.

She knew what he *really* wanted.

She wanted it, too.

Even then, her body arched intimately against him. The whiskered roughness of his jaw felt good against her skin. And she ached for him to touch her as he had out in the hall. Her body was begging for him to finish what he'd started. Slowly, intently, he lowered her to the mattress —

Deborah rolled out from under him. *What was she doing?* "Wait! We can't do this."

He looked at the mattress, as if surprised to find her missing. He frowned. "Yes, we can."

"No." Her bodice drooped, exposing her sensible cotton chemise and far too much cleavage. She stood, pulling her dress up over her bosom and feeling remarkably stupid. "I'm sorry. I've misled you. I'm not able to —" She stopped, stumped for the right word. "Well, *you know.*"

His smile turned knowingly lazy. He leaned back on the bed, temptation incarnate. "No, I don't know."

"You do, too!" She would have marched for the door, but he bolted up and placed himself in front of her.

Deborah attempted to step around him. He blocked her path. *Dear Lord,* even her hair was a mess. The pins had come loose, and half of it tumbled to her shoulders.

His hair was mussed, too, giving him a boy-ishly handsome charm. And his shirt was pulled from his breeches. She'd done that when she'd been groaning for more during their hallway tryst.

Her throat tightened. "I don't blame you for believing I am a woman of loose morals. I've behaved in a wanton fashion, and I must face myself. But I'm not what you think. No, I have an excellent reputation. People respect me."

"I respect you."

She looked into his handsome face and shook her head. "You want to bed me."

"But that doesn't mean I don't respect you." His candid words and the sparkle of laughter in his eye caught her off guard.

And his humor at her expense made her angry, an anger she wrapped around her like armor. "Good night, sir. I hope never to see you again." With those haughty words, she started for the door, but was jerked back.

Turning, she saw he'd grabbed her skirt and held tight.

Deborah frowned. "Let go of my clothing."

He moved around to sit on the bed. She had no choice but to follow. "Not until you tell me what I've done to offend you."

She pressed her lips together, not wanting to confront her own foolishness.

"Well?" he prompted. "Are you going to give me the earful you obviously wish to deliver, or shall we stand like this all night?"

"Oh, you'd let me go sooner or later," she assured him.

"Don't count on it." To emphasize his commitment, he yanked the skirt, causing her to take a step back.

Deborah reached down to pull the skirt from his grasp, but could not pry loose his fingers. It was as if he held the material in a vise. She was so close to him now, she stood between his legs.

"Talk to me, Deborah," he urged. "Tell me what mischief is brewing in that beautiful head of yours."

Beautiful? No one else had ever called her beautiful. She'd always been "too foreign" when compared to her blond sisters. She unbent a little. "I'm sorry, but I've changed my mind."

"Why?"

"Does there have to be a reason?" Exasperation gave her words force. If she didn't leave soon, she was in danger of losing her resolve. Her attraction to him was that powerful.

"Yes," he said resolutely. "We were having a good time. I must have done something to upset you."

She didn't want to answer. There wasn't anything she could say that wouldn't make her appear anything other than an immoral tease. She could blame the wine . . . but she'd be lying.

"Deb?"

His shortened use of her name made what had transpired between them all the more intimate. However, she was not a coward. He deserved to know why she blew hot then cold. "I don't usually make a habit of groping men in the hallway."

The tension left his face, and he smiled. "I assumed as much."

She couldn't meet his eyes. "I don't know why. I've given you no cause to believe me."

"You kissed like a virgin."

His blunt words shocked her into looking at him. "Well, I'm not one."

"Most widows aren't," he answered.

Her face burned with embarrassment. "I shouldn't have said what I did. The impropriety —"

"There is no impropriety, Deb." He wrapped both his arms around her legs and nuzzled his nose close to her belly button before looking up. "I want you in my bed tonight — and no, I don't believe you are a whore or a slut." The intensity in his dark gaze robbed the words of insult and held her mesmerized. "From the first moment I laid eyes on you, I felt as if I'd been waiting to meet you all my life. There's something between us, Deb, something rare. Couldn't you taste it when we kissed?"

Her heart thundered in her chest. He, too, had felt the strong attraction between them. He wasn't making love to her just because she was convenient. "I don't kiss well, remember?"

His lips curved into an endearingly crooked grin. "I find you a quick learner." He lowered her to sit on his knee. "Dear sweet Deb." His lips brushed the top of her breast.

Desire shot through her. Sweet, wicked desire.

"If you don't wish to do this, then, here." He opened his arms. "You're free."

But Deborah didn't move. She sat there, warring with herself. "I'm sensible," she admitted. "I always do what is responsible."

He nodded in understanding. "And it is a pain in the arse, isn't it? Always having to live up to others' expectations and walk a narrow line lest you fall from grace and they believe the worst of you."

"Yes," she said, amazed to hear her innermost thoughts spoken aloud. "But it usually doesn't make any difference. They all think what they wish to think."

"Which is usually the worst."

"Oh, yes," she agreed. "And if you bypass

their expectations, they take credit for keeping you on a short rein. Or if you follow your heart, your imagination, they cluck their tongues and predict your demise."

Mr. Aldercy rested his arm on her leg. His seductive humor had vanished. Instead, he said seriously, "You do know."

Deborah nodded. "Oh, yes."

"God, I hate them," he replied fervently . . . echoing sentiments she'd never let herself dare voice.

"They are so hard to please."

He frowned. "And is it because of them you won't act on wild impulse?"

"And because of my own common sense," she admitted ruefully. "Saying no to you is the most frustrating, difficult thing I've ever done in my life."

His brows came together. "Then don't say no," he answered, lacing his fingers in hers. That was somehow more intimate than anything they had done so far.

She stared at the sight of her hand joined in his. "I must. I feel the pull toward you. But if I give in to desire and anyone finds out, I'm ruined. I could not disgrace my family in this way."

"No one will know," he vowed.

"Unless there is a child. That is always substantial proof."

Offended, he said with confidence, "I've yet to sire a child out of wedlock —"

"You aren't married, are you?" She tried to jump up, struck by a new fear.

He held her close, quieting her with a shushing sound. "I'm not married. And I'm not some Lothario who beds every widow he meets. This night is special. You are special." He released his hold and started pulling the loose pins from her hair. "There are ways, Deborah," he said in a low, confidential tone, "to avoid getting a woman with child." He began combing her hair with his fingers. It felt good.

"But if someone found out what I'd done . . ." The consequences were too terrifying to voice.

"No one will." He cradled her closer. His body heat cocooned them. "Listen to the rain," he whispered. It beat hard and steady against the house. "It's as though we are the only ones in the world. Let me make love to you, Deb. Let me show you all of what there is to know between a man and woman. Then, in the early hours of the morning, I'll carry you back to your bed. No one will be the wiser."

No one will be the wiser.

He kissed her, fully, hungrily on the lips.

Deborah gave in to Temptation.

She could not save herself. Not with Parson Ames and another dull marriage waiting for her back in Ilam. Not when she was growing older with each passing day.

Tomorrow, she would return to being the moral, responsible oldest child. But tonight — ?

She kissed him back with all the hidden passion of her soul. He rolled her down onto the bed. His hands started undressing her. She reached for the knot in his neckcloth and tugged at his jacket.

For the next several minutes they were busy undressing each other and kissing. Mr. Aldercy made a game of it, one he was better at than she. He stroked and kissed each newly revealed expanse of flesh while she'd merely untied his neckcloth and barely gotten one arm out of his coat.

His kisses lowered until he covered her nipple with his hot mouth. He sucked gently — and she feared she had caught on fire.

She had to have him. Then. That very minute.

The Royal Army could have marched into the room, headed by Dame Alodia — and Deborah could not have stopped her fingers from curling in his black hair and urging him on.

His head dipped lower as he pulled her chemise and petticoats down over her hips. He unfastened her garters.

She'd never been completely nude in front of Mr. Percival. She'd always worn her nightdress. But this felt perfectly right.

Mr. Aldercy kissed the inside of her thigh, and Deborah sighed contentedly. How sweetly delicious.

Then he lifted her legs on either of his shoulders and kissed the most intimate part of her.

For the blinding space of several heartbeats, Deborah couldn't think. She couldn't move.

A part of her was embarrassed beyond thinking; another part said, *oh, yessssss* and surrendered.

Mr. Aldercy feasted, and she was powerless to stop him — as if she wanted to. She arched toward him, need, needing, needing —

Her body tightened. Her fingers clutched his hair. "Mr. Aldercy?"

Then, it happened. Sharp, piercing . . . devastating. She cried out, a sharp gasp of surprise ending on a coo of pleasure. Wave after relentless wave of sensation flowed through her.

She couldn't move. She didn't want to do anything to disturb this incredible sense of well-being.

He lifted his head, pleased with himself. "Your husband never showed you that, did he?"

She could only whimper a response.

He stood. "Wait until you see what we are going to do next." Tall, proud, undeniably handsome, he began undressing.

"Another trick like that may kill me," she confessed.

He chuckled, pleased. "I'd like to see us both die happy, then," he said, and tossed his shirt aside. Sitting on the edge of the bed, he began to remove his boots. The glow of the fire cast a golden light over his skin and highlighted the flex and play of strong muscles.

He stood. Facing her, he slowly undid first one button, then another. Hooking both hands in his breeches, he slid them down his legs.

Dear God, he was huge and very ready for her. She'd never seen Mr. Percival's. They'd had separate rooms and when he did come to her, she was already under her sheets and half-asleep. He would climb on top of her, fiddle a bit, grunt, and get off. Most of the time, Deborah could pretend nothing had happened.

Now, she hummed her appreciation.

He liked her reaction. "Touch me."

She came up to sit on her knees. Her hair tumbled down around her shoulders. Her breasts were tight and full. Carefully, she ran the back of one finger up the length of him.

He was smooth and soft like a newborn's skin, and yet, he felt warm and alive.

"Deb?"

She raised her gaze. He cupped the side of her face with his hand and drew her up to kiss her. At the same time, he placed her hand around his shaft and showed her what he liked.

Their kiss grew greedy. He leaned her back on the bed. She opened her legs, her body feverish with anticipation.

He didn't waste time but in one strong fluid thrust, filled her.

And it was heaven. *This* was what she'd been missing. This strength, this virility. She wrapped her legs around his lean hips. He began moving, his lips finding hers. Soft moans of pleasure escaped from her.

"You are so tight," he murmured. "I can't hold myself. You feel so good."

His praise served to open her more to him. He was thrusting deep now, his movements demanding. It was as if he were possessing her. In truth, she no longer recognized the shameless, lustful creature she'd become. She pleaded with him, begging for more, wanting it all.

As before, her body spiraled higher and higher, only this time, she was bringing him with her. This was better than before. More alive. More real.

Suddenly, like a shooting star, her desire hit the pinnacle. She shattered into crystal-bright pieces of passion.

Fulfillment. She was no longer herself but an ethereal creature fashioned of light and happiness as bright and sparkling as the afternoon sun shimmering off water. He'd taken her to the heavens, and she now floated gently to the earth with a sense of completion and contentment she'd not known existed.

She'd almost forgotten he was there.

His muscles tightened. He gasped, "Can't," and pulled out of her body. He rolled away quickly.

His abrupt movements disrupted her well-being. She started to turn toward him, but he threw his arm over her to hold her in place. His eyes were closed tight. His sex was spent, his seed on his leg.

He'd kept his promise. She was so stunned with satisfaction, she didn't know how he'd managed to keep his wits.

They lay like such for a several long moments.

He was the first to stir. He moved his arm and slid it around her shoulders to keep her near. Humbly, he said, "Not a very noble sight, hmmm? But I did manage to pull out in time. No babies. It was hard though." He pressed a hard kiss to her forehead. "You're brilliant. Incredible."

She laid her head on his chest, her ear over his heart. Already, she knew the smell and taste of his skin better than she did her own. She held her hand up. He again laced his fingers in hers — knowing without words what she had wanted.

She'd just compromised all her principles, but she didn't want to consider her actions too closely. Not yet. Everything, her reactions, the whole experience was still too new for her to contemplate objectively.

"I didn't hurt you, did I?"

She wet her lips, self-conscious. "No." A beat. "I should go to my room now." She didn't move. She couldn't.

His arm came around her waist, holding her in place. "Stay here. With me. I'll wake you with enough time to put you in your bed before anyone is the wiser."

"Is that wise? I mean, we're both leaving on the morrow."

Mr. Aldercy hugged her closer. His warmth felt so comforting. "Listen to the rain. They won't have the bridge back up by morning."

The sheets felt good against her bare skin, and she was suddenly very tired. And yet, she didn't go right to sleep.

Neither did he. Instead, his hand stroked her hip and her thigh.

"You are very special, Deb."

His praise pleased her. "I had no idea it could be like that." Then, quietly, she whispered, "Thank you."

He bent his head down to her shoulder. She could feel the curve of his smile. That devilish smile. Without it, she might not have succumbed to temptation.

"The pleasure was all mine," he answered.

Sated, she fell asleep.

Tony was the first to wake the next morning. Deb slept on as if she were drugged, her head in the crook of his arm. The rain still came down steadily.

She'd surprised him last night. What he'd anticipated to be a pleasant diversion on a rainy evening had astounded him with the force of its passion. Here was no jaded widow happy for a quick roll on the sheets. Nor had the sex between them been perfunctory. She was liquid fire, mercurial, responsive . . . gorgeous.

And he wanted another go with her. Already, he was hard and ready. He'd slide into her while she was still asleep and watch her face wake with desire —

A sharp knock sounded at the door.

Deb raised a sleepy head, her eyes still closed.

"My lord," Marmy's sweet voice was edged with irony, "do you know where Mrs. Percival is? We seem to have misplaced her."

Chapter Five

Deborah's eyes flew open, and she shot out of the bed. Tony reached for her, grabbing her wrist before she could escape. He warned her to silence with a finger over his lips.

She was gloriously naked, her beautiful whiskey-colored eyes wide with embarrassment and apprehension. As if expecting an army of rulemongers to come charging through the door, she leaned back toward him for protection.

And he was enchanted.

"My lord?" Marmy said from the other side of the door to remind him she was still there and expected a response.

"I have her," he replied softly.

Deborah started, like a wild doe scrambling to hide or flee. He pulled her back against his chest before she could bolt. She smelled of woman and sex.

"We thought as much," Marmy said crisply, but, surprisingly, without censor. "Well, please tell her the bridge is still washed out. She'll not be going anywhere today, and mayhap tomorrow as well." There was a wise pause, then, "Will you be wishing breakfast to be sent up?"

"Yes."

"Your usual?"

Marmy was being deliberately pert. It was a trick of hers. She was scolding him, warning him to be careful.

"Yes . . . and something for my guest." He kissed the top of Deb's hair. She dug her elbow in his side, demanding to be let go. He tightened his hold.

"And what of your usual bath? Do you wish Roald to come up?"

"A bath would be perfect."

"Roald will bring breakfast up in a thrice."

Tony listened to her halting footsteps move away from the door. The sound mixed with the double-time beat of Deborah's heart. He needed to soothe over the awkwardness of the moment — but the moment he loosened his hold, she slid down out of his arms and off the bed.

Hurriedly, she started picking up her clothes — her stockings off the bedpost, her dress from a far corner. "I shouldn't be here. What was I thinking? I'm a fool. A complete fool." She dropped to her knees to reach for her chemise under the bed, affording him a tantalizing glimpse of her fetching bum.

Heedless of his own nakedness, he leaned over the edge of the bed. He couldn't let her leave. Not like this, mumbling and full of regrets. He tapped her bum. "Deb, it's all right."

She righted herself immediately, her cache of clothes protectively covering her breasts, her hand covering the place he'd touched. "All right?" she repeated as if he'd just asked her to kill the King. "My lord, it's not all right to be caught in a gentleman's room after a night of, of, of —"

"Passionate sex?" he offered helpfully.

"*Irresponsible* behavior," she corrected. She ran a frustrated hand through the unruly tangles of her hair and came to her feet. Last night, Tony had buried his fingers in that wonderful silken mass as he'd pushed himself deeper in her.

Immediately, his errant body responded to the mental image. What was it about this woman that attracted him like no other had?

Deborah noticed his erection — it would have been difficult not to — and groaned in exasperation. "*I* behaved like a common strumpet last night, but *you* are *hopeless.*"

"How the devil has this turned on me?"

Her answer was to give him her back and start to pull her dress over her head.

Tony didn't like being ignored. Not when he wanted to talk, and have sex. He grabbed the hem of the dress, refusing to let her don it.

For a second, they were locked in a tug-of-war. "Give me back my dress," she demanded through clenched teeth.

"Dress? I thought it was a hair shirt. And you may have regrets over last night, but I assure you, I have none."

"Of course," she agreed dryly.

His temper sizzled. He released his hold.

"What has come over you? We did nothing wrong. Nothing at all."

Her response was a short, "Ha!" as she scrambled to pull the dress over her head.

Tony rolled off the bed and snatched his breeches off the floor. He pulled them on without bothering with the buttons.

But he wasn't done with her. Not at all.

Barefoot, shoes, petticoat, and stockings in her arms, she started toward the door. Before she'd gone two steps, he swung her around and plopped her bottom down on the edge of the bed. "Very well," he said, lording his height over her. "We are both decent. Now tell me what is gnawing at your conscience. A hundred other couples did what we did last night, and they aren't flogging themselves for it this morning."

Deb couldn't even meet his eye — but grew even more agitated when she stared straight ahead at his unbuttoned breeches. With a sound of impatience, Tony did himself up. "There. Now, explain yourself."

The crease of a small frown appeared between her eyes. Her gaze met his briefly, then dropped to some point on his chest. "Those other couples are no doubt *married*. I behaved wantonly last night. Shamelessly. I — I owe you an apology for my uninhibited behavior. I assure you I am not usually of that mind. Now please, sir, let me leave."

"Sir? Why are you treating me like a

stranger?" The idea infuriated him.

She lowered her head, refusing to answer. He could have shaken her he was so frustrated — and then two huge tears rolled down her cheek and dropped to the floor between them.

His temper evaporated. "Deb?"

She averted her face. Another tear fell.

Tony felt like a bloody scoundrel. He dropped to his knees. "Deb, what we did was not terrible."

"I've betrayed my family, my upbringing. If anyone in Ilam were to ever discover —"

"The good folk of Ilam are snug in their beds on a day like this and not giving a care to what is happening in Derby."

"But I expected better of myself," she said, her voice hoarse. "If you only knew . . ." She didn't finish the thought but shut her eyes tight, holding back more tears.

Tony gathered her in his arms. She buried her face in his chest, struggling to not lose control — and had to give it up. He stroked her hair, holding her close, letting her cry.

Was he not more culpable than she? He was betrothed to another. Granted he and Lady Amelia had barely exchanged a half dozen words, but he was not the sort of man to take his commitments lightly.

The truth was, the spark that had flared into flames between him and Deborah last night startled him as much as it did her. He never lost control or forgot who and what he was.

That is, he hadn't, until he'd found himself in her arms. Even more astounding, he wasn't ready to leave her.

Nor did he want to inspect his motives too closely. When he married, he'd be faithful — unlike his parents. However, now . . .

"What we did was not wrong. You are taking the joy from it, Deb."

"I feel horrible," she muttered into his chest.

"You shouldn't. Ah, Deb, I'm no rake any more than you are a whore. The truth is, what happened between us last night, well, you aren't experienced to know . . . but it doesn't happen like that with just anyone. The attraction we felt toward each other was overpowering. We could not have stopped ourselves."

She raised her head. Her tears made her eyes brighter, her nose redder . . . and she looked adorable.

He ran his thumb down the smooth line of her cheek, brushing a tear away. "There's fire between us. A genuine passion. I can't explain why, but we fit well together . . ." He let his voice trail off. If he kept talking in that vein, he'd have her back on the bed with her skirts over her head — and she was too upset to forgive him for it.

The realization that he cared for her opinion was a revelation.

A knock sounded at the door. Almost with relief, he said, "Roald's here with breakfast.

Why don't you go behind the screen while I let him in?"

She nodded, the expression in her eyes thankful. He let her up, and she quickly did as he'd suggested.

Tony pulled on his shirt and answered the door. Roald stood there as he'd expected. "Miss Chalmers bid me to bring your breakfast, my lord. I'll have your bathwater warmed in half an hour." Tony nodded and indicated for the lad to put the tray on a small desk by the window. Roald left.

When Deb came out from behind the privacy screen he noticed she'd combed and plaited her hair with her fingers into one loose braid over her shoulder. A cool cloth had done much to repair her spirits. She appeared very young, very defenseless. An unexpected protectiveness welled up inside him.

He turned a comfortable padded chair toward the desk. "Would you care to sit?"

She didn't answer but moved to sit down. He pushed her chair in and sat in the hard-backed chair across from hers.

For a second, they were silent. She sat with her hands in her lap. He lifted the cover off one dish. To cover the awkward silence, he said cheerfully, "Ah, Mrs. Franklin has sent up sausages and buns. My favorite breakfast. Do you prefer coffee or tea?"

"Tea."

He poured her a cup, carefully keeping the

conversation centered on mundane things — the rain, her comfort, Mrs. Franklin's cooking. At the same time, he observed her closely, noticing things about her that unbridled lust had prevented him from seeing last night.

Slowly, with each sip of tea, she began to relax enough until she managed a bite or two of the bun he'd put on her plate. He admired her natural grace. Even stirring her tea, her movements were elegant. Hers was a timeless beauty. High cheekbones, dark, expressive eyes, an inborn graciousness, and golden skin.

He had to ask, "So you have Castilian blood in your background?"

Her gaze lifted in surprise. "My grandmother was Spanish. From Cadiz."

Here was a topic he could use to draw her out. He wanted to know more about her. He wanted to know everything. "And how did she end up in the wilds of the Peak District of all places?"

A becoming blush spread across her cheeks. "Actually, my mother's family is French — Lyonnaise. They were *émigrés*. They escaped the Terror," she said, referring to the French Revolution, "with nothing more than their lives. My mother met my father in London. He was studying law and brought her home with him."

Tony buttered a bun. "I imagine she had stories to tell."

"I didn't know her. She died of a fever

shortly after I was born. Her parents were dead, and she had no other family. What little I know is what my father told me. Unfortunately, he said they had been too busy being in love to learn much about her past history."

"And your sisters . . . ?" He offered half the bun to her, pleased when she accepted it.

"Are really my half sisters. I'm on my way to London to see one of them. She's recently been blessed by a child." She took a bite of the bun, then added as an afterthought, "My lord."

Tony hesitated. "My lord?"

"I'm neither deaf or addle-brained. I heard both Miss Chalmers and Roald this morning." She pinned him with those fathomless eyes. "Why are you pretending to be who you are not?"

"I am Mr. Aldercy. It's the family name." He leaned an elbow on the desk.

"But you have a title. One you didn't wish me to know. Why is that?"

"If you had known my title, would you have been as relaxed as you were last night?" he asked, turning her question on her so he wouldn't have to answer.

She blushed at his reminder of the previous night, but she didn't flinch from saying, "Some women would be flattered with a noble's attention."

"But not you," he said with certainty.

Her chin lifted with interest. "How do you know?"

"Because we're very much alike, you and I. We have our facades, the faces we put forth to the world. However, last night, we both let down our guard."

Her gaze dropped to her plate. "I fear I let down more than just my guard."

Unwilling to let her indulge in self-pity, he asked, "So, how did your mother fare in someplace as remote as the Peak District?"

Deb lifted her teacup. "She was never accepted. The Matrons of Ilam had already decided my father should marry a local girl. When he returned from his London studies with my mother, there were eyebrows raised. The Matrons do not like being thwarted."

"Ah, those formidable Matrons are everywhere, are they not?" he said in acknowledgment of another common bond. "Do they meddle as much in Ilam as they do in London?"

"Probably more so. And they were in all likelihood satisfied when my mother died and Father could marry the local girl who had been their original choice."

The bitterness in her declaration caught his attention. "Did they arrange your marriage?" he hazarded.

The muscles around her lips tightened. "My first and perhaps my next." She tapped a finger on the handle of her teacup, a thought not to her liking passing across her face. "They have decided I should marry again." She didn't hide her resentment.

"To a man you would not have chosen?" he ventured.

"Never," she returned fervently, then shook her head as if to dismiss the subject.

He didn't like her withdrawal. Where she was concerned, he had an insatiable curiosity and desire to know everything. He reached across the table, hooking her finger with his own, bringing her attention back to him.

Her gaze met his. "Talk to me," he said.

"I don't want to marry Parson Ames. I don't want to chase after his unruly children. They are hellions."

"Did the Matrons do as poor a job choosing your first husband?"

Beneath the table, she tapped her toe impatiently on the floor. "He was a good man. He took care of us. He . . ." Her voice trailed off as if she was reconsidering the weight of her words.

"What?" he prompted.

She didn't answer but sat up and poured herself another cup of tea.

Tony pressed. "He took care of you and what?"

"I don't want to speak ill of him." She reached for the cream. "My dissatisfaction was not his fault."

And she'd obviously not been in love with him or pining his death. The thought pleased Tony.

She poured cream into her tea, then paused.

"He took good care of my stepmother and saw my sisters married well. He wasn't a rich man but gave us what he could and let my sisters choose their own husbands. They married for love."

Love. There was that word again. But this time, Tony didn't mind discussing the issue.

"But you didn't marry for love," he stated, and she did not disagree.

"No. Perhaps that is why I — ?" She broke off her thought, a blush staining her cheeks.

"Why you came with me last night?" he suggested.

Her gaze met his. She shrugged, then nodded. "It wasn't Mr. Percival's fault. He was much older than I."

Tony had to ask. "How much older?"

She answered, "About thirty-seven years. I was sixteen; he was fifty-three."

He about fell out of his chair. "Good God! What possessed them to marry you off to such an old man?"

"He had money. We had nothing," she said, defending herself, her face reddening with embarrassment. "Father died leaving us barely two shillings to our name. My stepmother was sick with grief, and we needed a place to take care of her until she could face the world again. Mr. Percival wanted a young wife — he and his older children were fighting, and he hoped for another son to make up for the angry one. He approached Dame Alodia, and, before I knew it, I was married." Her voice grew pensive. "Of course, we didn't have children, and the majority of his estate went to his son by his first wife anyway. I received my widow's portion, of course, but Mr. Percival's true wealth was in his property."

Tony was shocked. No wonder she'd been naïve in bed. The old man had not shown her the joy in loving. "I'd wager he thought himself a lucky man."

"Well, on any household concern, Mr. Percival usually addressed my stepmother, not me. She passed away a year before he did, and he truly mourned her. He and I had little to say to each other nor did we entertain company. He didn't like to go out and about very much."

"So no parties. No visiting. No outside chance of you catching the eye of a younger man."

She blinked in surprise. "Are you saying he kept me close because of jealousy?"

"I'm certain he did." What man wouldn't want to keep a jewel such as she hidden from the covetous eyes of others? "So now that you are widowed, the Matrons have put their collective heads together and searched for the first expedient husband. Can't have an attractive unattached female roaming in their midst. Too much of a threat."

She appeared truly shocked. "You think they are jealous of me, too?"

"Absolutely. They want you safely tucked

away where their husbands won't be tempted to touch you."

His words startled a laugh out of her. "You are being absurd. You don't understand. My sisters are the beauties. They have blond hair, and their skin is the color of fresh cream. You wouldn't look at me twice if they were here."

"Do you truly believe what you've just said?" He'd never met a woman who didn't know exactly her impact on men — especially one as lovely as she. "Even after last night?" He reached across the table and pulled her hand to his lips.

"Last night was lust," she whispered huskily.

"Yes," he agreed, and kissed, then lightly sucked the tips of her fingers. She caught her breath in her throat. Her nipples tightened, pressing against the bodice of her dress.

A knock sounded at the door. It had to be Roald with the bathwater. Deb started to withdraw her hand, but Tony wouldn't let go.

Instead, he stood, his arousal obvious. "Tell me, Mrs. Percival, have you ever bathed with a man before?"

She was shocked. Her eyes widened but there was interest in them, too. "Can you do that?"

"Let's see," he suggested.

"It sounds wanton, my lord."

"It is very wanton," he assured her. "And call me by my given name, Tony. I believe we are beyond titles, don't you?" He rubbed his thumb across the inside of her palm. A small delicate contact and yet, it was enough to flame passion.

"Yes," she agreed softly. "We have gone beyond many things."

He smiled in triumph.

And they managed to bathe together very well.

Chapter Six

Deborah and Tony spent the day in a sensual haze, alternating between making love and reading a Maria Edgeworth novel Miss Chalmers had in her library. Her conscience was eased slightly by Miss Chalmers treating her with the same courtesy as the night before, which was very polite of her.

She almost *had* to be close to Tony. She craved his touch, his warmth, his presence. He was everything she had imagined a lover should be, attentive, thoughtful, and unfailingly careful that she should not be burdened with an out-of-wedlock child.

They also talked about anything and everything. She didn't think she'd ever talked to any one person so much in her life. But for all they had to say to each other they didn't mention the future or a moment beyond this bedroom. She refused to consider right or wrong. For once, she was doing exactly as she wanted. The experience was both thrilling and frightening.

What amazed her was that he seemed to feel the same way she did. When Miss Chalmers relayed the news that although the rain had finally stopped, the bridge would not be repaired until the morrow, neither expressed regret.

Their second night together, in the wee hours

of the morning as Tony slept soundly beside her, Deborah realized she could never marry Parson Ames. The thought of giving herself over to another loveless marriage was now intolerable. She didn't know what she was going to do when she returned to Ilam. Everyone, including Dame Alodia, expected her to fall in line.

But she couldn't.

Not now.

She was in love.

Her heart almost stopped beating at the thought. What in the world was she thinking?

She couldn't be in love. She'd just met Tony. He was, for all their laughter and shared confidences, still a stranger. And while she was considered gently raised, even looked upon as gentry in the Valley, they were of different classes.

Yet, there was also that irresistible pull between them. Every time he touched her, her resistance, common sense, and pride melted. She liked being this close to him, hearing him breathe, feeling the warmth of his skin.

She was beginning to know him as completely as she knew herself. She even trusted him, although she sensed he didn't trust easily. He was too guarded. Perhaps at one time he'd been betrayed —

His sudden cry surprised her. He jerked and then withdrew the hand across her waist to flail at the air. As he rolled onto his back, his movements grew increasingly agitated and sweat formed on his brow. He was having a nightmare.

Rising, Deborah shook his shoulder. "Tony, Tony, wake up. You are dreaming."

He mumbled something, then attempted to turn away from her. She cradled his face in her hands, forcing him to wake.

His eyes opened. They were red-rimmed and glassy. He stared as if he'd never seen her before.

"You had a nightmare," she whispered softly. He didn't respond. "Tony, what is it?"

His brow wrinkled in a frown. "Deb?" His hand touched her hair.

"Yes," she answered, encouraged.

He lay back. "My father's not here?"

She shook her head, confused.

Tony wet his lips. "I haven't had the dream in a long time. Not since school. I thought I'd laid that demon to rest." His arm came around her and pulled her close. His heart was racing against his chest.

"Did I say anything?" He seemed desperate to know.

"Nothing I could make out." She placed her palm against his forehead. He'd been sweating.

He turned away, his expression troubled.

Deborah placed a soothing hand on his arm. His muscles were tight with tension. "Sometimes, it helps if you talk about it."

He remained silent . . . and she feared she'd

overstepped some unseen boundary. She wished she could call back her words —

"He killed himself. I found him. He used to visit me in my dreams. He hasn't come in a long while. Now, he's back."

She rose to look down into his face. He was staring at the ceiling. The horror of his father being a suicide, of his being the one to find him chilled her. "Does he speak to you in these dreams?"

His gaze swung to hers in surprise. His expression softened, and he hugged her close. "No one has ever asked me that question." His hand stroked her hair. "Your directness caught me off guard. In my family we always pretend everything is all right. But it isn't, is it?" he whispered, his question more for himself than her.

"What do you see in your dream?"

His hand stopped moving. "I don't remember. I never remember."

Or else the dream was so disturbing, he erased it from his mind. She'd had dreams like that before but never a recurring one.

"Talk to me," she urged.

For a moment, he debated within himself. Then, "When I was in school, the other boys heard me cry out in the night. The headmaster warned me to be quiet at night. That's the only comment anyone made to me. 'Be quiet at night.' There wasn't even a funeral or a mourning period. His grave is unmarked and not on holy ground. It was as if he had never existed."

"How did you handle all of it?" she asked, feeling compassion for the child he'd been.

"I told myself to go forward. There's nothing to do but go forward."

She placed her hand on his chest. "Do you dream of a funeral?"

He shook his head. "I don't know. The devil in not remembering is that people wonder if I'm not a bit like him."

She heard what he didn't say . . . that he had those fears, too.

The line of his mouth flattened. He wasn't pleased by something. She slid down into the bed beside him, placing her arm across his chest. For long moments, she waited.

"He was a weak man."

"In what way?" she prodded.

He shrugged. "He gambled. Lost it all. My grandfather gambled, too, so by the time I came along, there was hardly anything left save a pack of hungry relatives."

"Who needed a roof over their heads?"

He nodded.

Deborah ran a thoughtful finger along the line of his collarbone. "I suppose we are much alike."

"How so?" he asked.

"We've both had to sell a bit of our souls for our families. Now I know why you under-stood."

He lightly touched her hair with his hand. "Aye."

"So, your father had debts and decided the easiest route was to take his own life?"

Tony gathered her in his arms and held her very tight. "It was more than that. He was unstable," he admitted, his voice quiet in the dark. "He'd have fits. He feared my mother would have him locked away."

Now, he was speaking to the heart of his dream. Deborah sensed it. "And you pray his madness is not in you?"

His hold on her tightened. He brushed his lips across her cheek. "Yes. My grandfather suffered, too." He paused. "He spent the last years of his life in an asylum."

Shocked, she struggled to sit up. "Do you ever behave as your father did?"

Tony's eyes were bright in the dark. "I won't let myself."

"But if the madness is in your blood, it could be out of your hands."

"Not if I fight it," he vowed. "Of course, they both showed signs in their midtwenties. Here I am, past thirty and of sound mind." He gave her a small smile. "I hope." The smile turned bitter. "Then again, maybe the rumors are right and I'm not my father's get. When your mother has lovers, people wonder."

Deborah placed her hand against the side of his face, overwhelmed with compassion and wanting to ease the pain she heard in his voice.

Now she grasped why Tony kept himself aloof. She understood pride . . . and the insecurity of sensing you are different from others. "What of your mother? Could she not relieve your concerns?"

"We don't speak," he said brutally.

Anger radiated from him — and in that moment Deborah knew who her lover was. "You're Lord Burnell." It was said the line was tainted and the rumors of his mother's infidelities, of the family's excesses were almost too fantastic to be believed. Even a rustic like herself had heard rumors.

He sat up, his back against the headboard. "You've heard of me?" Cynicism etched his words.

Deborah hesitated. "Not about you, but your parents." She didn't add she'd heard the son was rich. Very rich. His wealth, *true* wealth made her uncomfortable.

Suddenly, desperately, he reached for her hand and drew it to his lips. He placed a kiss in the center of her palm. "I'm sorry. We shouldn't have discussed this. I didn't mean to frighten you. There is nothing wrong. Nothing at all."

"I see no madness in you," she said truthfully . . . because she didn't. And the rumors didn't matter either. Nothing mattered, save the man, and she had faith in him. Simple, unwavering faith.

His hand came round her neck to draw her

head to his lips. "There isn't," he whispered. "Not when I'm with you." He rolled her onto the mattress and willingly she opened herself to him.

But later, she lay awake, thinking on what he'd said.

Late the next afternoon, while Deborah bathed, Tony went down to the sitting room to search the bookshelves for a new book. His quest was interrupted by Marmy's entrance. She relied heavily on her cane today.

"Roald went to the inn for news," she said, "and learned the bridge will be ready on the morrow."

Tony put the book he held in his hand back on the shelf, no longer interested in it. "The mails and stages will be running again."

"And just in time. The town is overcrowded with stranded passengers." There was a pause. "And you and Mrs. Percival must part."

He didn't like the thought. "Of course." The words sounded stiff even to his own ears.

"She's a lovely woman." Marmy crossed to her chair before the hearth and sat with a soft sigh of relief. "It's unfortunate you are already betrothed." There was a studied nonchalance in her words.

For the first time in days, he remembered Lady Amelia. He didn't like the reminder. "Mrs. Percival and I are —" He stopped. He didn't have words to describe their relationship.

They were enjoying themselves, but she was coming to mean more to him, so *much* more.

"My lord, you know I do not approve."

He had the good grace to wince at the harsh verdict. Marmy continued, "The heart is a delicate instrument. I know what it is like to have a heart broken, and I shall not be pleased if you break Mrs. Percival's."

What of mine? The unspoken question shocked him.

Marmy's watery gaze turned shrewd. "Have you informed her of your betrothal?"

He didn't answer.

She didn't need one. "I didn't think so." She picked up her embroidery. "Matters between men and women are never simple. But whatever you do, don't hurt her, or I shall be very angry."

"It isn't what you think," he said defensively.

"I only know what I observe," she responded.

"I wouldn't harm her. And I'll not let harm come to her."

Marmy smiled, the expression not meeting her eyes. "I shall hold you to your promise, Lord Tony," she replied quietly.

"But you distrust my motives?" he challenged.

"I fear you are a man, my lord."

Tony took a step toward the door and then another. He shook his head. "I've never given you cause to doubt me."

"I don't doubt you, my lord, but I fear you

don't realize what forces you are playing with so lightly."

An uneasiness settled between the blades of his shoulders, a sign that often told him she was right. And yet, what did she know? He and Deborah were mature adults. They understood what was between them. That was all that was important.

"I shall see you at supper," he said stiffly.

"I shall look forward to your presence."

With a bow, Tony turned and left, frowning. Her reminder that mere hours stood between now and Deborah's departure did not sit well. He'd known they would part, but he wasn't ready. Not yet.

He took the stairs two at a time, anxious to return to their haven. Inside their room, he saw she'd finished her bath and had opened a window to capture the rain-freshened breeze, which she used to dry her hair. It fell like a silk curtain to her waist. She looked up at his entrance and gifted him with a radiant smile.

No woman had a smile as wonderful as his Deb's. He shut the door. "Miss Chalmers says the post and the stages will run tomorrow."

"Oh." She slid down to sit in the chair by the window. "Tomorrow." Another beat of silence. "Of course."

"If I had my way, I'd keep you captive here forever."

His declaration broke the gloom. Deb laughed. "Forever? No, you'd tire of me soon.

If anyone was to hold another captive, I'd have to be the one to tie you to the bed."

"Now that sounds like an interesting proposition." He pushed away from the door. She rose and met him before he'd halfway crossed the room, her arms slipping around his waist.

He slid his fingers through her hair. She smelled of fresh air and the hint of summer. "Let us hold each other captive," he suggested, and kissed her.

Her tongue, no longer shy, met his and, within moments, they tumbled onto the bed.

But the atmosphere between them had changed. The time to part was coming. Their movements took on a new urgency, a deeper need. The knowledge that they would soon part left questions between them — questions with no easy answers.

Questions neither wanted to ask.

That evening they ate in the dining room with Marmy. She made no effort to hide her approval of Deb. She liked her. Knowing Marmy the way he did, Tony knew she would not particularly care for Lady Amelia.

After dinner, Marmy asked Deb if she played the pianoforte, and to Tony's surprise the answer was yes. How had they not talked about music? They seemed to have discussed everything else. At Marmy's urging, Deb gave them a small concert of country tunes. Her voice was a smooth, mellow alto.

"Sing with her, my lord," Marmy pleaded. To

Deb, she said, "He has a wonderful voice, but his talent embarrasses him."

"Please join me," Deb pleaded and he did . . . because he found it hard to deny her anything.

Self-consciously, he joined her in "Barbara Ellen." Their voices made for a rich harmony, and when they were done, when they'd finished singing, ". . . And around the top growed a true lover's knot/And around it twined sweet-briar . . ." they stared at each other in amazement.

Marmy smiled with a wisdom known to her alone. "I believe I will seek my bed."

Tony muttered a perfunctory good night, his gaze not leaving Deb's. The older woman didn't seem to expect anything more.

Once they were alone, he admitted, "I don't want you to leave me tomorrow."

"I don't want to go. But this is not the real world, my lord. And we must each go our own way."

"Of course," he agreed, catching himself before he said something silly. Still, he needed to have something binding between him. A link, a possibility. From a drawer in a writing desk in the room, he pulled out one of his cards. In slanted print was the single word, *Burnell*. On the back, he wrote, *If ever you need me*. He offered the card to her.

"What is this?" she asked.

"Wherever you are, whenever you wish, send this to me, and I will be by your side as quickly as I am able."

"It's not necessary —" she started, but he cut her off.

"Please."

She took the card, the expression in her dark eyes somber. "Very well." She ran a finger over the engraved name, her head bowed. He wished he knew what she was thinking. She raised her gaze to meet his, opened her mouth to speak, then seemed to think differently of it.

That was fine. He understood. He didn't have the right words either.

Instead, he took her hand and led her upstairs. There, in the privacy of their room, their special haven, he removed the pins from her hair.

His Deb. His beautiful, willing Deb.

"I wish I'd met you sooner," he whispered, and he meant the words. These past three days had changed him. He was not quite certain how, but he felt different. An emptiness had been filled, a loneliness relieved.

"But we must part," she said sadly. "We knew it wasn't forever."

Forever. The word lingered in the air around them.

He buried his nose in her hair, drinking in the scent of her. With his lips, he found the curve of her ear. She laughed softly and stepped closer into his arms, fitting their bodies together.

He wanted to be in her. Now.

Swinging her up in his arms, he carried her

to the bed. Her arms came up around his neck, her lips locked with his.

They both knew their time was short. They practically tore the clothes off each other. And when they were naked, there was no hesitation. His need was hard, ready. He thrust into her with a demanding hunger.

She was hot, willing, tight and so perfect. She gave herself with abandon. Her soft cries of pleasure and the way she touched him, encouraging him, begging him for more drove him into a frenzy. She cried his name, pulling him closer, deeper . . .

He had to fill her, to give her all of him. He was done denying himself. He didn't want to let her go. Not without binding her to him.

So, in a single, selfish act, he did what Nature had intended. He buried himself to the hilt and lost himself in her. The pleasure of his release came in wave after damning wave. It was heaven.

And it wasn't until he settled back down to earth, that he realized exactly what he'd done.

What he'd *wanted* to do.

Chapter Seven

Deborah felt Tony release himself deep within her — and she wanted to cry out in joy. The act was complete. Whole.

She hugged him to her, their hearts beating as one, and she never wanted to let him go. Two had become one.

Tony moved first. He came up on his elbows and looked down at her, his gaze dazed. She lifted a hand to soothe back the sweep of his hair over his brow which furrowed with concern.

"I didn't," he whispered.

He rolled off her in a trice, coming up to sit on the edge of the bed, his back to her. Embers glowed in the hearth. Their light cast his long shadow sinisterly across the room's walls. He ran a hand through his mussed hair. "I've compromised you. I shouldn't have, but I did."

The implications of what they'd done became reality.

He'd always been so careful, but she'd pushed this night, knowing it would be their last.

Dear Lord, help her.

Deborah pulled the sheet over herself to cover her nakedness. Instinctively, she slid her hand down over her abdomen. A baby could already be forming there. A spark of life created by them during these last few moments of passionate madness.

His gaze followed the movement of her hand. The line of his jaw hardened. "I'm sorry, Deb. I would not for the life of me have —" His voice broke off. He looked away.

And she understood. Or thought she did.

He stood and began pulling on his breeches. She looked around the room. This magical time now appeared to her as it truly was — nothing more than a chance meeting with a man she barely knew. She'd been deceiving herself. Rationalizing her behavior. Justifying her actions by believing *she* was in *love*.

Deborah went very still, embarrassed by how easily she'd duped herself into such shameless behavior. What if she had a child? She could not raise it in Ilam. Dame Alodia and the other Matrons would shun it. Already a fierce protectiveness welled up inside her.

Tony leaned across the bed. "It was my fault, Deb. Mine."

"Not completely. I . . . " She drew a breath for courage. "I should have stopped." *She should never have begun.* "What am I going to do?"

He took her hand and kissed the back of it. The gesture was reassuring. "*We* are going to do what we must," he said. "Things happen for a reason in this life. If anything comes of this night, I shall take care of you."

She dropped her gaze to their clasped hands. "Then, you are not upset?" she asked, cautious.

"I should have been more careful, but then, this means you'll stay with me," he said.

His words filled her with indescribable happiness. "Stay with you," she repeated. He loved her! He *must*.

Suddenly, the world contained a million wondrous possibilities, all of them centering around him. And the best of all was that she loved him. She allowed herself to see the blazing truth of her feelings . . . and to confess them to him. But as she opened her mouth to speak, he cut her off.

"You don't mind, do you, Deb?"

"No, in fact, I —"

"You'll have my protection, Deb. Anything you desire will be yours. *Carte blanche*."

Carte blanche. The words rang in her ears like an alarm bell. *Carte blanche* wasn't marriage. He was asking her to be his mistress.

Tony scooted across the bed closer to her, his eyes alive with his excitement over the idea. "In fact, I don't care if there is a baby or not. I like the idea of my wealth and power protecting you. The Matrons of Ilam will never push you around again." He chuckled at his own joke.

But she heard no humor in his offer. He thought she was the sort of woman who would like to be kept. Like a candle quickly snuffed, all the joy in her heart left her. She, Deborah Seaton Percival, raised to know better, had been played for a fool. She prayed there was no child, because she would never accept his offer.

But he didn't seem to notice her sudden withdrawal. "A house, horses, money, whatever you want." He pressed his lips against her hand. "I want you under my protection, and not with some fat parson and his nasty children. You can travel with me, to London during the Season and then back to Yorkshire for the rest of the year. I'll buy you homes in each place. And we don't have to stay in England. I've wanted to see Italy, to tour Venice and see the cradle of civilization. I've even wished to travel to Egypt. How exotic is that? You'll come with me, wouldn't you, Deb? You and me, together." He laced his fingers with hers.

He was offering so much and yet, was not willing to give her his name. For all his fine posturing about her beauty and intelligence, he did not consider her good enough to marry.

Her humiliation was complete.

If one of her sisters had done what she had done, she would have been bitterly disappointed in her. She would even have told the erring sister she was fortunate to have received an offer of *carte blanche* for no *decent* man would ever touch her. Not even the desperate Parson Ames.

For many long years, even through a loveless marriage, Deborah had nursed and trusted the conviction that someday she'd find the kind of deep-seated love that her father had held for her mother — a love that crossed all barriers and asked for nothing in return. Perhaps that would explain why she had been so susceptible to Tony's advances.

However, while she'd been falling into love, he'd been satisfying his lust. Why else would he have just made such a dishonorable offer?

Pride had gotten her through bad times before. Pride would see her through this. But she would never let Tony — no, she amended, *Lord Burnell* know her true feelings. She'd never reveal that, like a green country girl, she'd fallen for the lord of the manor.

"I'm not certain I wish to be tied down." She rolled over on her side, away from him.

"Tied down?" he repeated dumbly. There was a long pause. "Do you mean, you don't want a house?"

His voice held a note of uncertainty. She drew a deep, steadying breath, and announced boldly, "I don't want a man."

Hers was a fatal thrust, and, for a long moment, silence reigned. She bit her bottom lip to prevent herself from explaining or from saying something she would later regret. She held tight to her pride.

He spoke. "Well." He blew air out of his cheeks. "That was a blow." He patted the bed. "What was this, fun and games?"

She hardened her heart. She could not afford to let down her guard. "It was," she drawled, "until you violated our agreement. You said you could prevent an accident."

Abruptly, he rolled off the bed onto his feet. She heard him pace toward the fire. He stopped. "You're angry at me."

"I am not."

"Oh, yes, you are. Something has happened here. Ten minutes ago, no, as little as five minutes ago you were crying out my name and now, you've turned your back to me."

Deborah punched her pillow. "I've never cried out your name."

The mattress gave as he crawled back onto the bed. "Yes, you did."

Well, perhaps she had. She'd not admit it though. "I'm tired." She gave an exaggerated yawn and closed her eyes.

He climbed on top of her, up on all fours, and looked down. She could feel him staring at her face. She refused to open her eyes. He nudged her back with his knee. "My offer of *carte blanche* is what set you off, wasn't it?"

She didn't speak.

He slid down, cradling her back to his chest. He kissed her hair. "Deb, it's the only sensible thing to do."

Sensible? Her heart was breaking.

Wrapping the warm heat of his body closer around hers, he moved a hand down to her abdomen. "You might already be carrying my child," he whispered in her ear. "You should at least stay under my protection until we are certain." He nibbled her neck.

For once in her life, Deborah didn't want to be reasonable. She didn't know why she was disappointed. He'd been honest with her from the beginning. She was the one who'd allowed herself to foolishly believe there was something more could evolve between them.

"Deb, I made a mistake, but I don't want you to suffer." He snuggled her backside. "You can't leave me. Not like this."

"I must." The words were the most difficult she'd ever spoken.

"Then you don't care?"

She hated the genuine disappointment in his voice and had to bite her lip to keep her silence. Time was measured by the beating of her heart in her throat.

He sat up. "I see," he said soberly.

Did he? She prayed, and waited . . . hoping for more. *Please give me more.*

Instead, he rose from the bed. She opened her eyes and turned to watch him cross to the window. He braced his hands on the windowsill and stretched out his arms, his gaze on the floor.

"Tony?"

"You have my card. If ever you need me, send it with your whereabouts, and I'll move heaven and earth to be by your side."

He did not look at her. He said nothing about love.

Nor did he return to bed. Instead, he stayed

by the window, staring out into the night.

Deborah did not speak further. She still had her pride. It would have to be enough.

She closed her eyes and pretended to be asleep . . . but sleep was a long time in coming.

Tony didn't know how he'd made it through the night. He sat watch by the window. He was so attuned to her every nuance that he'd known exactly when she'd finally gone to sleep. But he didn't know how he was going to let her go in the morning.

Since his father's death, he had carefully constructed walls around his feelings that protected him with a facade of indifference. A man needed a clear mind and an iron soul to navigate the world.

With Deb, he'd let those walls come down. She'd managed to slip under his defenses, to make him care.

And then, after he'd offered her everything in his power to give, she had casually rejected him with nothing more than a shrug of her shoulder.

A rooster was crowing the hour before dawn before he could bring himself to turn back to the room. He took a moment to dress. He didn't know if he had the courage to cross the room and wake her —

She stretched. She was an early riser, as was he. The morning before he'd made love to her as she woke. Now, he leaned against the window frame, wishing she wasn't so enticing, so innocently beautiful. High cheekbones, those full lips begging for a kiss, firm breasts. He wanted her now, in spite of her rejection.

His father had been played for a fool by a woman, too.

Sitting up, she started to smile a sleepy greeting, then the memory of what had transpired during the night returned.

Her smile died. She had the good grace to blush and pull the covers around her nakedness. She tossed her hair back as if challenging him.

He pushed away from the window. "I'd best give you privacy to get dressed. I'll send Roald to the inn to book your passage." He himself was already dressed save for shaving. He picked up his razor and kit and left the room.

Deb didn't take long to ready herself. Tony waited for her downstairs. Roald had hitched up the curricle, but Tony decided *he* would take Mrs. Percival to meet the mail coach. He didn't know why he wished to linger over seeing her off. Some perversity in his nature, perhaps.

When she came downstairs, she was wearing the bonnet she'd had on when they'd first met. The brim had been reblocked but was still slightly askew. He could buy her a dozen bonnets, one to match every outfit — but then, she'd refused his offer.

At the bottom of the stairs, she smiled, the

expression hesitant as if she wished a truce between them.

He didn't return her smile. His feelings were in too much of a turmoil. But he'd not let her see that.

Marmy wasn't up yet. The damp had been hard on her rheumatism. Mrs. Franklin came out in the hall from the dining room, wiping her hands on the apron tied around her ample girth. "You'll be wanting something to eat before you go," she said.

Deb shook her head. "I'm fine."

"Eat," he insisted sourly. After all, she might be carrying his child, even if she refused his largesse.

"I'm fine," she said firmly, refusing to look at him. Instead, she addressed Mrs. Franklin. "I need to settle my account with Miss Chalmers."

Mrs. Franklin's gaze slid to Tony. He took over. "You have no account," he said. "There is no charge."

Deb's back stiffened. "I will pay my bill."

"There is no bill," he answered.

She whirled on him. "I'd rather discuss the issue with the owner of the house."

"You are," he said, and enjoyed seeing the surprise on her face. "This is my house. I provided it for Marmy."

The color drained from her cheeks, and he realized a hollow victory. "Very well," she said in small voice. "I need to be leaving."

"I'm driving you."

She paused midstep. She didn't like the idea one bit, but she didn't question him. Instead, she took a moment graciously to thank Mrs. Franklin for her good service as well as to tip both her and Roald handsomely.

Tony held the door open for her. She sailed out like the Queen, pulling her gloves on as she passed so she wouldn't have to look at him. Roald started to carry her portmanteau, but Tony took it from him. He followed her down the steps.

Deb waited by the carriage, ready to give him a piece of her mind. "You should have told me outright that you owned this house. The impropriety of my staying under *your* roof —" She finished with an exasperated sound.

He helped her up into the seat next to the driver's and leaned in, his voice low. "Among all the things we did *to* each other and *for* each other these past days, your being under my roof pales in bawdy significance."

Her answer was a choking sound as she swallowed her fury. After that, she closed herself in, arms crossed against her chest, all the way to the inn.

Tony was willing to let her stay that way. Let her be tiffy the whole journey to London for all he cared — but the sight of the waiting mail coach in the puddle-filled inn yard, gave him pause. Wisps of fog rose from the ground. Travelers were anxiously boarding the coach while the horses stamped, eager to be off.

He reined in his team . . . and risked one last chance. "Deb —"

"No, don't say anything." She was still angry. "You don't understand how I feel. You don't care —"

"I do care! I've offered you everything I own."

Her clear gaze met his. "Except — ?" she prodded.

"There is no 'except.' I don't want you to leave."

There, he'd made a strong declaration . . . but it obviously wasn't enough for her. However, instead of biting his head off, a great sadness come into her eyes.

"I *must* leave." She placed her gloved hand over his. "I —" She stopped and drew a deep breath. He waited, anxious for what she had to say. "I won't ever forget you." She leaned over and kissed him on the cheek.

A small peck.

After what they'd been together.

"I don't understand," he ground out.

"I know," she answered evenly. Before he registered her intent, she grabbed her portmanteau and hopped to the ground.

"Good-bye, my lord." She would have turned and strode away, but he stopped her.

"You have my card?"

She shifted the weight of the portmanteau from one hand to the other, then nodded reluctantly.

"You *will* contact me if you need me, won't you?" He had to know.

Suddenly, she was back beside the carriage. She reached up, hooked her hand around his neck, and pulled him down for a hard, bruising kiss. Right there in the middle of the inn yard for the whole world to see. "Thank you," she whispered, then turned and hurried away.

He sat, dumbfounded. Did any man understand women? She paid her fare and climbed into the coach. Within what seemed like seconds, the driver and guard climbed aboard. The horn was blown; the whip snapped over the team of horses' heads. The coach pulled out of the yard, heading toward London.

He felt as if an important, irreplaceable part of himself were leaving. He told himself his feelings were from his concern that she might be carrying his child. If so, he would have responsibilities to her.

But his rationalizing did not ease the fact that she'd turned his life upside down, then walked away.

He slapped the reins and drove home. By the time he'd handed the curricle over to Roald and entered the hall, he'd halfway convinced himself Deb's parting was all for the best. He had his life mapped out. Soon, he'd be married to the most beautiful woman in London, and her father would further his ambitions. Once the marriage took place, he'd never be sniffed at or publicly "cut" again.

The chemistry he shared with Deb had been an aberration. To celebrate her leaving, he opened a bottle of whiskey and sat down in front of the fire in the sitting room, determined to obliterate all memory of Deborah Percival.

Of course, the devil of it all was that he was here alone . . . and she'd left him for London with little more than a thank-you.

Tony woke to find Marmy sitting in the chair opposite his. A fire burned in the grate. His mouth tasted like cotton. A headache pounded his brain.

"How long was I asleep?" he mumbled.

"About nine hours."

He sat up and eyed the level of the whiskey decanter on the table beside his chair. He'd made better headway than he'd thought, but it wasn't worth such a wicked headache.

"You shouldn't drink before your breakfast, my lord. Bad form. Tea?" Marmy poured a cup from a pot on the table next to her chair. "It's black tea, and I believe it will make you feel right side up immediately."

"I need something."

"Breakfast?" Marmy chided sweetly.

He frowned his answer and took the cup from her. The hot brew did much to relieve his headache.

"You let her go?"

He didn't need to ask Marmy whom she meant. Deb. The house felt empty without her.

"I asked her to stay. She wouldn't. On second thought, is there something to eat?" he asked, changing the subject. Rising, he walked toward the dining room. He didn't want to jaw about Deb any longer. He'd already wasted enough time. There was no sense in his delaying his journey to Yorkshire. He had business to attend, crops to inspect, people depending on his decisions. People who wouldn't shut him out on a whim.

"I'll have Mrs. Franklin make something for you," Marmy said, following him. She gave an exaggerated sigh. "Well, it is for the best Mrs. Percival left. After all, you will soon be a married man."

Tony didn't want to talk about this.

"And it was obvious she was in love with you," Marmy continued. "Silly emotion, love. Makes people do foolish things. You are much better off without her." She started out of the sitting room.

It took a moment for her words to sink into his brain. He grabbed her arm, pulling her back. "Love?" He shook his head. "She didn't love me. She left me. She was glad to leave."

"Do you really think so?" Marmy quizzed. "I suppose. But then, we'll never really know, will we? She's on her way to London, and you are left here drinking whiskey."

"I was thirsty," he said abruptly. He was no child to be questioned for his actions.

"Ummhmmm," she agreed, undeterred by

his anger. "Do you even know where she is in case you wish to contact her again?"

He made an impatient sound. The sudden realization that he hadn't asked where she was going did not set well with him. "She has family in London. She went to see them."

"But you do not know their address? What of their names?" Her disappointment was clear.

Tony raised his hands and then let them drop in defeat. "She did not want me." There, he could not be more brutally truthful.

"Funny, but I had the opposite impression," Marmy said. "Oh, well, I suppose if you *wished* to find her, you could. You have the resources, the money. You should put them to good use." Now *she* was the one to change the subject. "I'm going to the kitchen to consult with Mrs. Franklin about dinner. I'll have Roald bring you some cold beef and toast. That should tide you over." She started down the hall.

Tony should have let her go, but he couldn't. "You don't understand," he called after her. "I offered Deb *carte blanche*. She refused me."

Marmy jerked to a halt in her tracks. *"Carte blanche?"* she repeated incredulously. "And not marriage?"

"I can't marry. I'm promised to another."

"You've already pointed the fact out to me, my lord . . . several times. I'm old but not feeble-witted. You meet a woman that you are instantly attracted to, that you can't keep your hands off —"

"Ah, there see? What kind of morals can she have?"

"The same as yours, my lord," Marmy said crisply. "And I see no morality in marrying a woman for her money alone. Especially a woman whose eye color you can't remember."

"Blue," he lied. "Lady Amelia's eyes are blue."

"You are a fool, Lord Tony."

He could not answer her. He feared she might be right.

She made as if to go on her way, but had one last bit of advice. "You may not countenance this, Lord Tony, but a woman has pride, too. Your offer was an insult to one such as Mrs. Percival. Oh, please understand, I did not approve of what games the two of you played. However, I sensed she was behaving out of character and was unselfish enough to sacrifice herself. Someone, something has to snap sense into you — or else you *will* end up like your parents."

"Never." He backed away. "That will not happen."

Marmy followed him. "Lord Tony, please. I know how hard it is for you to let down your guard. I allowed you and Mrs. Percival to —" She paused for the right word.

"Play games," he said flatly, using her earlier description.

"But they weren't really games, were they?" she countered. "It's been a long time since I

136

saw you trust another person even a little."

"And I was dealt handsomely for it, wasn't I? I made a bloody fool of myself."

"Love does that to each of us at one time or another."

"Love?" He reeled from the word. Love was a fool's game, a dangerous emotion. It had been the impetus behind his father's madness. "I'm not in love with her."

Marmy knew when she'd gone too far. She stood silent, her hands folded in front of her. He didn't know why she didn't speak. He was certainly not going to say more on the subject.

"Very well, I understand," she said quietly at last, her disappointment clear. "You've already delayed your trip to Alder House long enough. Perhaps it was best the two of you parted."

He grunted an answer. He sensed no matter what he said, she'd not believe him. Love. What a stupid idea!

Her smile was sad and sweet, as if she could read his mind. "Let me see to supper, my lord." She headed toward the back of the house and the kitchen.

But Tony didn't move. He was thinking.

Love might not be his motive . . . but he certainly wanted Deb. What if Marmy was right, and she had fallen in love with him? Her mood had changed after he'd made his offer. Marmy's theory about Deb's pride made sense.

His business could keep him in Yorkshire for several weeks. Besides, if Deb discovered she was with child, she would need him, and it might take weeks, months even, before he'd receive word. Important months.

He could not leave her alone in the world. Especially if Marmy was right, and Deb's feelings ran deeper than she'd led him to believe. After all, he'd hidden behind pride most of his life . . . and there was that one last kiss she'd given him. What had she really been trying to say to him?

He went down to the kitchen, where he found Marmy inspecting a huge ham with Mrs. Franklin. Roald was putting a plate of cold beef on a tray.

"I'm leaving," he announced. "Wrap up the beef in some bread and I'll take it with me."

"Leaving at this hour of the afternoon, my lord?" Mrs. Franklin said.

"It's not yet four o'clock, and I don't mind traveling at night."

"But the Yorkshire road might be difficult after all the rain," Marmy reminded him.

"It's not to Yorkshire I'm going, but to London." He caught the triumphant gleam pass between the two women, but he was too distracted to care.

He had to find Deb.

He *must* find her.

And when he did, he was going to demand she explain that last kiss.

Chapter Eight

Deborah's first impression of London was of the noise and crowds on top of crowds. There was such a din, a cacophony of what seemed to be thousands of voices shouting, arguing, haggling and of twice that many animals' snorting, braying, barking. All was punctuated by the rumble of coach after coach, cart after cart.

Staring out the coach's window, Deborah marveled she'd never seen such numbers before or so many shapes, sizes, and colors. A man smoking a pipe walked up the street with, of all things, a parrot on his shoulder. A grand lady whose bulk threatened to overflow her sedan chair harangued her carriers for not being more fleet-footed. Small boys darted their way through the adults, one of them deftly picking a pocket as Deborah watched from the coach. She started to cry out but was already too late. The crowds swallowed both thief and victim, and the victim was none the wiser.

But Deb wasn't quite ready to handle any adventure. From the moment the stage had pulled out of the yard in Derby, she'd been weepy and depressed. The other passengers had made commiserating noises, certain she must be mourning a close death.

In a way she was.

The hardest thing she'd ever done in her life was to walk away from Tony's offer. The temptation had been great, and her pride was now cold comfort.

She couldn't wait to be in Lizbet's comforting presence, so she could have a good cry in peace — not that she'd *ever* tell her sister what she'd done. Oh, no, it was her secret and hers alone.

In the London inn yard, a fellow passenger, an older woman with grandchildren, noticed Deborah's confusion and took pity. She helped Deborah hire a hack to drive her to Lizbet and Edmond's house located in a modest but genteel area off of New Road. The driver charged an outrageous fare of twelve shillings. At those prices, Deborah feared, her small horde of funds would not last.

Twilight's long shadows darkened the street by the time she wearily climbed the step up to Lizbet and Edmond's door. No candles shone a welcome in the windows, not that she'd expected them. She'd written to tell Lizbet to expect her but she'd had no way to pinpoint a date, let alone an exact time.

She pulled the bell. The sound echoed overloud. She waited. When she heard no footfall on the other side of the door she wondered if Lizbet was home. She pulled out her sister's letter and rechecked the address.

Deborah pulled the bell again. Nothing. Her heart hammered in her throat. Perhaps she could approach one of the neighbors, but all of their houses appeared locked up tight. The people who walked past her moved with a sense of purpose, their heads low, avoiding any eye contact.

However, when she reached for the bell a third time, the door opened. With grateful sigh, Deborah fell through the entrance, but came to an abrupt halt.

She had been expecting a servant. Instead, she almost didn't recognize this woman for her sister. Her memory of Lizbet was of a laughing girl with merry blue eyes and hair the golden color of ale. This woman was shadowy and sad. Her hair hung to her waist in a single plait as if she'd not had time to style it, her skin was pale. She held a baby at her shoulder.

"Deborah? Is it really you?"

"Yes." Deborah nodded inanely, trying to adjust her mental picture of Lizbet with this new creature. "Did I arrive at a bad time?"

"You couldn't have arrived soon enough!" Lizbet threw her free arm around her sister's shoulders. "I've missed you. I've missed *all* of you. Tell me about Rachel and the Valley and all my friends. I want to hear the news. It's been so long since I've talked to anyone who could answer me with intelligence." She jiggled the baby on her shoulder as she spoke, her movements nervous.

"Well, first, let us close the door," Deborah said.

"Of course," Lizbet agreed, shutting it . . . and what little light had been was cut off into a murky gloom. "Here, hang your cloak on this hook and let's go into the front drawing room." She walked ahead of Deborah into a room off the right of the short hall. No candle burned there, either, and there was no cheery fire in the grate. Nor did Lizbet offer to light any.

Deborah untied the ribbons of her bonnet, deciding to keep any comments to herself — for the moment. She held out her hands. "Here, let me see my niece."

Carefully, Lizbet passed over the baby. Then, with a weary sigh, she collapsed on the settee, but her hands were still fidgety. She touched her hair, her face. She crossed and uncrossed her arms.

The child was asleep. She smelled of milk, and the wisps of blond curls gave her the air of an angel.

Deborah's maternal instinct swelled inside of her. She could be pregnant even at that moment . . . and, for the first time since leaving Derby, the idea did not give her distress.

"She's beautiful. What did you name her?" Deborah asked, charmed.

"Pamela."

"After Mother?" Deborah said with a smile, referring to her stepmother. "She would be pleased."

"Yes, I thought so." Lizbet pulled her braid over her shoulder and rubbed the ends.

"Is there a candle we can light?"

Lizbet roused herself. "Candle?" She shook her head. "Edmond doesn't think we should spare the expense in the front parlor. In fact, I'd been heading to bed when you arrived. If I can't burn a candle, there is no sense sitting in the dark."

Deborah slipped out of her cloak, holding the baby carefully. She laid the cloak over one of the two chairs across from the settee. The room was threadbare — no colorful rugs or pictures on the wall. The atmosphere was as somber as a funeral's.

She sat in the other chair and placed the sleeping child in her lap. "Lizbet, can you talk to me about what is happening?"

Her question opened a floodwall of emotion. "Deborah, everything is wrong, wrong, wrong!" Her sister choked back sobs. "Edmond doesn't know you are coming . . . He'd told me not to write . . . He will be very angry —"

"Then I shall endeavor to soothe his nerves." The baby had startled at her mother's voice, and Deborah rubbed a soothing hand across her back to lull her back to sleep.

"Yes, yes, you will. You'll make everything right. You always do." Lizbet continued, "He didn't want anyone to know how desperate we are. He's embarrassed and *I* know how he feels, but I couldn't go on this way. I want to go home, Deborah, but he refuses to consider the idea. Everyone in Ilam believes he has this wonderful position, and he doesn't want anyone to know he's been sacked."

"What happened?" Deborah asked.

"The duke doesn't want him. He threw Edmond out without so much as a by-your-leave!"

"No explanation at all?" Deborah was doubtful. After all, a duke should be a reasonable man.

"None!" Lizbet came to her feet and began pacing the room. Color was returning to her cheeks.

"Surely, Edmond has an idea."

Lizbet stopped. "He believes he was terminated over a speech the duke gave to the House of Lords. The duke insisted on writing it himself and it contained some rather lurid ideas about the place of the middle classes. Suffice it to say, the speech was not well accepted. He became the butt of many embarrassing cartoons. The cartoonists in this city are vicious and the populace takes up their taunts and, well, Society is cruel."

"Was the speech Edmond's fault?"

"No! He said he was surprised when the duke said some of the things he did. However, afterward, when everyone laughed at him, the duke blamed everything on Edmond. He painted him quite black to all his acquaintances. Deborah, before the incident, we were quite popular. Now, invitations have stopped coming in. Our friends have deserted us."

"I assume Edmond is looking for a new position?"

"Yes, but the duke will not give references. Deborah, my husband is *determined* to stay in London. He feels his future is here. But we have *no money!* What little we've had extra, Edmond has needed to keep up appearances while he searched for a new position. As you can see, things *are not good.*"

Lizbet waved her hand to encompass the room. "We've sold all the furnishings. I've even sold the jewelry Mother left me. I had no choice. Now, there is nothing left, and I don't know how we are going to eat or how I shall care for Pamela." Tears rolled from her eyes. "Deborah, I'm a terrible mother. I know nothing about babies. She's quiet now but before you arrived, she'd been crying and crying, and I don't know what to do for her!"

As if to give truth to her words, Pamela woke, doubled a tiny fist, and let out a complaint. It was a weak sound, and it alarmed Deborah more than any of the words she'd heard from her sister.

She lifted the baby in her arms. Pamela took one good look at the stranger and cried in earnest.

Lizbet was right, she did have healthy lungs.

"Perhaps she is hungry?" Deborah said, bouncing the baby a bit to make her happy. "Have you nursed her recently?"

"I can't nurse!" Lizbet wailed, the sound

joining the baby's. "When she was born, Edmond said it wasn't the thing to do, so we hired a wet nurse."

"A wet nurse? Was there something wrong with your milk?"

"You don't understand," Lizbet countered. "In London, Fashion is everything."

"And it is out of fashion to feed your baby?" Deborah was incredulous.

"It's out of fashion to nurse your *own* baby," Lizbet corrected.

Deborah hummed her opinion, deciding to keep the words to herself.

Lizbet heard the criticism. She crossed her arms. "You wouldn't understand. You're from the country. Besides, what does it matter now? My milk's dried up."

No wonder Pamela screamed. Hungry and no mother to comfort her. "So what are you feeding the baby?"

"We have a goat."

"A what?"

"A goat. Edmond says a nanny's milk is much like a mother's, and Pamela quite likes it, but I'm not good at milking goats. They don't like me. You know that."

Yes, Deborah did know Lizbet always avoided tending animals. In fact, the idea of her sister managing a London household alone was beyond Deborah's imagination.

"Edmond milks Nanny before he leaves in the morning, but Pamela was very hungry today," Lizbet said.

"So the child can't eat until her father comes home." Deborah was dumbfounded, but not surprised. Her precious youngest sister had always been coddled by everyone. Deborah decided to take charge. "Take me to the goat, and I'll milk it." The baby had to have something to eat.

Her words were a tonic to Lizbet. She threw her arms around Deborah. "I knew you'd make everything all right. Edmond may be furious, but everything will be much better, and then he'll be happy."

Deborah wasn't so certain. Poor Pamela was whimpering in her unhappiness. "Take me to the goat and light a candle before I trip and kill myself."

Dutifully, Lizbet did, using a candle stub from several on the hallway table. Then, to Deborah's surprise, Lizbet did not go outside but started down a narrow set of stairs leading to the kitchen. Deborah had never been one to enjoy going down to the root cellar. The kitchen was not much larger than one, although the ventilation was better . . . which was good — since in the middle of the room was a nanny goat, a gray-spotted beast with a loud bleat and stomping hooves, standing in a pile of muck and surrounded by dirty dishes.

The whole kitchen disgusted Deborah. Dishes were stacked waiting to be washed. The air was stale and sour. But then, Lizbet had never been good at keeping house either.

Nor did Nanny appear too happy about the situation.

Deborah held her breath. "Lizbet, goats do not belong in the house." She handed the baby to her sister. Pamela was so upset she was sucking on her wee fist.

"Edmond doesn't want the neighbors to know we don't have a wet nurse."

"Won't they assume you don't have any servants *at all* when *you* answer the door?" Deborah was growing tired of Edmond's edicts.

"I never have to answer the door," Lizbet said, swaying to and fro with the baby on her hip. "It's not like we have many visitors."

"Where is a pail?"

Her sister handed her one that was none too clean. At least, Deborah would have a project to keep her from mooning over Tony. She cleaned the bucket and then set to work milking the goat. "Boil some water for tea, will you?" she tossed over her shoulder. will need fortification."

Somberly, Lizbet did as bid although she warned Deborah they'd have to scrape the tea drawer for enough leaves. Deborah was at a point she'd drink hot water if need be.

Not much later, while Lizbet fed the baby, Deborah shoveled out the goat's muck. A set of stairs led up to a small yard, and that's where she tossed it. Tomorrow, she'd worry about the niceties outside. Back downstairs, she attacked the dishes. There was no doubt a pile of laundry to be done and Lord only knew what other house chores awaited her. She also wondered what her sister had been eating. In the pantry, all she found was a half-sliced loaf of bread and some cheese. She prepared a serving for both of them.

"I'm so happy you are here," her sister said, polishing off her bread and cheese, the baby in her lap. "You can help me convince Edmond to return to Ilam."

Her suggestion sounded like an excellent idea. "Where is he now?"

"Oh, out meeting important people who can help him," Lizbet said vaguely. "He leaves every morning for the government houses. Sometimes, someone invites him to supper at his club, and he must go."

Deborah pictured him dining on beef while his wife and child ate like mice.

She couldn't wait to see her brother-in-law.

As if she'd conjured him, footsteps echoed across the bare wood floor over their heads.

"He's home!" Lizbet said. She came to her feet, her movements frantic. "Please, Deborah, tell him you decided to come to London as a lark. Don't say anything about my letter. He'd be furious if he knew I sent for you."

"Why would he be upset?"

Her sister frowned. "You don't understand. He's changed. He's . . . he's not happy. Nothing

149

makes him happy." Without explaining more, she lit a candle stub for Deborah and started up the stairs.

Deborah untied the towel she'd wrapped around her waist to protect her dress and followed. Upstairs, she could hear Edmond's voice complaining. She walked down the hall to a back room. It had a row of windows that probably overlooked the yard. In the morning it would be full of sun. Tonight, a single burning candle highlighted the young couple and held back a sense of foreboding.

". . . he acted like he didn't know me," Edmond was saying. He stood in front of the windows, a boyishly handsome man with blond looks. His blue eyes burned with humiliation. Holding her child, Lizbet sat in a comfortable chair although the room was as sparsely furnished as the others.

"Gave me a direct cut," Edmond continued. "Right there, in front of everyone. Liz, I was . . ." His voice trailed off as if he feared putting his feelings into words.

"Perhaps, he *didn't* see you," she offered.

"*He saw me.*" The finality in his statement was disturbing.

Deborah decided to let her presence be known and give him something else to fret about. She took a step into the room. "Good evening, Edmond."

There was a beat of surprised silence. "What is Deborah doing here?" he asked. Slowly, he confronted his wife. "You told her. You told *all* of them."

"No, just Deborah. She's the only one I wrote."

"And you don't believe she blabbed everything to Rachel and Henry and the whole Valley?" Spots of red colored his pale cheeks. "I wouldn't be surprised if she didn't run right over and spill all to Dame Alodia!" The Dame had been a generous benefactress to Edmond and took great pride in his London success. He would be embarrassed to disappoint her.

Deborah sought to soothe his ruffled feathers. "I wouldn't betray you," she said . . . although she wasn't about to confess Henry had opened the letter and he most certainly would have told his aunt everything by now. "I can appreciate your not wanting anyone else to know. After all," she continued, thinking of Tony, "we all have secrets we wish to keep."

Edmond snorted his opinion. "You? Saint Deborah? The Sacrificial Lamb upon the Altar of Marriage for the good of your family?"

His sarcasm stunned her. "You make me sound like a perfect prig."

"You are," he replied ruthlessly.

"Edmond," Lizbet warned.

" 'Tis nothing you haven't said yourself," her husband shot back.

Lizbet made a distressed sound. She rose from the chair, lifting the baby up to her shoulder. "Her being here is *my* fault. I need help. The baby takes all my time, and I can't do anything right around the house. We once had two maids, Edmond. Now I'm expected to do all their work while you are out for hours." Tears threatened. "I'm lonely, Edmond. I knew if Deborah was here, everything would turn out all right. I had to write her!"

To his credit, his whole manner changed. He was by her side in an instant. "Lizbet, please, don't cry. I let my temper get the best of me. I'm so sorry, so sorry." He ran a distracted hand through his blond curls. "I'm such a failure. I believed I could survive, that I could make things better for us but after today . . ."

Lizbet's tears vanished. "You can," she said loyally. "I know you can." She moved into his arms, putting her arm around his waist, the baby between them.

Deborah was touched by their commitment to each other. It was what *she* longed for.

She crossed to Lizbet and held out her hands. "Here, let me take the baby up and put her to bed. The two of you need a moment alone. And, Edmond, I'm not here to disapprove. I'm sorry if I've given the impression I was some sort of martyr."

He started to contradict her, but she wouldn't let him. "No, I appreciate your honesty." Edmond had been right. She *had* been a bore. Whereas she'd thought she'd been cheerful, she'd also spent years steeped in self-pity and resentment, so much so, she'd stopped living — until Tony.

For a second, a sense of loss threatened to overwhelm her. "Perhaps we don't know each other very well," she told Edmond tightly.

"I know you would not have let Lizbet down as I have."

Deborah shook her head. If Lizbet ever learned of her scandalous behavior over the last three days, she'd be horrified. "You may not know me as well as you believe." She took the baby from her sister's arms. The sleeping baby's weight felt good in her arms. "Either way, I'm here to help. If my presence is a hardship, I will return home and speak to no one about your personal circumstances. However, I would like the opportunity to help if I may."

"Please, let her stay," Lizbet begged. "Deborah is a good housekeeper. Why, when she was married, she had only one servant and took care of all of us. You'll be happier when everything is in order again. And I need her. Deborah will make everything right. You'll see."

Deborah didn't feel like a miracle worker. She was exhausted. The day had been very long. "You two need to discuss the matter alone. I'm taking the baby to her room and I'll retire for the night."

Edmond didn't answer. He was still defensive. Lizbet lit a candle stub for her and told her to put the baby in her crib in their room, the one at the far right of the upstairs hall.

"There are two other bedrooms. Make yourself comfortable in whichever suits your fancy."

Deborah nodded and left. Upstairs, Lizbet and Edmond's room was a disaster. It appeared as if neither knew how to fold or hang clothing since breeches, dresses, and other articles were stacked everywhere. She had only to follow her nose to find the baby's dirty nappies.

Pamela was a darling. She slept without waking as Deborah changed her nappy. Lizbet was blessed.

For a second, Deborah was riveted by fear and desire. On one level, she dreaded the thought of pregnancy. On another, she secretly craved a child — a link to Tony. It was time. She was seven-and-twenty and would not grow younger.

"A link that would need to be clothed and cared for," she reminded herself. Futhermore, what did she have to offer a child? The Matrons would publicly ostracize her; her family would be shamed. She and babe would both starve to death.

Disturbed by the thought and threatened by a case of self-pity — something she despised — she picked up her portmanteau and chose the room the farthest from Lizbet and Edmond's. It took her a mere five minutes to unpack. She undressed, put on her nightgown, and brushed her hair. The hour was late, but the bed was not inviting.

She didn't like being alone. Not anymore.

Nor did she want to climb into a cold bed.

She'd opened a Pandora's box, one filled with things she should not have seen . . . because the idea of being a lord's mistress — especially in light of Edmond and Lizbet's problems, the work ahead of her, and a myriad other fears and worries — was all too tempting.

She pulled Tony's card out of her reticule. The bold slash of his handwriting reminded her so much of the man.

Thoughtfully, she pulled out the letter from Lizbet. The back of the second page was blank. In the small writing desk by the bedroom window, she found ink and a pen. She sat down.

"Why I Will Not Contact Tony —" she wrote as a header on the back of the letter, then crossed out "Tony" and penned in "Lord Burnell."

Edmond and Lizbet came up the stairs and walked toward their room. By their whisperings and hushed cooing, they were no longer angry with each other. Jealous, Deborah listened. She waited. There was the sound of a kiss, and then the door to their room shut.

She forced her vivid imagination away from her sister and back to her reasons for refusing Tony's offer of *carte blanche* —

Self-respect.

Honor.

Independence. All her life, she'd either lived with family or a husband . . . a man who'd been older than her father. Now she realized she was enjoying this touch of rebellion that had driven her out of Ilam. She did not want to be hurried off by Dame Alodia and the others to Parson Ames. But what did she want in its place?

Self-respect. She underlined the word twice because of the guilt she still carried for her reckless behavior in Derby — although she did not regret the affair. But she would not ever do it again. No, no, no. She wished fervently to return to the "respectable" Deborah who didn't flirt with disaster.

And, she decided, she wanted — *Love.* She stared at the word. No more arranged marriages. She wanted passion. She wanted laughter and fulfillment. She wanted everything she'd experienced with Tony —

Marriage!

She'd not be any man's mistress. From a wellspring of reliance she did not know she'd possessed, she decided if she was pregnant, she would not turn to him. Not if he couldn't offer *her* honor, self-respect and — most of all — love.

She folded the paper and placed it and the card back in her reticule.

She felt good. She'd made her decision. She could live with the knowledge of her affair.

But she hoped no one she knew ever found out. It would be her secret, and she'd carry it to the grave if need be.

But, as she curled up between the cold sheets of her bed, she prayed she was not pregnant.

Tony arrived at his London home shortly after dawn. He slept a few hours and then contacted his man of business Allendale to come for an immediate appointment.

"My lord, I thought you'd be at Alder House," Allendale said by way of greeting. He was a short, neat man with a bald pate and an accountant's eye for details.

"My journey was postponed," Tony answered. "Sit down."

"Lord Longest will be happy you've returned. He has accepted the marriage contract and the banns have been posted."

Tony dismissed the information with a noncommittal grunt. Instead, he launched right into the topic foremost on his mind. "How could I find someone if I don't have an address for her?"

"Is this person known to you?" the secretary asked, sitting in the chair across from Tony's desk.

"Yes, although I don't know where she is right now. I mean, I know she is in London. Or I suspect she is."

Allendale lifted an eyebrow in surprise at the word "she." Tony didn't flinch as he met his gaze. Allendale cleared his throat, and suggested, "We could hire a man skilled at tracking. I'm certain Bow Street may have such a person."

"I want this to be most discreet."

"I'm certain that can be arranged."

Tony smiled. As Marmy had said, money could buy anything. He had piles of the stuff. Why shouldn't he finally use it for something he really wanted — Deborah.

"I want to meet with a Runner today," he told Allendale. "I want this person found. It is important to me."

"Yes, my lord," the secretary answered, and left the room.

Tony sat silent a moment. He shouldn't have let her go. But now he would make up for it. He'd find Deb and convince her she had only one option, and that was to be his.

Chapter Nine

By the end of her first full week in her sister's house, Deborah was questioning her decision to stay.

Lizbet did nothing but sleep. She could be roused to feed the baby or change a nappy, but she always returned to bed when the task was done. While she was awake, all she did was reminisce how good life had been before Edmond had lost his position.

Edmond acted ignorant of his young wife's shortcomings. Nursing the belief that with a bit of luck, he could overcome being blackballed by a duke, he left the house every morning at eleven to make what he referred to as his "rounds." He often didn't come home until late in the evening.

The task of running the household fell on Deborah's shoulders. She exhausted herself the first day with the laundry. The second and third, she applied elbow grease to cleaning and airing.

The goat was quickly relegated to the back-yard. Her brother-in-law was too engrossed in his own worries to care about past edicts . . . especially once he realized Deborah had a little money.

She'd bought vegetables and a hare for their

dinner. Edmond ate well without even questioning how the meal appeared on his table. Finally, Lizbet said, "Was it not generous of Deborah to buy this meal for us?"

"Deborah bought everything?" Edmond wiped his mouth with his napkin.

"Of course," his wife answered. "We've not had the money for anything more than bread, cheese, and boiled potatoes in weeks." She smiled at Deborah, obviously pleased that a member of *her* family could help.

His answer was noncommittal, but Deborah sensed he viewed her with new eyes. She discovered how much so the next morning. He came to her before he left the house. He was dressed for the day, his shirt pressed, his neckcloth tied in the latest style. "Deborah, um, I wonder if you could lend me a half crown or two?"

She didn't know what to say. Relations were strained between them, and she feared refusing his request would make matters worse. She gave him the money.

When he asked again the next day, she again complied, but this time with a sour look around her mouth.

Edmond didn't like the subtle criticism, but he did not withdraw his hand.

She gave him the money, but not before saying, "This is ridiculous, Edmond. Why don't we all return to the Valley? Henry and Rachel will take us in."

The suggestion incensed him. "Henry is an ass. I'm not some woman to be at his mercy."

His comment pricked her pride. Still, she pressed, "I'm not suggesting it be forever. Perhaps you were meant to leave London. There may be a benefactor in the country who would admire and appreciate your qualities."

"I have offers," he replied stiffly. "These matters take time."

"I'm certain," she murmured, frustrated by his ridiculous refusal to see matters as they were.

The one bright spot was Pamela, a completely happy baby. Deborah worked while she napped and usually took her on her daily shopping forays for food. She loved the sound of the baby's laughter and delighted in stroking her tiny hands and feet. How perfect Pamela was!

She was saddened that both Edmond and Lizbet seemed too wrapped up in their own worries to enjoy their daughter. And she was further scandalized when she learned neither attended church, a mandatory custom in Ilam. She went by herself and spent a good deal of time in prayer.

There, in the holy sanctuary, her loneliness for Tony grew strongest. It wasn't as if he hadn't hovered in her mind throughout the week. He'd even haunted her dreams. But now, in the cool stillness with the scent of incense in the air, she finally admitted to herself she would not get over him easily. He'd been more

161

than a brief love affair. He'd been a kindred spirit.

She wished he were there that very moment. If he had been, she would have confided how worried she was about her sister, how she wanted all of them to return to Ilam and a simple life — but she would not contact him. She refused even to touch his card. She'd folded it carefully in her list of reasons to avoid him and tucked them both in the very bottom of her reticule.

Sitting in the quiet church long after the service was over, Deborah knew she was paying penance for the hubris of her affair. If she'd known parting from Tony would be as if a piece of her was missing, she would never have let him have that first kiss. It might have tasted like heaven, but it had stolen her soul.

And what good were noble principles when you didn't like waking alone in the morning?

She rose from her seat and moved out from the pew into the aisles. A deacon fussed with candles in the back of the church. She nodded farewell and stepped out into the afternoon light.

At home, Edmond and Lizbet were in the back morning room. They had the baby with them. Deborah did not want to disturb the family moment and went on up to her room.

It was there she learned she wasn't pregnant.

For a second, she was euphoric with relief . . . followed by an indescribable sadness. There was her last pretext of a link with Tony. It was God's answer to her prayers.

With a heavy heart, she went down to the kitchen to prepare dinner.

Several days later, Edmond was thinking he did not like having his sister-in-law around, even though she worked hard and his wife was in a better frame of mind with her present. He would have preferred for Lizbet and himself to solve their own problems. It was too bad Lizbet didn't have some of her older sister's resourcefulness.

Of course, what he hated most was that Deborah had money and he didn't. Every time he asked to borrow a few miserable shillings, he sensed she saw him as less than a man.

So, was it any wonder that when he noticed her reticule on the top of her wardrobe and knew she was down below stairs preparing breakfast, he decided to slip a few quid into his own pocket instead of going through the humiliation of begging?

Lizbet was busy with the baby. She would not approve of what he was about to do. *He* wouldn't approve either — if circumstances had been different. However, he had asked Geoffrey Rolland to lunch. Rolland had the power to appoint Edmond a tax collector. Edmond would rather do anything other than collect stamp duties and yet, what choice did he have? Nothing was coming his way. He had to find a way to stay in London.

Although it was likely that, once he became a taxman, few would hire him for a better position. But it was preferable to returning to Ilam.

In Deborah's room, he tugged open the drawstrings and stuffed his hand inside. To his dismay, Deborah didn't have more than five pounds left to her name. He turned the small purse inside out, praying there was more.

There was nothing else . . . except for a letter stuffed in the bottom of the bag. Nosy, he pulled it out and recognized Lizbet's handwriting. This had to be the letter his wife had written his sister asking her to come, and he wanted to know what she'd written. He unfolded the sheets of foolscap. A calling card fluttered to the ground and landed at his feet. Edmond stooped for it and caught sight of the word *Burnell*.

What was a calling card from the most notorious and certainly most wealthy man in London doing in his sister-in-law's reticule?

He turned the card over and saw the words "If ever you should need me" in a bold sprawl.

Edmond stood. He looked from the card to the letter and noticed the list on the back written by Deborah. Closing the door to her room, he took his time reading it with a growing sense of excitement. He didn't fully understand the list's import, but he sensed all the way to his bones that the card he held in his hand was something he could turn to his advantage.

Whenever Tony invested time and money, he expected results. He was not happy with what Mr. Bayford, the Bow Street man had to say. The man had been searching for Deborah for a week and a half. Tony wanted progress.

"My lord, if you had more information, then perhaps we could find this young woman. I've had two of my best men on the matter for the last three days, and they say it is impossible to find this Mrs. Percival based upon the sketchy bit we know about her activities in London."

Tony drummed his fingers on his desk. He shouldn't have let her go. "Tell me what you have done."

Mr. Bayford cast a nervous glance at Allendale and referred to a sheet of paper. "We made inquiries in all the major marketplaces in the city. You know, the shops where women go for their laces and parasols. I personally checked all inns and hostelries —"

"She wouldn't be there. I told you she was staying with her sister and her husband."

"Yes, my lord, but my thought is it never hurts to be thorough," Mr. Bayford countered. "After all, what if there was a family argument? I also hoped to catch word of her arrival in London."

Now, here was something of interest to Tony. "Did you?"

"Unfortunately, no. After that flooding rain, the schedules were confused. Passengers were coming and going with no one being the wiser."

Tony pushed back from his desk and stood. "Go on," he ordered Bayford. He paced the room, listening but too tense to be idle.

"I had a man posted at all the churches. I'm assuming from your description of Mrs. Percival, she would be a religious person. Most folks from the country are."

"That was a good idea." Tony stopped. "And?"

"I'm sorry, my lord, nothing. Of course, London is full of churches. We shall continue to check."

Where the devil was Deb? Tony wanted to believe he could find her. He knew in his heart that if she did carry his child, her pride would not let her contact him. "Where else have you looked?" he demanded.

Mr. Bayford folded the paper. "Nowhere. Short of going from door to door or posting a man on every corner of this city, we have no other options. I fear to say, my lord, that the more time that passes, the colder her trail grows. I'm sorry, but I believe in speaking plainly."

There was an awkward silence as Tony hashed out the matter in his mind. He knew Allendale was curious about this mysterious Mrs. Percival. However, his secretary kept his questions to himself.

Suddenly, Tony had an inspiration. "Have you been to Ilam, where Mrs. Percival is from?"

"No, my lord," Mr. Bayford answered. "We have kept our investigations to London. That is where you said she was."

"But Ilam is where she is *from*. She must return there sooner or later." A growing excitement colored Tony's voice. This idea had merit.

"To send someone across the country . . . well, the expense would be considerable, my lord."

Tony sat in his chair. "I didn't ask your opinion on my expenses, Mr. Bayford. I ordered you to find her."

The Bow Street man said stiffly, "I will do as you wish, my lord."

"Good." Tony leaned forward. "Don't worry about the cost. Your mission is to find Mrs. Percival."

"Yes, my lord." Mr. Bayford came to his feet. "I will report back to you next week? At the same time?

"Absolutely."

Allendale showed the Runner to the door. Alone, Tony stared out the window next to his desk. The view overlooked manicured lawns and an elegant fountain. He wondered what Deb saw when she looked out her window? Was she miles away or in the next block?

For a second, the need for her overwhelmed him —

"My lord?" Allendale stood in the doorway.

Tony looked up with a frown.

"I don't wish to disturb but you are to attend Lady Longest's musicale this afternoon."

"Yes, that's right." Tony rose from his desk.

Lady Amelia was known for her lovely voice, and her mother enjoyed these exhibits of her daughter's talent to a select, exclusive group of friends. This would be Tony's introduction to these people, a circle to which his parents would never have had access.

However, as he listened to Lady Amelia's lilting soprano later that day, his mind wasn't on the important connections he was making or on the beauty of the girl he had agreed to marry in two months' time.

No, his mind was on Deb.

And the crucial question — where was she?

He spent the afternoon going through the motions, smiling, being polite — conscious that several people disapproved of the match. He heard the whispering. Those who remembered his parents' scandals clued in those new to the gossip. For once, he really didn't care what the scandalmongers said. His mind was preoccupied.

He and Lady Amelia stood together for a few moments.

He told her she had a lovely voice.

She thanked him prettily but without enthusiasm.

He left.

However, when he returned home, Allendale met him at the door, his expression anxious. "Lord Burnell, there is a gentleman who has been waiting to see you most of the afternoon. I believe you will find what he has to say of particular interest."

"How so?" Tony handed a footman his hat and coat.

Allendale held out a card. Tony's card. The one he'd given to Deb.

"He says he is her brother-in-law. I had him wait in your library."

Without another word, Tony charged back to meet this man.

Deborah had braided her hair and then tied it up in a kerchief before she went out into the backyard to attack the laundry. She'd put off the chore of nappy washing long enough. The day was spring fresh, and she didn't mind being outside, but she hated doing the wash.

However while swirling the clothes around in the hot soapy water with a paddle, she had a sense something was out of order. She couldn't quite put her finger on exactly what but the awareness that all was not as it should be nagged at her.

She paused, resting on the paddle . . . and then it came to her. When she'd gone to change into her gray working dress she'd spied her reticule on the top of the dresser drawer where she usually placed it. However, she always folded the drawstring ties on *top* of the purse and this time, they were folded *beneath.* Immediately, she knew Edmond had been going through her reticule for money. He hadn't asked her for any the last two days. She would have told him no, and he knew it.

But would he really go through her personal things and help himself — ?

Astounded rage shot through her. She put down the paddle, ready to go check, when she heard footsteps coming from the kitchen stairs. Lizbet came running up, her eyes alive with excitement. Since arriving in London, Deborah had not seen her sister look so animated and hopeful.

"Deborah, at last I've found you. Come quickly! Edmond has found a position!"

"He has?" She wiped her forehead with the back of her hand.

"Yes, and with the most remarkable, *generous* employer. Edmond promised everything would work out, and so it has! The gentleman is here now, in my sitting room, playing with the baby."

"Who is he?"

Lizbet laughed, giddy with happiness. "I'm cautioned not to tell you. Edmond wants to see the surprise on your face."

Now, Deborah was leery. "Why would *I* be surprised?"

"Oh, come. Humor him. Please, he's had such a hard time. And this gentleman is the answer to our dreams. Deborah, he is the richest man in London, and Edmond says he is the one man with the influence to defy Etheridge. The duke's long arm can't harm us now."

Curious, Deborah dried her hands on the towel she'd wrapped around her waist for an apron. "Very well. I should go brush my hair and change." She pushed the pins she'd used to pin her braid up off her neck.

"Just remove the kerchief from your hair. You look fine as you are. Come, Edmond urged me to hurry, and warned me to not let you out of my sight." Lizbet practically danced with excitement. Her enthusiasm was infectious. Deborah followed. Her dress was work-worn and her hands red from the soap and water but what did it matter? The gentleman was here to honor Edmond and Lizbet and not some country relative.

They entered the house through the morning room. From up the hallway, Deborah could hear male voices. There was Edmond's and then —

She stopped. The other voice sounded more than familiar, its deep resonance rolling straight to her soul.

But it couldn't be.

"Come," Lizbet urged, and hurried ahead.

Deborah held back at the corner of the staircase. Her feet had turned to lead weights. Lizbet blocked her view into the sitting room, giving Deborah no choice but to go forward.

She had to know, to see for herself.

She came to the door. Lizbet turned with a glorious smile. "Here's my sister now." She stood aside, and Deborah had no choice but to enter the room . . . and there he was. Tony. Looking more handsome than she had remembered.

He was wearing his customary dark blue jacket and leather riding breeches that seemed molded to the length of him. The strength of his presence filled the room. But what truly caught her off guard was that he held sweet little Pamela in his arms as naturally as if she'd been his own.

For a second, Deborah couldn't breathe, let alone speak.

Edmond stood back, watching. *He knows.* She didn't know how he knew, but he was aware of her connection with Tony. Immediately, intuition told her just what had happened — he had discovered the card when he was stealing her money.

If Tony had said a word to Edmond about the personal nature of their relationship, she'd never forgive him.

Lizbet, the dutiful hostess, was busy introducing Deborah to Lord Burnell, Edmond's new employer.

Tony bowed. "Mrs. Percival."

The sound of his voice echoed through her. She'd missed him so much.

She opened her mouth to answer, but the

niceties wouldn't pass her lips. They couldn't.

She wasn't one to pretend. And she didn't trust his reason for being there.

So, Deborah did the one thing she could do — she ran.

Chapter Ten

Edmond Warner and his lovely wife stared after Deb in astonishment as she ran down the hall toward the back of the house.

Mrs. Warner turned to Tony. "I'm sorry. I don't know what has gotten into her. Do you?" she asked her husband.

"I don't know," came the gruff reply, "but I'll not have her walk out on a guest in my house." Warner would have charged after Deb but Tony stopped him.

"No, please, let me speak to her." He didn't wait for an answer but moved toward the door. Then, pausing a moment, he held the blue-eyed baby up. "You don't mind if I take her. I may need her support."

Mrs. Warner appeared befuddled by the request, but Warner hurriedly said, "Of course, of course. Anything you wish, my lord."

As Tony left the room, he heard Mrs. Warner say to her husband, "He took Pamela? He *wanted* to take the baby?"

"It's fine, Lizbet. Fine," was the placating answer.

Pamela stared wide-eyed up at Tony as he walked the path Deb had taken. "You must help my case, pretty girl," he whispered. "Your aunt is going to want my head on a pike. You must soothe matters between us."

The baby pursed her lips and let a bubble form. Tony didn't know if she was commenting on her desire to help or if she shared her aunt's ability to see right through him.

At the back of the house, Tony entered a morning room with its bank of windows overlooking the sparse yard. At one time, it had been a pretty garden, but not much had been done to it this season. In the corner of the garden, a nanny goat munched grass as if she could never be filled. On the other side stood Deb.

She used a paddle to stir a tubful of laundry with the ferocity of a witch casting a spell. He knew he could be taking his life in his hands, but he had no choice. Now that he'd found her, he would not walk away.

"Come along," he said to the child, who held his coat lapel with her tiny hand. He went out the door leading to the garden and made his way down the steps.

The moment Pamela saw Deb, she held out her hands and made anxious noises as if she wished her aunt to rescue her. Deb refused to acknowledge either Tony's or the baby's presence. Her arms moved with agility and grace as she turned the laundry over and over. She appeared thinner and more tired than he remembered, but just as lovely. The simple plait of her hair emphasized her high cheekbones, her straight nose, and determined chin.

Dear God, he'd missed her.

He stopped less than three feet from where she stood and waited. Let her say the first word. Then he could gauge her mood.

Pamela kicked her feet and began crying. He knew Deb could not ignore such a plea for long.

"I didn't send for you," she said brutally, refusing to look at either him or the baby. "There is no . . ." She let her voice trail off.

He understood.

There was no child between them.

He looked down at the squirming baby in his arms, the one who wanted her aunt to pay attention to her. She raised tearful eyes up to Tony, beseeching his help . . . and he knew how she felt. Instead of being satisfied he had not compromised Deb, he felt deprived of something he'd needed, something he'd dearly wanted.

"Edmond took your card without permission," Deb said, stabbing the water viciously with her paddle. "That's how *desperate* he is for work." There was no respect in her voice.

"He admitted such."

The paddle stopped moving. "Does Edmond know?" Deb's tense words spoke volumes.

"He isn't a stupid man," Tony said, moving Pamela up to his shoulder, "but I didn't say anything. He hopes to use a connection to his advantage."

"And it has worked," she said, her disgust

clear. "Unless you go so far as to make my brother-in-law's employment with you weigh in the balance of my doing your bidding."

Tony felt his temper rise. "You believe I would do such a thing?" he replied heatedly.

For the first time since he'd come out in the yard, she met his gaze. "I believe I don't know you well enough to say one way or the other."

Tony stepped back as if she'd hit him. She knew she'd insulted him. She glared at him defiantly, daring him to walk away — and he would have . . . until he recalled Marmy's admonishment to be careful of Deb's pride.

Pride was something he understood.

The baby punctuated the silence with her whimpers. Instinctively, Tony started rocking the child. Pamela began to quiet, chewing. She laid her sweet head on his shoulder.

Deb's hard gaze softened as it dropped to the child he held. In her eyes he read hunger and regret. Whatever she claimed, she was not as callous toward him as she wished to pretend.

He spoke from a place deep within him, a place he'd not known existed until that moment. "You say you don't know me, and yet, I feel as if I've known you all my life. As if I've been waiting for you."

Now she was the one to step back.

Tony continued. "When I look at you, Deb, I see more than just flesh and blood. In your dark eyes, I see your compassion, your honesty. Your strength and resolve to prevail against any odds is etched around the corners of your lovely mouth. Your sense of purpose is in the set of your shoulders. Your determination in the strength and grace of your hands. I suppose most lovers would not sing praises to those things and yet, to me, they are the soul, the essence of you."

Her grip on the paddle she'd been holding protectively in front of her loosened. Huge tears welled in her eyes. She held them back.

He pressed on. "It's not that you aren't beautiful. You are. I ache just looking at you. But what pulls me to you, Deb, what lies between us, is more than mere lust. Other women pale in comparison to you. And when they leave a room, I don't feel like they are taking a piece of my soul with them."

She dropped the paddle. It flipped out of the tub onto the ground splashing water as it went, but she didn't give it a care. Instead, she lowered her head, clenching her fists around the apron upon her waist. Two large tears fell.

Tony would not let her shut him out. "I'm not going to let you go — not without a fight."

His declaration hovered in the air. On his shoulder, Pamela sighed and fell asleep, one arm over his back. Tony waited, wanting, willing Deb to come back to him. She must.

She raised her head. Her expression was anything but conciliatory. "I won't be your mistress."

"I —" he started, then closed his mouth.

What could he say? He had nothing else to offer.

He couldn't offer marriage. He was promised to another.

For a second, words of explanation were on the tip of his tongue — but he held them back because Marmy was right. Deb didn't know the rules, and she wouldn't understand that even though he was to marry another, she would have first place in his heart. He was going to have to break her in gently. He could not go back on his word to Longest, not with everything he'd spent these last years working toward at stake.

But he didn't want to give up Deb, and telling her the complete truth would be tantamount to cutting off his own hands. He would tell her the truth, but later, when she would be more receptive. Now was not the right moment.

So here they were. And he knew neither of them could yield.

The baby sleeping on his shoulder had become an unwelcome weight. A reminder of what they could have had . . . and didn't.

He handed her the child. "This isn't over between us." He left the yard.

Deborah watched him leave, and it was like having her insides torn from her.

Why could things not be different? If he cared as much as he did, why did he not offer marriage — ?

Unless he did not consider her his class equal.

Shame consumed her. She regretted ever meeting him and suddenly, she needed to be someplace private.

Not wanting to run into her sister or her loutish brother-in-law, she ran down the stairs into the kitchen and took the back way upstairs. She put Pamela in her crib and then escaped to her own room. Once there, in this private haven, she shut the door, threw herself on the bed, and, burying her face in her pillow, gave in to the luxury of tears. She needed them to cleanse her soul . . . and to help her find the strength to go on.

She cried until there was nothing left inside. Then, exhausted, she lay on the bed wondering what would become of her. She'd rather die than to be Parson Ames's next wife.

A timid knock sounded at the door.

Deborah was too spent to respond.

The door opened. Lizbet peeked in. "Deborah, may I speak to you a moment?"

Covering her red-rimmed eyes with her arm, Deborah turned away. The light of day was fading fast. She wished she could fade with it.

The door quietly closed. The bed moved as Lizbet sat on the edge beside Deborah.

"Do you wish to talk about it?"

No, she didn't — especially with one of her sisters.

Several moments of silence passed, then

Lizbet said, "You are usually the one to comfort me. This time, let me help you. I hate to see you in such distress."

"I'll be fine," Deborah managed to choke out. Her throat was raw from her tears. "Don't worry about me."

"I do worry," Lizbet countered, "in the same way you worry about me. Please, Deborah, don't treat me like a child. It's clear Lord Burnell didn't come here because he wished to meet me, he wanted to see you. The two of you have met before, haven't you?"

Deborah didn't want to answer. Lizbet sat patiently, no judgment in her gaze — but a woman's sympathy. Realizing her behavior was more that of a stubborn child than a woman, Deborah sat up, taking a moment to arrange her skirts before saying, "We've met."

"He's smitten."

When Deborah opened her mouth to take umbrage, Lizbet said, "Please, give me credit, big sister. I was the Belle of the Valley, remember? I received no fewer than eight offers. I know when a man is smitten."

"But, Lizbet . . . it's not what you think." Hot color burned her face. "Does Edmond still have a position or did Lord Burnell withdraw the offer?"

"Withdraw it? Whyever would he do that?"

Deborah straightened, confused. "Do you mean, he said nothing when he left the house?"

"Lord Burnell? Nothing other than the usual

pleasantries. He told Edmond he'd see him on the morrow."

"Then he didn't say . . . ?" Deborah let her voice drift before she revealed too much. She was thankful Tony was not going to make her sister's family pay for her mistakes. Now she could leave, return to Ilam, and try and resurrect something out of the muddle she'd made of her life.

"Say what?" Lizbet prodded.

Deborah shook her head. "It was unimportant." She would have gotten off the bed, but Lizbet's hand on her arm stopped her.

"No, he didn't say anything to us about the two of you being lovers."

Deborah's world came to a sudden halt. Slowly, she turned toward her sister. "How do you know?"

"Edmond told me what he'd found in your purse." Lizbet soothed a nonexistent wrinkle in her skirt. "I didn't condone his actions, mind you, but once he knew he could not let opportunity pass."

"Ummmm," Deborah said noncommittally, seeing her youngest sister through new eyes. Lizbet had a bit of her husband's expediency. Leaning back against the headboard, she summed her feelings neatly by saying, "I feel such a fool. But then, maybe I got what I deserved."

"Which is?"

Deborah frowned and decided to confess.

"Lord Burnell asked me to be his mistress. He offered *carte blanche.*"

Lizbet's blue eyes widened. Her mouth dropped open. Deborah understood her shock. "I know," she agreed. "Father must be rolling in his grave. And I hope no one in the Valley hears of this. I'd be ruined."

"No, you wouldn't!" Lizbet answered.

"Well, of course not, because I'm not going to take the offer —"

"But you must!" Lizbet cried. "This is wonderful news! I'm so happy for you!"

"Happy — ?" Her question was cut off by Lizbet's arms around her neck. The bed bounced with her enthusiasm.

"Yes, I'm happy!" Her sister drew back to look in her face. "Lord Burnell is a fantastic catch. You are very fortunate. Oh, granted, there is all that gossip about his father killing himself — you *knew* Lord Burnell was the one to find the body? I think he was no older than twelve" — she waved her hand — "or something like that. And his mother —" She frowned. "Talk about scandalous behavior! They say she had a different lover every week. Some whisper Lord Burnell isn't his father's but another man's child. They say that is why the man killed himself and not over some nonsense like gambling debts. His mother used to be quite a fixture in town, but has since remarried, and I suppose is happy. She's bad *ton.* Lord Burnell suffered from her reputation and, of course, no one can condone a suicide. But they also say his father was, hmmmm, how to put it? Emotional. I've heard he used to do outrageous things on a whim. No one ever knew what would set him off. He'd have these fits — actually cry in public or go into terrible rages."

The information was coming so fast, Deborah had trouble grasping it all. "Tony is nothing like that."

Lizbet cocked an eyebrow in interest. "Tony, is it?" She smiled. "He's very rich you know."

"All England has heard of Lord Burnell's wealth."

"Edmond says more and more people are wooing Lord Burnell. They are attracted to his ability to make money. I don't believe he's vulgar about it, although, he's never been admitted to Almack's, and there are many who openly snub him. Some members of the *haut ton* are such sticklers they'd even turn up their noses at Wellington. Can you imagine?" She paused, before saying thoughtfully, "Of course, Lord Burnell is rumored to walk the straight and narrow. That is, when compared to the other men of his class and of his age. I've heard of many women who have set their caps for him but he's not been known to take a mistress."

Deborah held up a hand, begging a moment's break in the monologue. "Excuse me, Lizbet, are you saying you are *not* averse to my accepting his offer of *carte blanche?*"

"I believe you would be wise to do so."

Her frank agreement almost sent Deborah tumbling off the bed in surprise. "Lizbet, we were raised with more pride in ourselves than that. Tony made a dishonorable offer."

"That a clever woman might be wise to consider." Lizbet leaned one hand on the bed. "You do like him, don't you?"

Here was fragile territory. Deborah was uncertain how much to reveal to this sister who was surprising her by the minute. "He's above my touch," she replied stiffly.

Lizbet shook her head. "I forgot how provincial the Valley is. Here, in London, sex blurs class distinctions. Let us pretend that you admire Lord Burnell very much, and that if your principles and your fear of the gossips in the Valley didn't stand in your way, you wouldn't mind being his mistress."

Her accuracy was unnerving. "I could never. What would Rachel and Henry say?"

"Oh, I imagine Henry would give you an earful — at first. However eventually, like Edmond, he wouldn't mind having a sister-in-law with such an important benefactor. Lord Burnell is an earl, after all." She drummed her fingers on the bed. "You'd not be invited to Dame Alodia's for her afternoon tea parties, but since she uses those occasions to bully people into her meddling designs, what would you care? Besides, you'd be in London living in a house grander than hers. And beyond the Valley, who cares what Dame

Alodia thinks? Not I."

Not Deborah either. It would be a heaven send to be free of the dame's overbearing nosiness.

"But I would be living outside of Society," Deborah protested.

"You already are, dear sister. Unfairly, but it's true. *Your* mother was not English, and in Ilam or any other country village, there are small minds. Why else do you think Mother let them push you into a marriage with Mr. Percival? She could sacrifice you. She'd not have let Rachel or me make such a marriage."

Deborah had never dared to let herself think such thoughts. Now, here was Lizbet bluntly telling the truth. An anger she'd not known was lurking deep within her raised its ugly head. She crossed her arms tightly.

"But you are free now, Deborah," Lizbet reminded her. "And if I were you, I would be asking myself what did I want out of life? You are still young and certainly not ready for the shelf."

"No, I'm not," Deborah agreed quickly. "But I don't know what I want," she confessed. "I know I don't want Parson Ames or to be confined to living off the benevolence of others." She struggled for the right words, the right meanings for her secret desires. "I want to feel independent and valued. I want to be able to hold my head high and not feel like some afterthought."

"Have Rachel and I made you feel that way?" Lizbet said with alarm.

"Oh, no. But you just admitted you were aware Mother saw a difference between us. And both your marriages are too new. Your husbands do not always appreciate my presence. I feel very much the outsider."

Lizbet leaned forward to deliver her point, "With Lord Burnell, you need never be sacrificed again. And his protection can give you a great deal of freedom. I saw the expression on his face when he left. Whether you realize it or not, he's yours."

Closing her eyes, Deborah pictured herself with him. In her mind's eye was the powerful image of him holding Pamela. He had a good manner with her. Edmond rarely carried the baby, but Tony had been quite at ease . . . and she was sorry they'd not created a child together. The regret centered deep within her. "I'd rather have marriage." There, she'd said it. She'd spoken her wildest dream.

Lizbet sat silent. Deborah opened her eyes. "Am I a fool?"

Her sister scooted closer for confidences. "You're not a fool, not if you've truly hooked him. More than one woman has brought a rich man up to scratch. And you aren't entirely unsuitable. Your mother was nobility, even if she was French. I've even heard of actresses, who are little better than whores, to have accomplished the feat."

"You would compare me to them?" Deborah said flatly, the burden of guilt still heavy on her shoulders.

"I mean no insult," Lizbet said quickly. "I'm being practical." She reached out and started loosening Deborah's braid with her fingers. "Of course, we are going to need to work on you a bit. Over the years, dear sister, you've become a bit too drab." She paused, then observed, "Many women say being a mistress is preferable to being a wife."

"Not me."

Lizbet shrugged. "Then we must encourage Lord Burnell to change his offer to the real prize — marriage."

She said this with such confidence, Deb wanted to believe it could happen. She wanted Tony, but on her terms. "What must I do?"

Putting her legs over the side of the bed, Lizbet stood. "We'll plot something. Bringing a man up to scratch calls for careful strategy. Why don't you splash some water on your face and freshen up while I prepare a pot of tea? I'll meet you in the morning room." She left, humming busily with ideas.

Deborah followed her advice. She took a moment to brush out her hair and wash her face before following. Lizbet had been very successful garnering offers from young, eligible men before she'd settled on Edmond. If anyone could help, she could.

However, before going to the morning room,

she sought out her brother-in-law. She caught him as he was leaving the sitting room and confronted him.

"You went through my personal things."

Edmond had the good grace to blush, but he did not apologize. "This is my house."

"You wanted my money."

He looked down the hall as if wishing Lizbet would interrupt them. When she didn't make an appearance, he said briskly, "We are family. I did not think you would mind."

"Oh, I mind, Edmond. I mind very much."

"But it is all going to work out for the better, isn't it? I talked to Lizbet. One way or the other, everything will work to your advantage," he answered smugly. "In fact, you should be thanking me instead of pressing the issue. Who knows what riches your future holds?"

Deborah shook her head. "Be careful, Edmond. I may not play the game the way you wish." With that word of warning, she turned on her heel and left him.

Tony spent a restless night. He'd always gotten what he wanted. Either through hard work, money, or persuasion, he'd *always* succeeded. No one had ever refused him.

Save Deb.

Nor could he accept the idea that she was not as captivated of him as he was of her. It was simply not possible . . . and yet, she'd rejected him.

He came to the breakfast table heavy-lidded and tired. Food held no appeal, and he had no enthusiasm for the day ahead.

While he sipped a cup of strongly brewed coffee, Allendale knocked on the breakfast room door. Tony invited him in and offered him coffee.

"Warner came by early this morning, my lord," Allendale said. "I told him I didn't really have time to deal with him until Monday, but he was insistent about going to work immediately. I sent him to the merchant office for the day to help with ship schedules." He paused and then admitted, "Perhaps I was too harsh in my assessment of him. He seems a bright and capable man and is very willing to make a mark for himself."

"Yes, that was my thought, too," Tony agreed. And, in turn, he would also receive word from time to time about Deb.

"He brought this in, my lord, and asked me to deliver it to you personally."

Allendale placed a vellum envelope sealed with red wax on the table by the morning papers. Tony did not recognize the distinctly feminine handwriting . . . but could it be from Deb? His heart in his throat, he gave a disinterested nod. "I'll look at it later. This morning, I plan to look at some broodmares Catlett has for sale. Do you wish to join me?"

"Unfortunately, I'm detained here, my lord."

For the next fifteen minutes, as was their custom, they discussed the business of the day. Tony might have pretended otherwise, but in reality he could not wait for Allendale to excuse himself.

The moment he was alone, he ripped into the envelope. His eye scanned to the signature. *Deborah.*

Dear Lord Burnell,

You are right. There is a bond between us. I pray you forgive my contrary female mind and accept my apology for my behavior yesterday afternoon. I fear I was overwrought with the emotion of seeing you again because, in truth, you hold my heart.

With every fondness,
Deborah Somerset Percival

He held her heart!

Suddenly, the world was a wonderful place. For the first time that morning, he realized how beautiful the day was. Yes, the sky was overcast and dull, but nothing could mar his joy. He was full of energy and hope. *He* held her heart. She was agreeing to be his mistress.

Ideas of work vanished.

He threw down his napkin, rose from the table, and paced the room three times to control his excitement. Deborah wanted him.

He had to see her, to *celebrate* with her. They needed to do something momentous so they'd never forget the night when she'd agreed to be his. Someplace romantic. But entertaining, too.

191

Sitting, he drummed his fingers on the table. Then, an idea struck him. He would take her to Vauxhall Gardens. He'd heard much about the pleasure gardens. He'd not been there before because he'd never been willing to take the time. The stories of its fireworks and music fetes had all seemed too frivolous.

Vauxhall would be the perfect spot.

He marched to his study and wrote out an invitation. He instructed his footman to wait for a reply, then proceeded to walk the floor until the lad returned.

"She says she'd be honored, my lord."

With those words, all was right in the world and Tony vowed that, given a second chance, he'd never let her go.

"Vauxhall Gardens," Lizbet said with approval after she'd read Tony's letter outlining his plans. "It is the perfect place for a liaison. Come, dear sister, you are to wear one of my dresses. I have an emerald green that will be spectacular with your coloring. Lord Burnell will not be able to resist. He'll probably devour you on the spot."

"Marriage," Deborah reiterated. "I want marriage."

Lizbet smiled, the expression that of the cat being caught in the cream. "Of course. Come."

In a daze, Deborah followed her sister up to her room.

Chapter Eleven

Tony counted the hours until he would see Deborah.

Never in his life had he looked forward to something with as much anticipation. His appointments, his schedule, his routine — nothing mattered more than his seeing Deb.

And his feelings involved more than his lust.

Yes, he wanted to bed her . . . but he wanted something else, too. Something he couldn't describe. In truth, he'd not opened himself to many people in his life. Friends were fickle and family jealous. However, Deb did not fit in either of these categories. She was unique, separate, and alone from others in his world.

More importantly, he trusted her.

He could not wait to have her alone where he could plead his case. She would come round. He had faith in his powers of persuasion. However, to help his chances, he made a trip to the jeweler's.

Tony had rarely visited a jeweler's. He considered such nonsense a waste of money. Now, he took pleasure in picking out the perfect present for Deb, one that would properly commemorate their arrangement.

Nothing caught his fancy until the jeweler held up a blood red ruby cut into the shape of a heart. It dangled from a heavy gold chain, the sort seen in a Renaissance painting.

You hold my heart . . .

Tony didn't even ask the price.

He held the jewel up to the light and could picture it hanging around Deb's neck. The stone would enhance her coloring, and he could tell her she wore his heart around her neck. He was no poet, but he was pleased, very pleased.

At half past six, he presented himself on Warner's modest doorstep. Surprisingly, Warner himself opened the door.

"Please, come in, my lord."

Tony did, removing his hat as he entered. The velvet pouch holding the necklace weighed heavy in the pocket of his coat.

For a second, an awkward silence reigned. Tony didn't know what to say to a man in his employ whose sister-in-law he wanted for his mistress.

"Would you care for a drink, my lord?" Warner asked.

"No. Thank you."

Warner crossed and then uncrossed his arms. "Let us go to the sitting room and wait. I know Deborah will be down shortly."

Tony shifted his weight from one foot to the other, then followed the shorter man into the next room, but neither moved more than a few steps beyond the door.

Again, there was silence. Then, Warner

asked, "You will take care of her?" He did not meet Tony's gaze with his own.

Tony did not pretend to misunderstand him. The man had willingly traded his sister-in-law for a position and now felt guilt. "She'll lack for nothing."

Warner nodded as if that was enough.

They were saved from having to make further small talk by the sound of a footstep at the door. Both men turned at once — and Tony caught his breath.

Deb stood there, her beaming sister by her side . . . but this was not the Deb he knew. Gone were the sensible sprigged cotton and drab colors.

Instead, she wore an emerald green dress, the bright, vivid color of the finest stones. The high-waisted bodice was practically nonexistent and when she dropped a graceful curtsy, he gaped like a fool. He remembered all too well the silken feeling of her breasts, their nipples dark and inviting. Just then, only a minuscule amount of material hid them away from his touch.

Her lustrous hair was pulled back in the Spanish style to emphasize the long line of her neck. Pearl earbobs highlighted the creamy color of her skin. She lifted her dark gaze to meet Tony's. "My lord."

It took him a second to unscramble his brains enough to answer. "You're beautiful." He blurted the words out. Right there in front of Warner and his wife. He didn't care. He spoke the truth.

A becoming blush tinged her cheeks.

He couldn't wait to get her alone.

Offering his arm, he muttered excuses and farewells while walking her to the door. Her sister stopped them. "Here, Deborah, you'll need a shawl this evening." She handed her sister a wrap of the finest Indian muslin. Spangles had been woven around the edge, and they shimmered and reflected the light with her every movement.

Deb draped the shawl elegantly over her hair. "Thank you." She kissed her sister's cheek. "For everything." Then slowly she turned to Tony, who already held the door open.

His coach and driver waited for them on the street. Deb pulled back when she saw the elaborate burled-wood vehicle pulled by a set of matched bays. His coat of arms was emblazoned on the door.

"Oh, dear," she murmured.

"What is it?"

Wide-eyed, she confessed, "Edmond said you were powerful . . . but I had not imagined exactly what he meant until I saw this."

His footman stood holding the door for them. "Let me help you in," Tony said, proud to have impressed her. "Wait until you feel the ride."

Inside, she ran a palm over the nap of the velvet seats before she sat and took a moment to look around at every convenience provided. There were a brass oil lamp and a holder for glasses and a brandy bottle. The windows were glass and slid up and down. "This is quite plush."

"It's the latest design." He was speaking in inanities, too taken by her scent of jasmine to think clearly.

Her lips formed an "oh." He knocked on the ceiling, a signal he was ready. There was a shout from the driver, and the coach started.

Deb sat back in the seat. "I barely feel we are moving."

"No small task on London streets," he answered, then reached in his pocket and pulled out the velvet jeweler's bag. Unexpected shyness overcame him. He'd rarely received gifts and so, consequently, had rarely given them. "I have something for you." He offered his gift.

She looked down at the velvet pouch. Her brows came together. She did not move. "For me?"

"Yes. It's a gift. From me."

"I don't know what to say." She raised her gaze to him, and he saw she was genuinely touched. "Thank you."

Her simple words of gratitude humbled him. And in that instant — Tony fell in love. Head-over-heels, never-to-be-the-same in love.

Love surprised him. It wasn't anything as he'd imagined. Years ago he'd gone calf-eyed over an Arabella Smythe. And there had been another woman or two who had caught his interest, but what he'd felt for all of them combined paled in importance when confronted by this new emotion. The feeling welling inside of him for Deb was something deeper, richer, finer . . . and more settled.

He needed her like he needed air to breathe.

She was water for his soul. A reason for his being.

His eyes suddenly burned with emotion. He had to look away. "Take it now. Open your present."

With trembling fingers, she tugged at the pouch's drawstrings and poured the necklace out into her hand. The light from the last rays of the late-afternoon sun fell on the chain and made the gold gleam. Her mouth dropped open on a quick intake of breath . . . and her stunned reaction was everything he could have hoped for.

Reverently, Deborah held the chain up so she could see the pendant. It was a heart, a ruby heart the size of her thumbnail set in gold. The weight of it surprised her.

"Let me help you put it on," Tony said.

She nodded, still too stunned to speak.

"You like it." He smiled, pleased. "Turn around," he ordered, his own manner slightly bemused.

Deborah didn't know if she could move she was so rattled by the gift. Lizbet had to be right. Tony would not have purchased something so rare, so expensive if he did not care for her.

Dutifully, she swiveled in her seat and lowered the shawl to offer her neck. Tony's arms came around her. He placed the chain around her neck. The pendant rested between the crests of her breasts. His fingers brushed her neck as he fastened the chain, and, instinctively, she leaned back toward him.

He did not pull away. He slid his hands down along her arms. His breath tickled her neck. "Deb," he whispered. His lips touched the sensitive spot right below her ear.

Her nipples tightened. His hands came round, cupping her breasts. "You're so beautiful." His hushed words hummed through her. She wanted to melt into him. Lazy, heavy desire drummed through her veins. She arched her back, pushing her breasts into his hands.

He kissed her, his lips following the curve of her jaw. One hand now dipped down over the flatness of her stomach, moving slowly, steadily to the center of her need. She placed her hand on his muscled thigh, her thumb inches away from him. She knew he was hard and ready for her. It was the way between them. She turned her lips to meet his. *Dear God, she wanted him. Right there. Now —*

Their only warning they were about to stop was a shout from the driver for some other coachman to move his horses. Quickly,

Deborah slid across the seat away from Tony. He leaned forward, needing a moment to compose himself. They both breathed heavily.

His amused gaze met hers. "I missed you."

She could only nod, her body aching with frustration.

The coach halted, and, a few seconds later, Tony's footman opened the door. "My lord," he murmured with a bow.

Tony got down first, then helped Deborah out of the coach. She placed a hand over the ruby heart. "Would that I could place a kiss there," he whispered, and her body heat rose.

They were beside the River Thames. Boats decorated with paper streamers and paper lanterns waited to row guests across to the Gardens. There were people of all ages and even all walks of life. The spangled shawl Lizbet had insisted she wear no longer seemed conspicuous. Everyone was dressed in the best. Some of the parties going over were even dressed in bold, outlandish costumes.

In spite of the low, threatening clouds, the evening was lovely. The air felt like warm velvet, the sound of water lapping against the boat was restful, and the merry spirit of the others traveling with them was infectious. One group had brought glasses, passing a bottle of wine amongst themselves. They offered some to Tony and Deborah, but they declined.

He leaned close, a protective arm around her. For a moment, she let herself believe they were man and wife. That he valued and loved her . . . because she was falling deeper in love. Every time he was near, her heart beat faster.

Lightly rubbing the ruby between her fingers, Deborah debated with herself. She could not accept the life of a kept woman, and she feared she could not give him up. She prayed she had the skill to make him offer marriage.

Music interrupted her thoughts. They were halfway across when she heard the first beckoning strains of a full orchestra. She'd never heard one before. She instantly recognized the music as a piece from Handel. It was one of his minuets, stately, noble, and absolutely perfect for the evening. She sat in awe, as did everyone else on the water. Even Tony appeared impressed.

The boat hit the shore. Men were on hand to help them step up onto private docks. Tony took her arm and guided her through the merry crowd. A buzz of excitement was in the air, a sense of magic, and as Deborah walked into the wondrous world that was Vauxhall Gardens, she began to believe this evening anything was possible.

Marble statues dotted the mazes of secluded alleyways, groves of exotic trees, and secret arbors. "Have you been here before?" she asked Tony.

"Never." He smiled, and it made the evening more special that this was a first time for both of them.

Several couples hurried off down gravel walks, but she and Tony moved toward the music. Strings of lanterns hung over the walks. Lights in the shape of stars were tucked into the shrubbery.

Then they walked into the central square, the center of Vauxhall. The orchestra played in an ornate open concert hall with its own dance floor. Around the hall were temples, pavilions, and rotundas in all shapes, where supper boxes had been neatly designed into every nook and cranny.

They were greeted by the head waiter. "Lord Burnell, this way to your box, please." He led them to one of the more private supper boxes. It was festively decorated in red and gold and set under the sheltering branches of a chestnut tree sporting a chandelier.

Couples sat in other boxes nearby, all too engrossed with each other to pay attention to Tony and Deborah. Farther down, what appeared to be a whole family had gathered to eat, be merry, and enjoy the music. The atmosphere reminded Deborah of the fair in Ilam.

Then, her gaze met that of an older gentleman in the pavilion across from theirs. He had snow-white hair and a strong nose. He'd been staring at her. She drew back, uncomfortable.

"What is it?" Tony asked.

She glanced back in the direction of the gentleman but he was now speaking animatedly to a woman sitting beside him. She, too, was older but obviously very frail. Her glance moved across the way toward Deborah, but then shrugged, disagreeing with her companion.

Deborah forced herself to dismiss the couple from her mind. "Nothing," she murmured, as an efficient waiter began serving a cold supper of chicken and ham. Tony had ordered the best vintages of wine, and she quickly lost her momentary sense of disquiet in the pleasure of good food and the company of the man she loved.

They entertained each other by watching the people who strolled past and pointing out the costumes some masked guests wore or laughing at the increasingly flamboyant behavior of others as the wine flowed.

Lizbet had been right. Vauxhall was the perfect place for a liaison. There, manners were more carefree and unrestrained. She and Tony did not have to worry about prying eyes. He could hold her hand, place an arm protectively around the back of her chair, or, beneath the table, brush his leg against her thigh.

More than once, she caught his gaze on the ruby heart resting in the cleft of her cleavage.

Evening faded into night. The candles, the fanciful lights, even the stars, seemed brighter and more festive.

"I have a surprise for dessert," he whispered in her ear. The waiter set a tray of strawberries and ice cream on their table.

"I've never had ice cream," Deborah confessed. With her first taste of the cold, melting concoction, she groaned in pleasure and finished the dish in a few bites.

"Here, have mine, too," Tony said. He pushed his stemmed glass of ice cream toward her.

"Oh, I couldn't."

He laughed, his expression so handsome he stole her breath. "You could. Let me help you." He dipped the spoon into his ice cream and held it up for her to taste.

But as she came closer, it was not the spoon her lips met, but his kiss — right there, in the semiprivacy of their supper box with the music of Handel in the air.

He tasted of strawberries and wine . . . a heady mixture. His hand slid to her waist — just as they were interrupted by the presence of the man who had been staring at Deborah earlier.

"I am so sorry. Please, I beg your pardon," a man said in a French-accented voice. He started to move back, obviously embarrassed.

Tony was not pleased. "You wished to speak to us?" he asked, his irritation clear.

"Not to you, my lord," the gentleman said, "but to the beautiful young woman with you. With your permission?"

Deborah pulled back, uncertain. He sensed her distrust. "I mean no offense. However . . .

you remind me so much of a woman I once knew. A Frenchwoman from Lyons. We were friends and with the Terror and coming to England —" His eyes misty, he beseeched her for understanding. "She meant something to me. And you, *you* are her image."

Tony resented the interruption but Deborah placed her hand on his arm. "Did you know her in Lyons?"

"We were childhood friends. Our families escaped together. She married an Englishman. This may be familiar to you, no?"

Now, Tony understood. He relaxed. Deborah leaned forward. "My mother was from Lyons."

The gentleman's face broke out in a wreath of smiles. He clapped his hands together. "I knew it. You are the daughter of Calandre de Cuvier."

"Yes. And you are?" Deborah asked, hearing for the first time how musical her mother's name was when spoken in her native tongue.

"Arnaud, Baron de Fontina. Your mother's family estate bordered mine. We grew up together, and both of our families escaped only moments before the bloodthirsty crowds attacked our lands. Tell me of your mother. How is she?"

For a stunned second, Deborah couldn't find the words. Then, softly, she said, "She is dead. She died right after I was born."

The baron made a distressed cry, then immediately apologized. "I am sorry. I am too old to

205

be so silly . . . but when one is in love — ?" A tear formed in his eye.

"Please, sit down and join us," Tony said standing.

The baron shook his head. "I would not intrude further." The sadness in his voice tore at Deborah's heart.

"You must have loved her very much," she said quietly.

"*Oui*, but — ?" He shook his head. "I wanted to marry her, but then she met her Englishman. Your father, no?"

"She was the love of his life," she said.

The baron nodded, his manner still distracted. "I must return to my wife." He forced a smile, in an attempt to recover his spirits. "She is not feeling well and has asked to leave. Her rheumatism makes her uncomfortable, and it is especially painful tonight."

"I hope it isn't a sign of rain," Tony said. "We've been lucky with the weather so far."

The Frenchman smiled. "The weather does give her pains, but I have discovered she is as often wrong as she is right." His gaze slid back to Deborah. "She is also a touch jealous. She knows how much I loved Calandre. You are very lovely, my lady. Your mother would have been proud."

Deborah was so touched, she couldn't speak until the baron said, "I have taken up enough of your time. *Merci* for your patience." He started to walk away, but Deborah called him back.

"Do you know anything about her relatives? Do I have family in London? Father always said I didn't, but perhaps — ?"

The baron stopped. "They are all gone, my lady. The duke and duchess, who would be your grandparents, were not strong. The Revolution robbed them of everything, and they died shortly after we arrived in London. There is no one."

"Perhaps she can have your name?" Tony suggested. "The two of you can meet. I'm certain there is much to be discussed."

Deborah could have thrown her arms around him for his suggestion. "Yes, please," she begged. "I know so little of my mother's life."

"I would be honored to tell you all I know," the baron said.

Tony took charge and gave the baron one of his cards. At the same time a waiter approached, saying the Baroness de Fontina requested her husband's presence immediately. She wished to leave.

The Frenchman shrugged. "I must go, no?" He bowed over Deborah's hand. "I have been blessed this night. It is good to know my beautiful Calandre lives on in her daughter." He left.

Deborah sat silent, needing a moment to take it all in.

Tony sat. He reached for her hand. "What are you thinking?"

She wasn't certain how to put her feelings

into words. "All my life I was not only the 'dark' one, but the child from a mother she never knew. Father spoke of her but not often. I can see now he didn't wish to make my step-mother jealous. And everyone else in the Valley acted as if she had never existed . . . except there was me." She looked up at the sky, covered with hundreds of stars. "If stars are angels, could one of them be she? Is she here now? Watching us?"

"If she is, then she knows how much I love you."

His words shimmered in the air between them. She could scarce believe her ears. "You love me?"

He lifted her hand and pressed a kiss on the back of it. "You hold my heart."

Deborah felt herself go numb. He repeated the words Lizbet had her write in the letter to him. Part of her was elated by his declaration; another part writhed with guilt. He thought she'd been the one to pen the letter.

But before she could form a confession, he rose. "Come, let's walk." He took her arm and led her toward one of the paths, a very private one without the festive lights of some of the others.

He laced his fingers in hers . . . and Deborah didn't want to confess she hadn't written the letter. What did it matter? The words mirrored those in her heart.

And she sensed there was a strong possibility

her dream of marriage was a very real possibility, especially when Tony pulled her into the secret haven of a rose arbor, the fragrant flowers perfuming the air. There, in the secret byway, they were alone.

Tony slipped his arms around her and began kissing her. Deborah kissed him back with all the passion she had in her soul.

She couldn't help herself.

Their kiss deepened. He pulled her closer, his tongue teasing hers. Between them, she could feel the strength of his erection. He was hard, ready. She pressed herself against him, as hungry as he was.

Then, suddenly, a high whistling sound filled the air, and there was an explosion of light.

Deborah broke the kiss with a gasp. Tony kept his arms around her as the night seemed to burst with stars.

Fireworks.

She'd heard of them but had never seen them. The orchestra was playing full force, its music carrying the night, punctuated by the fireworks. Wheels of flame and sparks spun and hissed in a whirlwind of light, while more rockets exploded in the air.

"It's marvelous," she said.

"Yes." He tightened his grip around her, and Deborah wished they could stay like that forever — locked in each other's embrace beneath velvet skies, surrounded by light and music. His lips brushed her hair. He bent down for another kiss —

A crack of thunder was their only warning before lightning split the sky. It was as if the fireworks had upset the gods. A heartbeat later, rain poured down. Tony ducked with her under the haven of the arbor, but it offered little protection from the rain. "We're going to have to run," he shouted over the din of rain hitting the earth.

She nodded.

He took her hand, and, together, they dashed down the path heading for the boats. They weren't alone. Couples came out from every walkway and crevice, some laughing giddily, others dismayed by the downpour.

At the docks, there was a teeming crowd of revelers anxious to board and go home. They all seemed to be young and full of high spirits. Deborah surmised that the older guests, like Baron de Fontina, had left earlier. The boatman had lanterns and there were a few gaslights still burning but the rest was dark.

The orchestra had dispersed, so some wag started singing a rousing folk tune, and others joined in. The rain let up a bit, then stopped completely as if it enjoyed the music.

Tony kept his arm around her as they moved forward in the crowd. With the crush, boatmen were taking whichever customers climbed aboard first. The most popular boats were the ones with striped canvas awnings.

Deborah worried to Tony, "Lizbet's dress is ruined."

"I'll buy her a dozen more," he promised. "And dresses for you, too." Then, he kissed her — right there. In public.

Of course, it was dark, and no one seemed to be paying attention to her. Instead, they all seemed as carefree as Tony. One man, laughing, jumped into the river, and two others jumped after him. The spectators roared approval at their antics.

Tony maneuvered her to a boat. She started to step aboard just as a woman giddy with laughter started forward. Both of them were forced to stop at the same time.

The laughing woman looked at Deborah. "Excuse me," she said. "You go first. I'll be second." She was a blond beauty, with long lashes and high cheekbones and dressed in a shepherdess's costume.

But suddenly, the mirth died in her eyes.

She look right past Deborah to Tony. Her gaze widened, and her lips parted in alarm. Even in the dark, Deborah could see the color drain from her face.

And Tony's reaction was just as surprised. He stood behind her, but Deborah sensed him stiffen and put a small distance between them.

"My lord?" the woman said.

"Lady Amelia."

Sensing something was wrong, Deborah turned to him. The expression on his face could have been etched in stone as he glared past her to her companion, a man dressed like a yeoman whom he recognized. "Bord," Tony acknowledged with unmistakable disdain.

"Burnell," came the curt reply.

Another young woman in costume barged between all of them. She grabbed Lady Amelia's arm, and said, "This way. We're all over here."

In seconds, the small group disappeared back into the crowd, and new people stepped forward in their place. The whole encounter happened so quickly, Deborah could have imagined it.

Tony guided her on the boat. The skies started raining again, but they found space under the awning and huddled together. He folded her wet shawl down, his manner all that could be loving and protective.

But then, he took a moment to look out over the water. The boat Lady Amelia's party had joined was loud with raucous shouts and laughter. The three men who had jumped into the river were part of their party and were making a great show of wringing out their coats and pouring water out of their shoes.

"Who was she?" Deborah asked offhandedly . . . but very interested in his reply.

He didn't answer immediately. Instead, he wrapped his arms around her, holding her tight in the warmth of his body heat. He nuzzled her ear.

She pulled away slightly. "Is she a friend?"

He didn't want to answer. She didn't trust his hesitation. She turned to look him fully in the face . . . he did not evade the question.

"She's to be my wife."

Chapter Twelve

Deborah wasn't quite certain she'd heard Tony correctly. Or if she'd *wanted* to pretend he hadn't actually said the word *wife*.

She was aware of their not being alone, of others in the boat although they were all involved in their own conversations. Her voice low, she demanded, "You're . . . going . . . to be married?"

He didn't answer immediately. His arms around her waist tightened their hold. He leaned his lips close to her ear. "Don't think about it. My marriage will have nothing to do with us."

The boat hit the pier with a bump, and there was no time to say more because she and Tony stood in front of the steps, and everyone in the overcrowded boat wanted to get out. Deborah moved as if sleepwalking. Tony protectively directed her with a possessive hand on her arm.

However, on the pier, the magic of Vauxhall was gone. She had returned to reality.

Other couples hurried past them, anxious to return home. Deborah had lost track of the boat carrying the woman who would be Tony's wife. It wasn't until they reached his coach waiting for them that she began to think and feel again.

And what she felt was *anger.*

Strong, resolute, ready-to-bite-someone's-head-off anger.

She dug in her heels. They had come to his coach, waiting away from the quickly dispersing crowd, and there was no way she would climb in with him.

Tony stopped beside her. "Deb?"

"It's Deborah." She yanked her arm out of his hand. "Deborah, Deborah, *Deborah.*"

"Not to me," he replied confidently. "To me, you are my Deb."

She answered him by slapping his face so hard that his head turned.

He had a very firm jaw. Her fingers stung.

"I'm not your *anything,*" she vowed. "You took me out this evening, in public, and you were already *promised* to someone else?"

He rubbed the side of his face. Now, in the light of the coach lamps, he looked her in the eye. His coachman gave a start but Tony waved him back. "I have a commitment. Yes," he said. "But *you* are the one I will care about, the one whose children I will value."

"Then why marry her?"

"Because I have no choice." He shook his head. "Deb, it is an arranged marriage. Her family's connections will offer me opportunities to advance myself."

She took a step back. He was little better than Edmond or Henry. Her damp hem dragged on the ground, and she felt common.

Angry questions formed on her lips, but she bit them back.

What gentleman gave a care what his mistress thought?

Head high, Deborah turned on her heel and walked away. Most of the other coaches were gone. The streets around the docks were dark, forbidding — but she didn't care. She had to get away from Tony before she revealed exactly how deeply he had hurt her. She'd trusted him . . . and yet, she had only herself to blame. From the beginning, he'd never offered marriage.

She was the one who had hoped.

Tears threatened. She choked them back. She wouldn't cry. Never again.

"Deb!" Booted feet crunched gravel as he came after her.

She kept walking, her back stiff.

"Deb, what the devil has gotten into you?" he demanded, his voice telling her he was much closer than she'd realized. Then, suddenly, he swept her up in his arms and started carrying her to the coach.

His long legs ate up the ground. Stunned, she took a moment to assess what was happening. He was taking her against her will!

She fought in earnest, twisting her body to be free, while striking out with her fists.

He tightened his hold until she couldn't move.

Turning her head toward his coachman and waiting footman, she started to shout for help, but he crushed her face to his chest. "Montvale," he ordered before practically tossing her into the coach and climbing in behind her. He shut the door with a resounding slam.

Deborah struggled to escape out the other side, but Tony was on top of her in a blink. The coachman set the horses off with a shout, and they charged through the streets of London.

She would have shouted for help, but he placed his hand over her mouth. His face mere inches from hers, he warned in a low voice, "Not here. Not now. You can wish me to Hades in a moment, but you will not create a further scene in front of the servants. They talk."

His vehemence surprised her into silence. He'd always seemed so implacable. Emotion ran high in him although she could not see signs of it in his face. Instead, the tension radiated from his body and appeared in the tight, direct movement of his hands.

Cautious now, she pushed back in the corner as far as she could go. She was not afraid, but she knew better than to bait him.

He noticed her withdrawal. "Deb — ?" he started, then stopped. Apparently it was not the time for talk. He watched her closely, his grip on her hands tight as if he feared she'd jump from the coach.

A few moments later, the horses were reined to a stop. Tony did not wait for the footman. He kicked open the door himself, pulling

Deborah with him as he got out. His arm around her, he hustled her toward the front door of a house blazing with light. His house. The steps were brick and the door a lacquered black decorated with polished brass. Inside, a chandelier with what seemed to be a hundred candles burned brightly from the high ceiling of the foyer.

A butler and several footmen greeted him. He waved them aside with a quick, "That will be all," and moved with her toward a curved staircase. The rugs were thick, the walls paneled with expensive woods. Deborah caught a glimpse of the ancestral portraits lining their way up the stairs, but Tony did not linger.

He whisked her up the first floor and down a hall toward a set of double doors. He threw open the doors. A valet rose from a chair before the fire where he'd been waiting. Seeing that his master was not alone, the servant practically disappeared, fading back into the shadows and slipping out a side door.

Deborah took two steps into the room and halted. They were in his bedroom. His private sanctuary.

The room itself was the size of the whole ground floor of Lizbet's house. The ceilings, at least twenty feet high, were painted with pastoral scenes and accented with gold-leaf medallions. The walls were cream; the rug patterned in golds and blue.

A canopied bed with huge posts at each

corner carved out of heavy mahogany dominated the room. The bed-curtains were gold-cut velvet. The mattress was so wide a family of six could have slept there and still had room. The bedclothes were the same cut velvet only in a marine blue.

Tony firmly shut the doors. "Now you can talk. Say anything you wish, no one will hear us."

"I'd rather leave," she announced proudly.

He shook his head. "Oh, no. I won't let you leave until you explain your behavior down at the piers."

"Explain *my* behavior?" she repeated, incredulous. "I've just met the woman you are going to *marry*, and you feel I owe the explanations?"

His expression turned bleak. "I never misled you, Deb. You knew I could not marry you."

"No, I knew you'd asked me to be your mistress and I told you no."

"You can't mean those words," he said, taking a step forward. "Not when you react the way you do to me."

She didn't back down. "I don't say what I don't mean. Why did you bring me here? To impress me with your money, your possessions?"

He made an impatient sound. "This is my home, Deb, but, yes, you need to see what I can offer. I can give you the world."

"But you can't give me your name." She raised a hand, then let it drop. "I'm sorry,

Tony, I want the one thing that you refuse to give me." She started for the door.

He stepped into her path. "You don't understand," he replied. *"I love you."*

When he'd said those words at Vauxhall, she'd been overjoyed. Now, doubt destroyed hope, to be replaced, in turn, with red-hot anger. A man who loved a woman didn't ask her to settle for *carte blanche*.

"My lord, you don't know the meaning of the word 'love.' "

Her barb hit its mark. Tony pulled back, and Deborah knew it to be her opportunity to escape before he challenged her further. Her resistance to him could only go so far.

She moved to the door. His hand shot out and caught her arm at the elbow. He swung her around. Anger and what looked like pain blazed in his eyes. "Damn you, Deb. Damn you for being the independent creature that you are. And damn you for testing me." His mouth came down on her lips.

It was no ordinary kiss. It was hard, demanding, unrelenting. He backed her up against the door. His tongue met hers.

She wanted to resist.

She couldn't.

His leg moved between hers . . . or did she open herself willingly?

The kiss deepened. Need, hunger, desire rose in her. She wanted to swallow him whole. He pressed his body against hers, pushing her until she fit against him.

Her blood pounded in her ears. She curved her arms around his neck and rubbed tight, full breasts against his chest. A moment earlier, she'd been proud and disdainful, but now she wanted him. She ached for him.

He tossed her wet shawl aside and lifted her skirts. She pressed toward his seeking hand. He unbuttoned his breeches. She didn't think she could wait a moment longer, yet a spark of sanity still reigned. "I shouldn't," she whispered struggling against her own desires.

He leaned into her. "Blame me, love, blame me . . . but don't turn me away."

And she couldn't.

He was already hard, and she was ready for him. He entered in one long smooth stroke — and for a second, she could barely breathe.

Holding himself still, he said against her hair, "Feel me?" He made himself move, and she gave a soft gasp of need. "Dear God, I want you." He slid in deeper. His lips brushed her hair, her neck as he made promises . . . promises she knew in her heart he could not keep, and she didn't care.

It was always thus with them. They were both powerless in the face of their own lust. He lifted her legs around his waist, the action taking him to the hilt until he filled her.

"Can you love me?" he begged against her ear. "Even a little?"

Oh, she loved him — but she would not

speak the words because he would never be hers, not fully.

Against the door, he began making love to her, and she met him, measure for measure. They found their own rhythm, one that was as old as time, giving and receiving, pleading and offering —

Suddenly, her body hit its release, and she seemed to shatter into a thousand sparkling stars.

Tony drove on, harder and harder until, abruptly, he pulled out of her body with a short cry. He sank slightly as if his legs could not hold his weight. Her skirts fell into place as she slid down the door to the floor.

He lowered himself to sit beside her. Lifting her arm, he kissed her palm, the back of her hand, the crook of her arm. She still wore her gloves.

"You are a wonder," he breathed against her neck.

"I'm wanton," she replied without self-pity. "You've changed me." She shook her head. "I was once so respectable."

Placing his hand against the side of her face, he forced her to face him. His gaze serious, he said, "You *are* respectable. I love you, Deb. I would never hurt you. And yet, you've not told me how you feel."

This was the moment she could answer him back in kind, where she should profess her love . . . but she wouldn't. She couldn't.

"Ah, Deb," he said sadly as if he could read her thoughts. He kissed her, a deep, satisfying kiss while his hands began to untie the laces of her dress. He pulled the pins from her damp hair and combed it with his fingers until it curled down over her breasts.

He took his time with the undressing until all she wore were the golden chain and ruby pendant. He led her to the bed. She lay back on the velvet covers and watched him disrobe. He was ready to make love again.

Stretching his body over hers, he settled himself between her legs and said confidently, "I know you love me."

And, sinful woman that she was, she opened her arms . . . but she did not speak the words.

Tony made love to her over and over until neither could move. They fell asleep in each other's arms.

However, several hours later, Deborah was awaken by his jerky movements and incoherent speaking. He was having the dream again.

She put her arms around him. "Tony, it's the dream. I'm here, Tony. It's all right."

He roused. "Deborah?"

"Yes."

He nuzzled her sleepily, never bothering to open his eyes. "My Deb." Lowering his head to her breast, he whispered, "I love you," and fell back into an easy sleep.

How much could a woman sacrifice for love?

As she stroked Tony's hair, the weight of his body on hers, she found herself thinking about her stepmother — the woman who had been her father's *second* choice. For the first time, she wondered if Pamela had been truly happy. Now, remembering her through a woman's experience, Deborah understood there had been a sadness about Pamela, a sense of disappointment.

For the first time, Deborah empathized. She did not want to share Tony with another woman. She wanted his heart, his presence, his name, and his children. She could settle for no less.

But it was going to be hard to leave him.

She pressed a kiss on the top of his head. In sleep, he appeared younger, more relaxed.

Carefully, she slid out of the bed. Tony slept on, his deep breathing even. Silently, she dressed in her damp clothes. She unclasped the necklace, placing it on his chest of drawers before draping the shawl over her head and shoulders.

She moved to the door . . . then paused. With one last glance to the man at the bed, she whispered, "I love you, too." Was it her imagination — or did he smile in his sleep as if he'd heard her?

She slipped out the door.

Downstairs, the candles of the chandelier had been snuffed, leaving a single candle burning by the doorway table. A footman slept in the chair, his wigged head resting on his chest. The hour had to be close to three.

Deborah hoped to tiptoe past him, but no such luck. He woke with a snort, embarrassed to have been caught napping. "I beg pardon, miss. Do you wish me to take you home?"

His offer surprised her. "You will?"

"Well, of course, I'd arrange it, if'n His Lordship don't mind. I'm to see to the door and His Lordship's guests."

The footman left his post to go fetch a coachman. Fearing Tony might wake and find her gone, Deborah didn't want to linger. She was relieved to learn that since she was an unexpected guest, the butler had ordered the coach to be kept on hand in case she needed to leave.

Within ten minutes, she found herself on her way to Lizbet's. Her sister's house was dark and silent. Deborah paused on the street, coming to a decision. She could no longer stay there. Both Edmond and Lizbet would make her uncomfortable for refusing Tony's offer. The time had come to leave.

She turned to the coachman. "May I beg a moment more of your time?"

"Yes, miss?" He was the same coachman that had driven them to Vauxhall.

"I need to be driven to the nearest coaching inn. Would you be so kind? Otherwise, I fear I'd be forced to walk. There's not another conveyance in sight at this hour of the morning."

The coachman appeared doubtful. "I know that Lord Burnell would not want you traveling the streets alone."

"I'd have no other choice."

"You're supposed to leave?"

"I must at first light."

With a resigned sigh, the footman agreed. "The coaching inn is on my way back anyway."

Deborah could have kissed him. Instead, she hurried inside Lizbet's and hastily packed her belongings. She thought about leaving a note, but there was no time. She'd write Lizbet from Ilam.

Without a backward glance, she left with no more than two pounds to her name, all she had in the world.

Tony woke later than his customary hour of the morning. With a sense of well-being, he reached across the sheets for Deb — and was alarmed to find her missing.

He sat up and searched the room with his eyes. Her clothes were gone. The necklace lay on his dresser.

A word to his valet and within minutes he learned that his coachman had driven her back to her sister's at around half past three. He was not pleased. Why should she leave? He'd brought her to his house because he'd *wanted* her there.

Impatient, he dismissed his fussy valet and dressed himself in riding clothes. He would ride to see her that morning. He was no fool. Her leaving did not bode well for him.

But he was not going to give up. Not until she admitted defeat and yielded to him.

He charged down the stairs, calling for his butler, Charles, to have his favorite horse saddled. The half hour it took for the horse to be readied and brought around seemed an eternity. He paced the length of the foyer until his butler tactfully suggested he have a bite to eat.

In the dining room, Tony didn't bother to sit but buttered toast and poured himself a glass of ale, ignoring the eggs, sausages, and beef set out for his enjoyment.

A footstep by the door caught his attention. He turned.

"My lord, Mr. Warner," Charles intoned.

Warner hovered in the doorway, his stance uncertain. Tony motioned for the butler and footman minding the breakfast table to leave the room. "What does Deborah have to say?" he demanded, thinking Warner was acting as an emissary from her.

However, the man's reaction was one of surprise. "She hasn't said a word to me. We thought she was here with you."

Alarmed now, Tony said, "She left last night." He strode to the door and shouted down the hall for Charles, who appeared instantly. "Fetch the coachman who drove Mrs. Percival to her sister's house last night. I want him here now."

"Yes, my lord."

Warner shifted, changing tack. "Please, my lord, I hope you realize I have no control over her. She's a headstrong woman. Difficult even. Far from biddable."

"Aren't you worried where she is?" Tony countered.

"Oh, yes," Warner agreed belatedly. "Very . . . worried."

"I see."

Footsteps out in the hallway signaled Charles's return. He had the coachman with him.

"This is Davis, my lord," Charles said.

Tony didn't waste time. "You drove a guest of mine to a house off of New Road?"

"Yes, my lord," Davis answered.

"Did she say anything about her further plans?" Tony nodded to Warner. "This gentleman is her brother-in-law and is most anxious about her."

Davis rubbed his palms on his breeches, obviously nervous. "Well, my lord, after I took her to the house off New Road, she ordered me to take her to the posting inn."

Tony straightened. "Did you stay with her until she left?"

Uncertainly, Davis nodded. "I thought it best rather than to leave a lady by herself."

"And do you know where she went?"

"She bought a ticket on the post bound for Derby."

"Excellent!" Tony looked to his butler. "Charles, I want you to find a new position for Davis. A step up, or two. He's pleased me."

"Thank you, my lord," Davis said, bowing.

"Send for Allendale, Charles. I'm leaving town today, and I'll need him to manage several matters for me."

"Yes, my lord."

"You are both dismissed." What Tony had to say to Warner, he didn't want overheard.

The man had the good sense to know he was in trouble. The moment the door closed, he pleaded, "I didn't know she was going to leave, my lord."

Tony held up a hand for silence. "Yes, but, Warner, if you were a better man, you would be calling me out instead of mewing about wondering where Deborah is."

The color drained from Warner's face. "I would think it is her decision."

"Ummhmmmm."

"And my position?" Warner asked hesitantly.

"Is still in my employ," Tony answered. "However, if I were you, I'd attempt to be more of a man."

His point was sorely taken. "You don't understand. If you had a wife and child and had been unfairly sacked, you, too, would have been desperate. Perhaps I haven't always acted wisely, but I had little choice."

And he'd done what was expedient. Had not

Tony been guilty of the same at one time or another?

He also knew Deborah would not be pleased if he baited her brother-in-law. "In the future, I will expect you to show more care." The silk in his voice ensured the man did not mistake his meaning.

"Yes, my lord." There followed a beat of silence, then Warner asked, "And what of my sister-in-law? What are you going to do?"

Her hushed words, spoken when she thought Tony was asleep, echoed in his mind . . . *I love you, too.*

He had thought her in the bed beside him. Obviously, she'd been on her way out the door. "I'm going after the Derby stage and take her off it."

Warner sputtered. "But you can't just remove a passenger from the post, especially one as stubborn as Deborah."

Tony laughed. "I'll find a way." He started for the door, but Warner stopped him.

"Why do I sense you are anticipating this encounter, my lord?"

"Because I am."

Their gazes met, admiration in Warner's eyes. "You'll be good to her?"

"In ways she has never even imagined," Tony promised. Fifteen minutes later he was on his way to Derby.

Chapter Thirteen

Cold and numb, Deborah sat on top of the overcrowded mail coach. Because of rain and delays, there were more travelers than normal. Of course, even if there had been a seat inside, she would not have been able to afford the higher-priced fare. So she faced the mists, the drizzle, and the possibility of heavier rain. The weather was not the best for traveling.

She was returning to Ilam a much different woman than she'd been when she'd left. When she'd started on the trip, she'd thought herself truly on her own for the first time.

Now, Deborah knew what alone really was.

Huddled among the nine other outside passengers, the only woman among males, she knew she had some decisions to make. She had already decided she would not marry Parson Ames. And never again would she obey a summons to an interview with Dame Alodia.

Nor would she ever allow herself to be dependent on her sisters and their husbands. She was going to have to find gainful employment. She thought of Mrs. Hemmings, Dame Alodia's companion, and a shiver of horror ran through her. Perhaps it would be better to find a position as a governess?

She attempted to picture herself schooling

someone else's adorable children . . . then she remembered the parson's ill-mannered brats.

Perhaps she shouldn't have let her pride turn away Tony's offer of *carte blanche.*

She tried to push that out of her mind and shifted away from the rotund gentleman over-crowding her seat on her right. He smelled of garlic and unwashed male. She held her breath, trying to pretend he wasn't there. She was exhausted from a lack of sleep, her head ached from the thinking, and she was tired of being wet and out in the open.

The thin gentleman on her left let out a huge sneeze — all over her. He had a red, bulbous nose. "So sorry, so sorry," he muttered, wiping his nose with the cuff of his sleeve. Then, he sneezed again with such force he rocked the bench they sat on. The other passengers around them frowned and turned away.

Not feeling too well herself, Deborah pulled her bonnet down around her face and hunkered into her seat. It was going to be a long ride.

"Hey there!" a passenger shouted to the mail driver. "There's a rider looks like he is trying to catch us back on the road there."

The driver ignored him but everyone else, including the guard, craned their necks to see. A man on horseback was less than a quarter mile behind them and gaining rapidly.

"Hold up," another passenger yelled to the driver. "He's motioning to us that he wants us to stop."

"Can't stop," the guard ordered from his perch at the rear of the coach, the precious mail tucked safely in the boot beneath his feet. "King's duty." To give importance to his words, he blew his brass horn.

It became a race then, and all the miserable souls packed like sausage rolls on the top of the mail coach had prime seats, provided they didn't topple off. The driver snapped his whip, the guard laughed, and they charged forward.

But the rider edged closer.

Even miserable as she was, Deborah was caught up in the contest — until she realized the rider was Tony.

She faced forward in her seat, momentarily stunned to imagine him chasing her, then she buried her face in her hands with a groan.

"You aren't under the weather, too?" her bulky neighbor asked. "Here, chew this." He offered her a clove of garlic. "It's an Italian cure," he confided. "I swear by it."

The man to her left sneezed again, too engrossed in the chase to wipe his nose.

Tony reached the corner of the coach. He was wearing a low-brimmed hat and a huge greatcoat. He shouted for the coach to stop.

The guard leaned over the side. "Go on with you! We've got the mail!"

"Five quid to each of you if you stop!" Tony answered.

The guard looked at the driver, who immediately started reining in the horses. The passengers laughed. The guard stood and warned they'd not wait long.

Tony brought his own mount to a halt while Deborah quickly slouched down among her companions, pulling the brim of her hat with her.

"Nice horseflesh," someone commented.

"Thank you," Tony tossed off before addressing the guard while offering money. "I need to speak to one of your passengers."

"Be quick about it," the guard said.

Deborah heard Tony open the door to the coach.

Around her, several passengers commented on the stylish cut of Tony's coat which sported no fewer than seven capes. "He's a nabob," Deborah's seat companion declared.

"Any man who offers money to stop the mail has more flow than I have," another gent answered.

The drizzle was turning to rain. A gentleman in the coach protested the delay to the driver, who ignored him. The coach door was slammed shut, then the coach swayed with Tony's weight as he climbed the ladder to the top.

Deborah sank even lower in her seat. She could see him. He'd reached the roof and scanned the crowd for her. His hat was set at a rakish angle, and the damp didn't seem to bother him at all. His skin glowed with vitality. He looked good, very good.

And then his gaze met hers. He grinned, that charming lopsided smile of his. It had already gotten her in more trouble than she'd ever even imagined.

He held out his hand. "Hello, Mrs. Percival."

"I'm not going with you," she stated flatly.

"You must."

"I won't."

"Here now," the driver said, standing. "You can't take a passenger off my coach if'n she doesn't wish to go. Now off with you. I've got a schedule to keep."

"She wants to go," Tony argued. "She's being stubborn."

"No, I really don't want to go," Deborah declared. "Now, leave me be. You are holding up the stage."

"You heard the lady, sir," the guard said. "We've got the mail to get through. I must ask you to leave."

"I'm not leaving without her," Tony answered simply.

The driver stood, one hand still on the reins. In his other hand, he held a wicked-looking pistol. He raised the sight on Tony. "I must ask you to change your position, sir. Now get down."

Tony looked right at him and said, "No."

Deborah panicked. What madness was this? The driver obviously didn't recognize Tony. "Please, this is Lord Burnell. You can't shoot him."

"My contract is to see the mail through, madam," the driver said. "I will not lose my commission because of him. Now, sir, lord or not, I'll give you a count of three to get off my coach. Let me warn you, my powder is dry, and I aim true."

Everyone ducked and moved away from Tony — save Deborah. She stood, frustrated by his interference in her life and his own foolish stubbornness. Below, the passengers with seats inside the coach had scrambled out to watch the unfolding drama.

"*One . . .*"

"Get off this coach. Leave," she ordered Tony. "He is deadly serious."

"I won't leave unless you come with me," he answered pleasantly.

She wasn't about to give in. "I'm not coming with you."

"Then I shall be shot," Tony answered.

"And die a fool!"

"Possibly."

"*Two,*" the driver said firmly.

Deborah clenched her fist. Did Tony believe this was some sort of joke? "I won't go with you." She bit each word out in frustration.

"So, you've said. But I'm not leaving without you."

She could have screamed at his implacable response. Had he lost all common sense? "And I'll not bend to your will," she shot back.

"*Three.*" The driver looked down the sight of

236

his gun — and Deborah couldn't stand it any longer.

She moved between the two men, raising her hand to ward off the confrontation. "Don't fire," she said. "I'm getting off the coach. Don't shoot him." She started down the ladder.

There was a collective sigh of satisfied relief and even a smattering of applause from the other passengers.

Tony was bold enough to take a bow. One would have thought he was aping on the stage instead of in danger of having a hole blown through him.

"Go on now," the driver ordered, and at last Tony complied.

At least he was in a good mood!

Down on the ground, with all the passengers gaping at her with round eyes, Deborah couldn't wait to give him a piece of her mind. However, her feet had barely hit the ground when the driver called out to the ogling passengers, "You all had better board quick. I'm not wasting any more time."

"What?" Deborah protested. "Wait! You can't leave me here!"

"You're off the coach," the driver announced.

"But my luggage!"

"Here, now, throw her luggage down," the driver instructed.

The garlic eater did as he said, tossing Deborah's portmanteau toward Tony, who caught it handily. But Deborah wasn't about to concede defeat. She ran up to driver's box. "I paid my fare to Derby!" she shouted up to him. "You can't leave me here, stranded!"

"I can and I will," the driver said, putting his pistol back under his coat. "Besides, you got His Lordship here. Work the matter out best between you."

"I'll take excellent care of her," Tony promised, even boldly giving a small salute.

"This isn't right!" Deborah said. She reached for the handle to the coach door, but the driver slapped the reins, and the horses started moving. She ran alongside the coach, the mud on the road slick beneath her feet. "I paid my fare. I'll write Parliament to complain!"

Her threats had little impact. The passengers inside the coach crowded to stare out the window, but no one offered help.

The vehicle picked up speed. Deborah could not stay with it. Forced to loose her hold, she stumbled and almost fell before the coach charged off, its wheels flinging mud at her skirts.

In seconds, it disappeared round a bend in the road and out of sight.

And she was left with Tony.

Slowly, she turned. He stood patiently, a pleased expression on his face, her portmanteau in his hands. His horse grazed contentedly a small distance away.

"If you think this changes anything between us, you are wrong," she said in a voice that could have chilled water.

"Oh, come, Deb," he countered reasonably. "You must like me, even a little. You didn't want to see me shot by the driver."

"I wouldn't want to see a dockside mutt shot by the driver," she flashed back.

He smiled serenely. "You said you loved me. Last night. You said the words, Deb."

So, he had heard! He hadn't been asleep.

Well, she wasn't about to admit to the words now. Not when she was so angry with him she'd rather picture him hanging by his thumbs. How in the world had she ever considered his grin endearing?

She marched right up to him and yanked the portmanteau out of his hands. He gave it up easily. "I don't know what you wished to accomplish by pulling me off the coach," she said, "but whatever it is, you will not get what you want, my lord."

"I want you," he responded, the line of his mouth turning serious.

"Well, you can't have me." She turned on her heel and started walking down the road, heading toward Derby. The dampness seeped into her shoes, wetting her stockings. The brim of her hat flopped forward, hopelessly ruined. She stopped a moment to fold it back from her face. Rain made her blink. She shivered and stifled a sneeze. She felt chilled all the way to her bones.

"Deb, I know you are angry with me." He approached, holding the reins of his horse.

She snorted her agreement and walked on.

He fell into step beside her. "But you do love me."

She said nothing.

He didn't need an answer. "I couldn't let you leave London, not now that we've found each other. I never believed in love until I met you. Granted, I'm not very good at it. I'm feeling my way . . . I know you are angry about this marriage nonsense —"

"Nonsense?" Deborah whirled to confront him. "You are about to enter into one of the sacraments of the church and you call it nonsense? *And yet,*" she continued before he could answer, "you improperly proposition me and call it *love?*" She shook her head and marched forward. "My lord, at this moment, I believe I should accept your offer of *carte blanche*. Then I'd spend every single penny you own and make your life miserable because I am so *angry* with you! How *dare* you not tell me you were promised to another? How dare you believe I was so bereft of all moral values that I would agree to enter into an indecent liaison with you?"

"Deb, I —"

She cut him off ruthlessly, warming to her subject. "Of course, how could you not think such a thing?" she asked the world at large. "If anything, my wanton behavior encouraged such a belief —" The sneeze she'd held back exploded out of her. She wished she had worn thicker stockings.

"Here let me hold that," Tony offered, reaching for her portmanteau.

She jerked it away from him. "I will take care of myself."

For the first time, he acted as if her words were getting through to him. "And is that what you want, Deb? To be alone?"

Was that what she wanted? She dared not answer him, afraid he'd talk circles around her. Her head ached from the emotion.

When she didn't speak but plowed on ahead, he said, "Well, at least get on Copper. No matter what you want, I'm not going to leave you alone in the middle of nowhere, and there is no sense in you walking in the rain, carrying your luggage."

She whirled. "What did you call your horse, Copper?"

"That's his name." The animal's ears pricked up as if agreeing — and suddenly, everything she was feeling crystallized.

"I've never heard anyone name a horse Copper unless it was flea-ridden or a child's mount," she confessed, and then admitted a bit hysterically, "You see, this is what you do to me. You are so big, so wealthy, so completely confident, and yes, a touch arrogant. But then, you disarm me with something you say, a look, a gesture, a little thoughtfulness." She raised a hand in wonder. "You name your horse Copper or are kind to a trusted servant like Miss

Chalmers or you hold Pamela in your arms as if she belongs there . . . and then, worse of all, you convince me there is no harm in one little kiss." She looked up to the heavens. "One little kiss? I rue the day I ever thought there was anything harmless in kissing!"

Tony took a step forward, his expression intent. "There isn't when you are with the right person."

She shook her head sadly, a shiver running through her. "The problem is I don't want to be in second place, Tony. I don't want to feel the stepdaughter anymore. I refuse to be the mistress. I won't be an afterthought or the one to make sacrifices. I want to be able to hold my head high and live my life on my terms."

"Those are radical ideas, Deb."

"I'm feeling radical." And it felt good to say so. She started walking backward, away from him. "I've behaved badly," she acknowledged, thinking aloud. "And whenever a woman behaves badly, there is a price she must pay." Oh, yes, there was a price. Her self-respect. Her dignity. Her place in society. Even her walking in this rain was a penance. "There can be nothing between us, my lord. Nothing at all."

He let go of the reins and hurried to catch her arm just as she started to turn away. The rain ran off the brim of his hat and wet his shoulder. "What must I do to make you realize *you are my life*. Deb, you are the only soul I've ever let myself trust, the only one I can. Don't say I don't respect you. You're everything to me."

"But I'll never be your wife!"

The moment she spoke those words, she wished she could call them back. She sounded so pathetic. She felt foolish for even having harbored the hope.

"I would marry you if I were free."

The words hung in the air between them.

"Oh, Tony . . ."

He opened his arms and she stepped into them, burying her face in the capes of his coat. Tears mingled with rain and her body was shaking. She was so tired. So very tired.

Holding her close, he murmured reassuring words and she wanted to believe them. Dear Lord, she wanted to believe!

"I wouldn't have agreed to the marriage," he was explaining, "if I'd known you were out there waiting for me. I barely know Amelia. Her father offered her, and I agreed because —" He broke off, but then admitted wearily, "I agreed because she's the catch of the Season. Also there was another man at the table, a man I thought I could trust, and when Longest made his offer, ugly words were said. It was my pride, Deb. I agreed out of pride. And now, my pride won't let me cry off. I'd ruin her. I'd ruin us." His lips brushed the top of her head. "Can you forgive me? Please, forgive me."

She wanted to. She wanted to burrow into him, to soak up his warmth, his belief that the future would be fine.

Then she thought of her parents. Would her mother have agreed to such an arrangement? Her father should be turning in his grave. He'd had little money, but great honor.

"Once there is an heir," Tony said, "Amelia and I will rarely see each other. She doesn't know me any more than I know her."

Jealousy raised its ugly head. An heir. He would make a baby with this woman, a baby who would have the right to his name . . . something her children would not have.

She pushed away, bone-weary. A darkness lingered around the edges of her mind. Her teeth chattered, and the only words she could utter were, "I can't."

His jaw hardened. An angry muscle worked there. "Because you don't want to," he accused. "Because you're stubborn, Deb. So very stubborn!"

Angry, she should be angry . . . but she didn't have the energy for the emotion. She picked her portmanteau from where she'd dropped it when he'd hugged her. "Good-bye, my lord."

She would have sidestepped him but instead of going forward, she started to fall back. Such a strange sensation . . . and then all turned to blackness.

Tony caught her before she fell to the ground. Copper came up, sensing something was wrong. He stamped but stood his ground.

The animal didn't like being in the rain any more than the humans did.

Biting the tips of his fingers, Tony pulled off his glove and felt Deb's forehead. Her pale skin burned with fever.

Dread laced through him. Why hadn't she said she was feeling poorly? He lifted her in his arms and placed her in Copper's saddle, not giving a second thought to the worn portmanteau left lying in the mud.

"Steady," he warned his horse as he mounted. The saddle leather was soaked. He shifted Deb's weight in front of him and removed his coat, covering her with it.

Copper anxiously pranced in the mud. Tony took a moment to look around. He did not recognize his surroundings and the gray rain made the hour seem later than it was. He'd passed several farms up the road a half hour's ride back. But there'd been no inn, no church, no sign of the kind of help she might need.

He had to get help for Deb. He had to take care of her.

But which way should he go? He decided to ride forward. *Always go forward,* he reminded himself.

Putting heels to horse, he charged on.

Chapter Fourteen

Deborah couldn't wake up. She was too exhausted. She wasn't certain where she was . . . and didn't care.

Anytime she attempted to rouse herself, her head was too heavy to lift, her tongue too thick to let her speak. There was warmth in the room, and she so needed to sleep. Deep, satisfying, healing sleep.

Movement came to her as if in a dream. There were voices. In the beginning, she'd been cold, too cold. Her teeth had chattered, and no amount of bedclothes seemed to have been able to keep her warm. Strong arms held her tight. Hands stroked her hair, holding her safe. A deep male voice hummed the tune to "Barbara Ellen" and she remembered being in Miss Chalmers's home and playing the pianoforte.

Then, she grew hot, too hot — feverish. She struggled, pushing her way out of the constricting arms and kicked the bedclothes off her body. Even her nightdress seemed too heavy for her. Sweat covered her body, making her restless and uncomfortable.

Someone applied damp cloths to her skin, but the heat radiated from the inside out. Nothing could relieve the discomfort.

She dreamed of water. Of rainwater

streaming down her face and over her body. She was naked and yet unashamed. Then the rain filled the earth, and she was floating in a swift-moving ocean. She attempted to paddle against the current . . . but grew tired. So very tired.

Deborah cried out for help. The water poured into her mouth, drowning her. She kicked her feet to keep afloat. A house floated by, along with chairs and logs. A whole tree, uprooted and on its side, sailed past.

Suddenly, she was surrounded by people. They stood on the water. Mr. Percival was there, and her stepmother. She waved and turned to face her father, who looked as he did when he was younger. In the distance, she could see her sisters, dancing with their husbands. She called for help. They turned their heads away from her.

She started sinking then, pulled down by the weight her skirts. She was so tired, she wanted to give up . . . and then there was Tony.

He swam beside and around her like a fish playing games. His arms circled her waist, and he kept them both up . . .

She woke.

At first, she thought she was in her bed back at the farm her husband had owned, the one her stepson, a man fifteen years older than she, had claimed. Funny, but he had not wanted his much younger stepmother to stay, and yet here she was . . . or so she thought.

A coal fire burning in the hearth was the only light. She wasn't at Mr. Percival's farm. He never burned coal since he thought it too expensive. Nor was she sleeping under a quilt of her making. And the mattress was softer and deeper than her husband had owned.

Memory returned. Mr. Percival was dead. She lived with her sister — no, she'd left for London and had met Tony. They'd fought . . . out in the rain. She'd meant to walk all the way to Derby.

Had she made it?

She thought not.

Deborah rolled onto her belly, the feather pillow bunched beneath her head. She stretched her toes to the end of the mattress. She knew she was sick. Her body felt weak, the taste in her mouth sour. Her hair was loose around her shoulders and stringy. She didn't like it that way.

She lifted her head. The room was not familiar. She let her gaze drift from the stand beside the bed with its bowls, spoons, and cloths. No rug covered the floor, but the furniture, though well-worn, was of good quality.

Then she saw Tony.

He slept in an uncomfortable wooden-backed chair, his head on his chest, his stocking feet propped up on the bed as if he attempted to make his large frame comfortable.

He did not look good. A heavy growth of whiskers covered his chin, and his hair was pushed every which way as if he'd been exasperated by something. He didn't wear a coat, and his shirt was open at the neck. A wool blanket had been thrown over his shoulders, and he appeared to have slept in his clothes for days.

Deborah remembered the mail coach, her anger, and how tired she'd been . . . and then she could remember nothing else. She didn't know how she had come to this place. And why was Tony here? She'd left him.

Her body as weak as a mewling kitten's, she attempted to sit up. She was thirsty. While there was no glass on the night table, a bowl held some sort of broth in it. She lifted it up and took a sniff. No, not broth — herbs, vile-smelling herbs.

In the corner on the other side of the bed was a privacy screen. She put her legs over the side of the mattress and unsteadily rose to her feet. First one step, then another. In spite of the fire, the floor was cold. She wondered if it was still raining? The windows were shuttered fast, yet she sensed it was night time.

Making the few steps to the privacy screen sapped her strength. She did her business and found water in a pitcher. She rinsed her mouth before pouring some in a bowl and washing her hands. Using a cloth beside the bowl, she cooled off her face and neck. She was tired, very tired.

She stepped out from behind the privacy

screen and realized Tony was awake. He took his feet down off the bed, sitting up. Concern was etched on his brow, and his eyes were dark, darker than her own right now.

"How are you feeling?" he asked, his voice hoarse.

She managed a weak smile. She couldn't answer. She needed to sleep. She had to sleep.

"I was worried," he said.

"Me too," she murmured, and crawled onto the mattress and beneath the covers. With a sigh, she laid her head on the pillow. Her last thought before drifting off into oblivion was how nice it was to have someone who cared enough to worry.

When next she woke, it was morning. The shutters had been thrown back, and the windows were open a crack. Sunshine flooded the room. A rooster crowed, and the warm promise of summer was finally in the air. It felt good after the rainy spring.

Deborah stretched. Her head felt clearer, and she was hungry. She thought of last night and immediately, she turned toward the chair where Tony had been sitting. He was gone, and the night table had been cleaned off.

A footstep sounded in the hall. The door opened, pushed by the shoulder of a mobcapped older woman with apple cheeks and a smile to match. She had to be a good twenty years older than Deborah. In her hands, she carried a pitcher and bowl.

She drew up short when she saw Deborah was awake. "Here now, I was hoping you'd be up, my lady. Your husband thought you might be feeling better this morning."

Husband? Tony had claimed they were man and wife, neatly sidestepping social proprieties. Did he realize how hypocritical he was being?

Her stomach growled.

The woman laughed. "Hunger is a good, healthy sign. I told your husband you'd pull through, and so you have. I'm Mrs. Strickler." She set the bowl and pitcher down behind the privacy screen and came to the side of the bed. "Here now, let me help you sit up. If you move too quickly, you'll make yourself dizzy."

Deborah was thankful for her help. Mrs. Strickler fluffed the pillows and arranged them behind Deborah's back.

"Where's — ?" Deborah hesitated. She'd been about to say "Lord Burnell." "Where's my husband?" The last two words sounded foreign to her ears.

"He's gone for a bit of air," the woman answered. "Pleased he is you are going to be fine. You've never seen a man more excited in your life than when he charged into my kitchen this morning and announced you had returned to your senses."

"Have I been that ill?"

"Oh, my lady, we thought you would die. 'Twas the influenza. It's a dangerous thing. I've three children, and my husband was not happy when His Lordship came knocking at our door begging for help. I recognized the fever immediately. It took my youngest brother years ago. He was dead before we could blink. I was afraid we were going to lose you, but your husband never gave up. Nursed you himself, he did."

Heat rose in Deborah's cheeks. She remembered the worry in his eyes last night. "I don't usually get sick."

"Sometimes the healthy ones get it the worst." Mrs. Strickler stirred the fire. "Your husband ordered in the coal. Purchased it for the whole house he did. I'm ashamed to say it was Lord Burnell's plump pockets that moved my husband to Christian charity, but there you have it."

Deborah wondered if she'd recognized Tony's title, but then again, her class probably didn't delight in London gossip the way Dame Alodia and the Matrons did. "How long was I sick?"

"Days. I feared His Lordship would take down with it, too. He rode himself through the rain for the doctor." She walked to the door. "Old Dr. James is a quack, and that's what we told His Lordship. Still, he had to see for himself. He didn't return with him. Dr. James must have sniveled about not traveling through the rain, and His Lordship vowed right then and there he'd cure you himself. When he came

252

back from that meeting, he was a sight to behold. Begging your pardon, my lady, but you are blessed to have such a man. He's devoted to you."

Yes, Deborah could imagine the scene. Once Tony made up his mind to do something, he'd move heaven and earth to accomplish it.

As for her other observation . . . Deborah pushed it from her mind, uncertain.

"Here now, let me fetch you some porridge," Mrs. Strickler said. "It's not tasty, but it's filling, and you don't need too much on your stomach right yet." She left the room, closing the door behind her.

Sinking down into the bed, Deborah reflected on everything Mrs. Strickler had said. Tony was nearby. She sensed his presence. When the door opened again, she was disappointed it wasn't him, but Mrs. Strickler with her porridge.

In spite of being ravenous, Deborah had trouble finishing all the food in her bowl. The part of her breakfast she most appreciated was a steaming cup of strong tea.

Mrs. Strickler fussed over her until the last spoonful of the bland cereal was gone. Afterward, she had two of her sons set up a tub and carry in hot water. They kept their heads low, and mumbled, "my lady," to Deborah when she thanked them.

"Do you need me to stay and help?" Mrs. Strickler offered.

"No, thank you," Deborah answered.

"Very well. Call if you need anything." The good woman shut the door.

Deborah had more strength after her meal. She made quick use of the bathwater. Mrs. Strickler's soap smelled of strong lye. However, it cleaned Deborah's hair, and she was happy.

The bath revived her spirits. It wasn't until she started putting on her nightgown that she realized the garment wasn't hers. This gown was made of the finest cotton, and the edges and hem were not frayed from many washings.

She searched the room for her portmanteau. She didn't find it anywhere. However, she did notice several dresses and a bonnet hanging from a peg in the wall. They were not hers . . . although they were all her size. There were stockings and a new pair of shoes, too.

Thoughtfully, she went back to bed. She would have to ask Mrs. Strickler where her clothes had gone, but once she lay down, she fell asleep . . .

When she woke again, the room was once again shuttered into darkness, and there was a low fire in the grate. A candle burned on the night table.

Tony had returned to the chair beside her bed, absorbed in a book. He'd shaved since the last time she'd seen him. His neckcloth was tied in a loose knot at his throat, and he wore his jacket and boots.

She didn't say anything, but he must have sensed she was awake because he looked up from his book and straight at her.

For a long time they held each other's gaze. Silence reigned. Then, she said, "Thank you."

He frowned, closing the book, marking the place with his finger. "For what? Dragging you through the rain? Almost costing you your life?"

That he blamed himself surprised her. Men usually didn't accept blame for anything.

"I'm the one who left London," she answered quietly, then changed the direction to the subject uppermost in her mind. "Mrs. Strickler believes we are man and wife."

He set the book aside on the night table. "I did what was expedient."

She hadn't realized she'd been hoping for a different answer until he didn't give her one.

Nothing had changed.

"Ah, yes," she agreed softly. "We must do what is expedient."

He leaned forward, burying his fingers in his hair before looking up, his expression haunted. "I would give anything to change what I've already promised."

For a long moment their gazes held. There were no easy answers.

Deborah looked away first. She studied the surface of the bedside table a moment before saying, "Let me tell you the dream I had. You can interpret it."

"I don't know if I believe dreams mean any-thing," he replied stiffly.

"They must," she said, her voice quiet. "Why else would God give them to us?"

He frowned his answer, but she was unde-terred. Repositioning a feather pillow behind her back, she started telling what she could re-member of her water dream. Tony listened in-tently. At one point he reached for her hand, lacing his fingers with hers. The power of that simple gesture spread through her.

She gave his hand a squeeze. "What do you make of my dream?"

"Other than it was raining when I brought you here?"

With an impatient sound, she said, "I under-stood your part of the dream. But what of all the rest?"

Tony considered a moment. "The water obvi-ously represents matters or emotions over which you have no control."

She nodded. His assessment made sense. Over the years, had she not felt weighed down or drowning under the expectations of others?

"Of course, you see me as a savior," he added, the light of a smile returning to his face. "Because I'm the one who kept you afloat."

"And the others are weights taking me down?"

His expression sobered. "Yes, they are all the people you have attempted to please in your life. Now they are powerless to help you reach a decision. That's what your dream is about, isn't it? You want to be with me, Deb. We belong together, but you are unwilling to trust me."

"I did make my decision," she returned. "I left London."

He reached for her hand, rubbing his thumb along her skin. Where he touched, she burned. "But you knew it wasn't over between us. In your heart, you knew."

"Tony —" she started, and would have pulled away, but he raised her hand to his lips.

"I was so afraid I had lost you. You are everything to me. Everything. Before I met you, I was walking through a life that held little meaning. I need you, Deb."

"Why? Because I'm something you can't buy?"

He let go of her hand as if it scalded. His jaw hardened. "No. Although I question your judgment of my character. I had thought you knew me better."

Hot tears stung her eyes. She held them back. "Sometimes I don't know you at all, my lord."

"Then ask," he dared. "I'll tell you anything."

"Like your betrothal?"

He hit the bedside in frustration and stood, walking several steps away from the bed until he turned. "I was wrong. But you must understand, Deb, I'd given no thought to marriage. Lady Amelia was a business arrangement. And then I met you . . . and my whole perspective of the world changed."

"Then cry off," she said, surprising herself that she could be this callous. If Tony cried off from the marriage, there would be gossip . . . and Lady Amelia, a young woman whom she'd seen only once, could suffer.

But was she not suffering herself now? And she feared the choice before her — a life without honor, or her honor and a life without Tony. She no longer trusted herself. Her principles were becoming easier to compromise.

"I would, Deb," he said soberly, "if it wouldn't come back and hurt you. Do you realize what kind of prison London can be when you are on the outside?"

"We don't have to live in London."

"Yes, we do. I have obligations and responsibilities to my title there." He returned to the chair beside the bed. "You would be shunned. No door would open to you. My public humiliation of Lady Amelia would reap a bitter harvest for years to come, even for our children. I've lived that life. I've fought and struggled against it. I do not want it for my sons."

"You'd rather have them branded bastards?"

"Yes. My money can provide compensation. They would be men of the world and not trapped by expectations."

There was a beat of silence. She understood what he was saying. Then, she said, "Better they not be born."

Her verdict tore at both of them. He turned away, staring into space. She struggled with her own demons.

He looked back at her, his expression tense. "Let me tell you my nightmare."

"The one you say you can't remember?" she asked, referring to the dream he'd had at Miss Chalmers's.

"I remember it." He didn't wait for permission but plunged forward. "I dream of that day. Only instead of being out riding, I'm standing at the window right outside the library and I can see my father. He puts the gun to his temple. I start shouting for him to stop. I pound on the window — beat it with my fist. But he doesn't see me. He looks right at me as if I'm not there."

"Then what happens?"

"He kills himself." He said the words as if from a distance. Then, he looked to her, and said, "Only I'm suddenly standing in the library, and the gun is in my hand."

"Dear God," Deborah whispered.

Tony's lips twisted into a cynical smile. "He doesn't hear. I've already asked Him."

She pushed the covers and reached for him. He didn't move, but she came to him, enveloping him in her arms, and he lowered his head against her shoulder. He was tight, everything about him so tight. If he'd been a child, she would have encouraged him to cry out his doubts and fears.

But he was man. Men held everything in.

"His death was not your fault," she said. "You were a child and not guilty. He *chose* to take his own life."

"I know." He pushed away.

"Then what is it?"

For a moment, she didn't think he would answer her. He appeared to struggle with some internal resistance. And then, he admitted, "I didn't believe I was his son. That's why he rode all the way from London to Alder House to do it. I've thought hard on this and it can be the only reason."

Deborah remembered Lizbet's gossip about rumors going around Tony was another man's child.

"Do you have doubts?" she asked gently.

"Absolutely none." He came to his feet. "And neither does Parliament and the king. I was granted the title."

"Then you should have no worries. Have you discussed this with your mother?" she asked, thinking that here was the one person who could set his deepest fears to rest. "I mean, I know you don't talk to her, but certainly on this matter — ?"

"I want nothing to do with her," he said flatly. "Or her husband."

"She's married?" Deborah asked with surprise. "I mean you've spoken so rarely of her, I'd pictured in my mind this tragic widow."

"Hardly," he said with a snort, and moved

260

around to the foot of the bed before adding contemptuously, "They married within months of my father's death. I told you there was very little mourning."

She understood his bitterness. She'd been too young to care when her father had remarried, but later, when she was older . . . she'd wondered how he could settle on another when he'd been supposedly so in love. Then, again, he'd had a baby to care for, and Dame Alodia probably did a bit of meddling.

"So you are estranged from her?" Deborah asked.

"We don't talk. I have nothing to say."

"Does she live in London?"

"Absolutely not," he answered. "The moment I hit my majority, I sent her a letter banishing both her and her husband from Society anywhere where I would be. They live in the country on her husband's estate."

"Your anger is well placed," she admitted.

"Yes, but I can't seem to avoid them. She married Sir Richard Adamson."

"The *general?*" Even she had heard of Adamson, who had fought bravely beside Wellington until he'd lost an arm at Talavera. It was hard to believe such a brave man would wed a hardened adulteress.

"Parliament likes him, too," Tony said, as if reading her mind.

"And you've never met him?"

"No, and I won't either. I don't give a damn

about him. Miss Chalmers was mother and father to me. *She* has my respect. Not them."

He had also rebuilt his family fortune and was now ready to marry a young woman whose connections he believed would repair the damage done to his title by his parents.

And what place did that leave for her?

Deborah couldn't face the question. Not now. She was still so very tired. Too tired to think clearly.

He noticed. "Here, lie back down. You need your rest."

"I'll be fine," she lied.

Tony would have none of it. He tucked her under the covers. "Don't worry. There will be a solution for us."

But Deborah wasn't so certain, especially when he placed a "brotherly" kiss on her forehead . . . as if he were putting distance between them. Perhaps he feared he'd revealed too much. Doubt took hold of her. What if *he* decided he did not want to be with her anymore?

She reached for his hand. "Stay with me tonight, here in this bed."

His expression softened. "The bed is too small for the two us to sleep comfortably, and you need your sleep. I want you well."

"I need you to be with me."

He sat on the chair. "What an odd couple we are. We so desperately need each other and yet . . . we can't have what we want?"

"Tonight, all I want is for you to hold me."

She meant the words.

Lightly, he touched her hair. "How can I refuse such a simple request?"

She smiled sleepily, curving the pillow to fit beneath her head. He started to undress, but she was asleep before he'd removed his shirt.

However, her last thought was it wouldn't be so bad to be a mistress.

Stretched out beside Deb on the narrow bed, Tony leaned on one arm over her, watching her even breathing in her sleep. He wasn't about to let anything happen to her.

She was the first good thing in his life. Had he thought he'd loved her before? No, he'd not even known what love was until he was faced with the fear of losing her to sickness.

What he felt now was deeper, more committed. He trusted her. Even with his darkest fears.

He had to keep her safe, to find a place where they could sort out what to do next.

Suddenly, he knew he wanted to take her to Alder House. There she would have the time to recover under his care. And he wanted her to see the estate, his home. He wanted her there beside him.

The next morning, he let her sleep until the sun was well into the sky, then woke her. Her color already appeared much better.

He'd taken the time to dress, so he plopped down on the end of the bed, one leg over the footrail, his foot swinging freely, and watched her brush her hair. "Do you feel well enough to travel?"

She shook her hair back from her eyes and nodded. "I'm hungry, too."

He laughed. "That is a good sign."

But she soberly said, "I must return home."

Tony took a deep breath and answered with a nonchalance he was far from feeling, "I want to take you to Alder House, my family seat."

Her dark gaze grew serious. "No."

"Yes, Deb."

She groaned her frustration. "Tony, this is no time to be stubborn. A man doesn't usually take his —" A small pause. She continued, her expression resolute, "— a man doesn't take his mistress to his family seat, does he?"

Mistress. She'd said the word. She'd accepted his offer.

He brought his feet down to the floor. "Do you mean this, Deb?"

She dropped her gaze to her hands holding the hairbrush in her lap. She appeared young and very innocent. "I believe I do," she said quietly.

Tony wanted to stand up and shout his joy — yet, he feared her changing her mind.

She raised her head. "But I don't believe taking me to Alder House is appropriate."

"No," he agreed. "It is necessary."

"Tony —" she started to protest, but he'd hear none of it.

"I do what I please, Deb. I'm the damn earl. Don't worry. There is no Greek chorus to drone on about proprieties. And I'm not married yet, so I don't have to answer to Longest. Please, I want you there. We can decide our future later."

She hesitated, her uncertainty clear. "I don't believe this is wise."

"Nothing about the two of us is wise."

He had her there. She didn't disagree. Her smile turned rueful. "I don't know why I worry. I have no place else to go now."

He understood. Accepting his offer meant she could not return to the simple world of her Valley. Her sacrifice humbled him.

He raised her hand to his lips. "You will not regret trusting me," he promised. "I love you, Deb, and I'll see no harm comes to you because of me."

She nodded agreement, but as she placed the brush on the bedside table, he noticed her hand shook. She caught him staring and clenched her fist. "I need to dress," she said. "And return this nightgown to Mrs. Strickler."

"It's yours," he said, and told her about leaving her portmanteau on the road in the rain. "I purchased a few dresses for you from the local seamstress. We took your size from the clothes you were wearing which I threw out. After all, I lost your clothes, I should replace them."

"Well," she said quietly, "I am truly 'kept'

now, aren't I?" Before he could respond, she said, "Please, Tony, give me a moment alone. I must get dressed."

He did as she asked, but his mind was very unsettled. In the front yard, pacing the length of it while he waited for her, he told himself he would not lose her. No matter what happened, he would not let her go.

What was his, he held.

Chapter Fifteen

Deborah had doubts about becoming a mistress. Grave doubts.

Yes, she'd given in. However, she was uncertain as to what he expected of her — other than the obvious. She knew what it was like to be a wife — but a mistress? The role sounded wicked and exotic. And no matter what Lizbet said, proper women from Ilam didn't enter into liaisons with men outside the married state.

However, out of her desperate love for Tony — should a mistress be in love? — she'd consented to be his.

And, as she pulled the cobalt blue merino wool dress Tony had chosen for her over her head and shook the skirt into place, she had to admit there were some good things about having a rich lover. The material was first quality. She'd never owned anything so fine and the local seamstress was very good. The dress was cut to perfection. He'd also purchased another cream-colored dress, a bonnet, gloves, petticoats, and even a pair of slippers made of leather so soft they molded to her feet.

But did finery compensate for the sacrifice of her good name?

Pushing one last pin into her hopelessly straight hair which she'd styled in a smooth chignon at the nape of her neck, she convinced herself that everything would work out. It must.

She picked up the bonnet and her gloves, and left the room. She came upon Tony and the Stricklers just as he was paying them handsomely for their hospitality. Outside a coach waited to take them to Alder House. His coat of arms was on the door.

"This is yours?" she asked, then wanted to chastise herself. If she was playing his wife for the Stricklers, she had just made a mistake.

"I sent a man to Yorkshire to fetch it when you first became ill," he answered smoothly. "If I had to race you to London for medical help, I wanted the fastest conveyance possible."

Mrs. Stickler gave a romantic sigh. Her husband was too occupied counting the money to care.

Even Deborah was humbled by his commitment. "You would do that for me?"

"And more," he said.

Perhaps being a mistress would be a lovely thing.

A coachman and a footman in the Burnell colors, blue and gold, waited for them to board. Tony handed her up into the vehicle, removed his hat, and joined her. His large frame took up three-quarters of the coach. She did not move away, but she was very conscious of his effortless crowding of her personal space.

With a knock on the roof, he signaled the

coachman to get started. The interior of the coach was of burled wood, and the seats were of buttery soft leather. The wheels were even better sprung than his vehicle in London.

For the first few minutes, she sat quiet, her hands flat on the seat feeling the smooth roll of the coach wheels. "This is nice."

"I'm glad you like it." His voice sounded carefully neutral.

She glanced up at him. He watched her intently. He was hers, and yet, not hers.

"Tony, I don't know if I will be very good at this. I've never been one to flout convention."

He leaned back in his own corner as if offended slightly. "Nor have I."

She almost laughed at that one as she removed her bonnet. "Your whole life has been breaking the rules. I can't imagine you cowed."

"I've had my moments." He set his hat on a hook by the door.

"And how did you handle them?" she wanted to know. "When everyone is disapproving, what did you do?"

Relaxing for the first time since they'd climbed into the coach, he smiled, cocksure and full of himself. "I brazened it out. There isn't much else you can do. Of course, with men, there is the threat that I might defend my honor. A wise man thinks twice before mocking a known swordsman."

"I don't see myself issuing challenges," she said. "Especially to Dame Alodia."

"Well, pistols and swords won't work for her. Come here," he said, "rest in my arms, and we shall devise a solution for the grande dame."

So here it was. His first request upon her person . . . Deborah did as he asked. And it did feel good to lean against him. He put his arms around her protectively. His lips brushed the top of her head. "I don't know what I'd do if confronted by the Matrons of Ilam," he confessed. "They are a formidable lot."

Of course, when he held her in his arms, they and all her doubts seemed far away, including the judgmental Matrons. His hand slowly rubbed up and down her shoulder, the motion relaxing her tension.

"I picture them as a flock of chickens," he said.

"Chickens?"

"Yes, biddy hens. You know, the sort that have to all eat at the same time and whenever there's a loud sound they all look up at once with beady eyes."

"Yes, well, I will seem odd to them because they have husbands." The moment the words left her lips, she regretted them. She lifted her head. "I'm sorry. I'm a relatively new mistress."

Something akin to pain appeared in the depths of his eyes. "Deb, if I could have it another way —"

She covered his mouth with her hand. "No. We've made our decision. Just hold me, and I shall be fine."

His arms around her tightened. Her head on his chest, she listened to the strong, steady beat of his heart.

"Boo," he said.

"What?" She looked up at him.

"Boo. That's what you say to the Matrons of Ilam. It's what I would say to biddy hens."

Deborah started laughing. She could see all the Matrons sitting in a circle during one of the dame's afternoon gossip sessions and her saying, "Boo."

"What is the matter?" Tony asked with mock dismay. "You said you can't call them out for pistols and swords. Boo is a perfectly fine challenge."

"Boo is a silly word."

"Well, they are silly women."

"They are important women," Deborah protested. "They are all married to the important gentleman of the valley."

Married. She'd said *married*, and the word seemed to linger in the air.

He knew she'd caught herself on it. She started to sit up, but he held her in place. "I love you."

"I love you," she answered, but the words sounded hollow, even to her own ears.

However, Tony did not press the issue. Instead, he changed the subject. "You still need rest. I don't want your sickness returning. Don't worry and let me take care of you."

She made herself relax and tried to keep her

doubts at bay. She was either successful or he had been right about her needing rest, because within minutes, she fell asleep.

Several hours later, she woke to find herself snuggled in Tony's arms while he stared pensively out the window at the passing countryside. His long legs were stretched out across the coach floor. His mind seemed to be hundreds of miles away.

He'd held her the whole time.

She let him know she was awake. "I was wrong when I said you didn't know what love is."

Tony had removed his gloves. He shifted his weight, his hand on her arm, his fingers inches from the curve of her breast. "Only because you've taught me its meaning. How are you feeling?"

Aware that if she moved, his hand could slip inside the low cut of her bodice, she whispered, "Better, thank you." It seemed an eternity since they'd last made love. She placed her hand on top of his thigh, feeling the muscles work beneath the material of his breeches.

His hand covered hers. His fingers stroked the sensitive skin right along the line of her bodice. "You're feeling much better."

She nodded, desire heating her blood. Raising herself up his body, she nibbled the line of his jaw.

"Deborah," he whispered. She moved her hand along his thigh and felt his growing arousal. Inside her, deep muscles clenched.

"Tony," she echoed, and found his lips. Their tongues met, entwined. Doubts fled. Reason ran . . . especially when his hand went unerringly to her breast. With his other hand, he pulled her up into his lap. She straddled his legs.

His hands slid up under her skirts. She started loosening his neckcloth. His lips brushed her neck, working their way up to her ear. His clever fingers slipped inside.

She sat up, surprised . . . and excited.

He stroked her once, twice. She tightened around him, her gaze not leaving his eyes. He smiled, pleased with himself.

"You do this very well," she managed to whisper.

"Oh, I believe I need more practice," he contradicted.

She could only whimper in reply. She wanted him. Now. She began fumbling with the buttons of his breeches, wanting them undone.

Outside the coach, the coachman said something to the footman.

They both froze, suddenly aware of the servants, the coach wall the only thing separating them. Deb met Tony's gaze. He smiled, wickedly, and kissed the spot on her throat he knew always defeated her resistance.

She moaned.

He shushed against her neck and helped her finish unbuttoning him.

The world beyond the confines of the coach continued on, but within, they were lost in passion. With one deft stroke of his fingers, he took her to the point where she wouldn't have cared if an army of Matrons surrounded the coach. She had to finish what they'd begun.

Tony lifted her up and slowly lowered her over him. They both caught their breath as he buried himself to the hilt. Slowly, she began moving, knowing what he liked, what they both liked.

She had missed this closeness to him. Whatever else lay between them, this was right and good. The movement of the coach added an extra momentum, and the presence of the servants so close added an element of excitement.

Tony pulled her bodice down to free her breasts. He took her nipple in his mouth, sucking hard — and she wanted to cry out from the pleasure of it even as she found her own release. In seconds, he joined her. They had to stifle their voices against each other's necks, and when they were done, neither could move.

Slowly, sanity returned. She heard the horses' hooves, the roll of the wheels over the road, the low voices of the servants.

Tony caught her eye, and then he grinned, his arms around her waist. She fell forward, feeling at peace. He hugged her. "Don't ever forget I love you."

She nodded, content, before moving off him. They took a moment to right their clothing. He reached into his pocket, and said, "Here." The ruby heart necklace dangled from his fingers. The gold of the expensive chain seemed to glow with a life of its own.

The jewelry, and his timing for giving to her, cheapened the moment.

Immediately, he sensed her change of mood. "This isn't a payment."

"No, I know." She looked away.

"Then what is it?" he prodded.

She took the necklace in her hand and slowly fastened the chain around her neck. "I've just not become accustomed to everything," she answered, her feelings too at odds for her to explain.

Tony was not satisfied, but he was wise enough not to press further. Instead, he pulled out a book. "Shall we read a bit?"

Idly rubbing the ruby heart between her fingers, she nodded and settled back into the far corner of the coach to listen to his deep baritone. She didn't know why she felt so unsettled. She knew it wasn't the expense of the gift. Although his comment the necklace wasn't payment disturbed her. What she'd once given freely, now had money attached.

Would Lizbet have such doubts? Or Rachel? After all, no one else wanted her.

Tony reached over to place his hand on her leg. His swordsman's fingers were long, tapered, capable. She wondered why she had doubts.

She was relieved when, two hours later, the coach finally slowed down to pull off the road into the yard of a well-appointed inn for the night.

Stable lads rushed out for the horses, and the innkeeper hurried out to greet his titled guest. The innkeeper's name was Hudgins. He had a round belly and a bald head, with a tuft of hair behind each ear. He was most anxious to please.

Tony got out of the coach first. "We need a good bed for the night and our dinner, Hudgins. One of your best meals, please."

"I have a nice pheasant," the innkeeper answered, "and a wine, new from France, that will make your palate sing."

"Perfect," Tony answered without even asking the cost of the meal. "A private supper room, please."

"Yes, my lord."

Tony turned to help Deborah down, but she hung back while tying the ribbons of her bonnet. "What is it?" he asked, his voice low.

"Am I pretending to be your wife again?"

Her question came out sharper than she'd intended it.

He wasn't pleased, and, yet, he didn't duck the question. "I'm certain that will be unnecessary. A good innkeeper is a discreet one."

"Hmmm, I suppose I'm being provincial," she couldn't stop herself from returning tartly.

"Not provincial, cautious," Tony corrected

and, taking her hand, kissed it. "Now, come, my love."

She forced herself to behave in the face of his patience. She didn't understand why she couldn't be more accepting and yet, deep within her was a kernel of rebellion, a disappointment that she could not have all of him.

Tony led her into the inn, with Hudgins bowing and scraping before them. He led them through a long narrow hall with the kitchen off to one side and a taproom to the other. "We've had a tidy bit of business this day," he was saying. "There were horse races in Connor Fields, not more than an hour's ride from here. Of course, most of the lads are gone, but we were busy this past week. Busy, busy, busy."

As if to punctuate the words, a gentleman came out of the taproom, his nose ruddy from drink. Immediately, he recognized Tony. "Ho now, Lord Burnell? Is that you?" the man's booming voice carried through the hall, and his sharp eyes told Deborah he didn't miss a thing, even in his cups.

Tony swore softly under his breath, then faced the well-dressed man, protectively standing in front of Deborah.

"Julius, it is good to see you. What brings you this way?"

"A man about a horse," Julius responded with a wink. Then, catching sight of Deborah, he said, "Wait now! I've heard you were tying the parson's knot. Don't tell me, this is your countess!"

She ducked her head, hoping the wide brim of her leghorn bonnet would conceal her identity. She did not want to be compared to Lady Amelia.

Tony didn't even flinch. "Julius," he said, "I'm in a bit of a hurry. You don't mind, do you?" He began to turn, moving Deborah ahead of him, but Julius was not the sort to be dissuaded.

He craned his neck for a curious look. "Come now, let me have an introduction. Then I shall beg her pardon before I draw you over to my friends. I really am here about a horse, my lord. We were just discussing that gray gelding you plan to race in Epsom. There's a German bloke with us who doesn't believe our claims. It'd be best if he heard it from you. Then perhaps he'll buy that filly I bred off the stallion to your gray."

"You hold up my end of the discussion," Tony said, edging away with Deborah. Hudgins waited by a staircase leading up to the rooms.

"I can't." Julius dropped his voice a notch. "I've got to pawn off that filly — what a pain in the arse she is! And the German needs a bit of tweaking. No one can sell a bill of goods better than you, Burnell. You could trade the king his own crown if you had a mind to. I'm certain your lovely countess wouldn't mind sparing you for a half hour or so. Or bring her in to meet the German. All of London buzzes about her beauty."

His comments praising Lady Amelia were like a burr in her shoe to Deborah. She'd seen Tony's betrothed. She knew she could not hold a candle to the younger woman's beauty.

Tony kept moving them backwards. "I'm sorry, Julius, you cannot. This is a private moment."

"Private?" Julius appeared stumped. Then, understanding dawned. "What ho! Private! Yes, yes, on with you, my lord! On with you." He strolled into the taproom and announced in his overloud voice, "Burnell can't join us. 'Tis his wedding day, and the man has better things to do than drink with us."

Laughter and several catcalls met his words. Tony gave Deborah a shove. "Hurry before they have the idea it would be fun to join us. There's no telling what a horse trader like Julius in his cups will do."

He didn't have to warn Deborah twice. She practically dashed up the stairs, bypassing Hudgins, who hurried behind her.

Of course, once they were at the top of the stairs, the obsequious innkeeper said, "I say, my lord, what an honor it is to serve both you and your bride." He attempted to get a hard look at Deborah. "And may I add, we've heard of her beauty even up here this far from London."

This was the last straw. If the earth had

opened up beneath her feet, Deborah would have happily disappeared.

Tony muttered some words to Hudgins, and they were enough to send the man scrambling to show them their room. The accommodations were spacious, but she didn't pause to admire the furnishings. Instead, she disappeared behind the privacy screen.

As soon as Hudgins left, she came out and said with what she hoped was irony, "Was that your idea of discretion?"

Tony wasn't amused. "Seeing Julius is bad luck." He'd removed his jacket and now loosened the knot in his neckcloth. "I'll talk to him. He won't gossip."

"The man dotes on nothing more than gossip," Deborah countered. "I know his kind. What are we going to do?"

"I'll talk to him," Tony repeated with a touch of impatience.

She sat on the corner of the four-poster. "Not about him. About us, Tony. I don't feel comfortable with subterfuge."

He crossed to her. "It won't be like that. Trust me, Deb. Please, trust me."

And she wanted to. Against everything she'd been taught and the morals of society, she wanted to trust him — because she was too selfish to give him up. Nor did she want to share him with another.

Dinner was a quiet affair between them. Neither had much appetite. Where words didn't work, touch did. In bed, he held her in his arms and she was content to be there.

Even though she sensed they both knew their days with each other were numbered.

The next morning, the sky was blue with nary a cloud in sight. Both of them woke at first light, edgy and ready to get on with the trip.

They didn't run into Mr. Julius as they left the inn. Tony's coach, horses, and servants were ready and so within an hour of rising, they were off.

They passed the hours playing cards or talking about unimportant matters. Tony seemed to need to hold her hand as if searching for reassurance. Cradled in his embrace, Deborah, too, wanted to pretend everything would be fine.

However, the closer they came to Alder House, the more doubts she had. Finally, when the coachman assured them they had less than an hour more on the road, Deborah voiced her concerns.

"We shouldn't be doing this. I should not go to Alder House." She was ready to climb out of the coach if need be and walk back to Derby.

"Nonsense. Everything will be fine," he stated firmly.

"Tony, what will your new wife say when she hears you've brought your mistress to your family seat?"

He turned in the seat and took her by both shoulders. "She won't care because she has no more concern for me than I have for her."

"She will care about the proprieties —"

"I *must* bring you there," he said, tightening his hold on her shoulders for emphasis. "You can call me foolish, but you are the most important person in my life. I feel like I'm walking blind here, Deb. One misstep, and I will lose you. But if I get you to Alder House, then I sense — without rhyme or reason — that we'll find answers there. And proprieties can go to hell."

The air around him was charged with tension. She saw now that this wasn't some lark on his part, that he moved with a purpose even he didn't understand. She leaned forward, resting her head on his chest, and he enveloped her in his arms.

"Trust me," he whispered.

She nodded. She would do as he asked.

He relaxed. "Here, we are close. Look, here is the crossroads. We are at the boundary of St. Gillian's parish."

Fifteen minutes later they entered the picturesque village of Morven. Neat houses with their front yards filled with roses lined the road. A medieval church marked the outskirts.

"That's St. Gillian's," Tony said with no small amount of pride. "My family has been attending services there for 350 years, ever since the first earl of Burnell took possession of this land."

"No claim to the Conqueror?" she teased.

"We were on the wrong side of that battle," he replied with no small amount of pride. "We were Saxons, but we managed to work our way up."

Several people stood in conversation by the church graveyard. They stopped and watched the coach roll past, but no one waved a greeting. Instead, their expressions were grim.

Tony ordered the coachman to halt. One of the gentlemen in the group approached the coach. Deborah slunk back in the corner, but Tony seemed not to care whether she was seen or not.

"Is there a problem, Vicar?"

The clergyman removed his hat. "A problem? No, other than to welcome you back, my lord."

"Thank you." Tony glanced back at the others, who had been talking with the vicar. "Why do I sense you've heard disturbing news?"

The vicar looked uncomfortable. Then, he said reluctantly, "You have guests at Alder House, my lord."

"Who are they?"

"I'd rather not be the one to say."

Tony frowned. "Well, I shall find out soon enough. Thank you for the warning."

"Yes, my lord." The vicar bowed and stepped back.

Tony signaled his driver to go on. He turned to Deborah, and said, "He isn't a shy man. I imagine there must not be good news. I hope it isn't bad news of Marmy."

"I pray it isn't either," Deborah agreed. "But, Tony, who could it be . . . and is it wise to take me there?"

"As to the first, I have no idea who would visit unannounced. As to the latter, my wanting you there is all that matters." And she could tell by the set of his face, the subject was closed.

Several minutes later, the coach turned down a long drive. Tony leaned forward. "We're here. This is Alder House."

She looked out the window. Everywhere she looked was lush greenery. She did not see the house immediately. Tall, stately linden trees lined the smooth dirt road. On either side were rolling pastures and herds of sheep.

Then they rounded a curve and came to the house.

A low stone fence separated the fields from the grounds and gardens. Rose beds in full bloom lined the fence. Beyond, was a circular drive and a stone house that, with the late-afternoon sun shining off its walls, appeared to have been turned to silver.

Tony turned to her with pride, his earlier disquiet vanquished. "What do you think?"

"I think I've never seen a more impressive estate," she replied.

Her words were true. Alder House was an old Tudor mansion built low, so it appeared to hug the landscape. Clay chimneys, too numerous to count, dotted the mossy stone roof. The entrance was of heavy oak surrounded by carved stone. The windows were narrow arches like miniature copies of those in a cathedral.

Tony hopped out before the coach had even rolled to a stop. He appeared younger, happier than he ever had before. He nodded to his coachman. "It's good to be home."

"That 'tis, my lord," the man answered. The front entryway opened, and liveried servants hurried out to help their master.

Holding out his hand, Tony said grandly, "Welcome to Alder House. Come, I want to —"

He stopped abruptly, never finishing what it was he wanted to do. Instead, his gaze was riveted on a woman who had come out of the house. She was beautiful and of an indeterminate age, with silver hair she wore loose to her shoulders. Her eyes were so blue they could have been black. Tony's eyes.

Behind her a gentleman almost as tall as Tony followed. His thick hair was the color of polished pewter. He wore his clothes well. His boots gleamed, and his jacket was cut of the finest wool. His bearing was that of a military man.

He had one arm.

Deborah knew the identity of the mysterious visitors — Sir Richard Adamson and his wife, *Tony's mother*. Concerned as to his reaction, she turned to Tony. He'd gone still, as if the life had drained from him.

285

His mother murmured a word to her husband and came forward, her step so light she seemed to float above the ground. Her smile was tentative, hopeful. "Are you surprised?"

"Constantly," Tony answered, his voice flat. "Now, pack your things and leave immediately."

Chapter Sixteen

Everyone heard Tony's harsh command.

The servants froze, uncertain as to what to do. General Adamson straightened and took a step forward, his eyes narrowing with malicious intent — but Tony's mother stayed him with a wave of her hand. He had the look of a caged panther — sleek, strong, lethal. He was not happy to be held at bay.

But Deborah was not interested in him. Like everyone else from the footman to the butler, her attention was on the drama between mother and son.

In spite of Tony's rebuff, she walked toward him, the set of her mouth determined, until she stood before Tony.

"I won't leave until we have found time to talk," she said.

"We have nothing to say to each other," he answered. "Now, excuse me, I have a guest." He turned to help Deborah from the coach. She wanted to shrink back, wishing no part of this scene.

"Please . . . my son," his mother said, her voice so soft on the last two words, Deborah could have imagined them.

His eyes met Deborah's. The set of his jaw was hard, unrelenting. He held out his hand.

"Let's go. They are uninvited and, whatever happens, watch your back." He spoke for her ears alone, but his mother had heard. A spot of color appeared on each cheek.

Deborah didn't know what to do. She couldn't hide in the coach forever. Feeling awkward, she placed her hand in Tony's, who would have whisked her away — save for his mother. She planted herself right in Deborah's path, and in a clear voice said, "I'm Sophia Adamson. You must be Mrs. Percival."

Both of them were shocked that she knew Deborah's name. He covered his reaction better because, as Deborah was beginning to understand, he would give no quarter to his mother.

Lady Adamson didn't need his permission. Almost defiantly, she held out her hand to Deborah. On the surface, she appeared composed, but in the depths of her blue eyes, Deborah saw her plea for understanding and, God help her, Deborah didn't have the heart to be rude. She took Lady Adamson's hand and made a small curtsy.

Tony went rigid. His hand on her elbow tightened, a silent command for her to rise . . . but Deborah had her own mind in this matter. Her loyalties were mixed. She did not admire his mother, but empathized with the woman's very private anguish. How did a mother continue on after she'd been so thoroughly rejected by her child?

Deborah released Lady Adamson's hand, aware she now stood between mother and son. Tony's expression was inscrutable.

Lady Adamson didn't waste a moment but took full advantage of Deborah's generosity. "Please call me Sophia, and let me introduce you to my husband. Richard," she said, raising her voice to call him forward.

But Tony wanted none of it. Ruthlessly, he said, "We have no desire to meet him. And I'm telling both of you to leave. Now." He strode off, his hold on Deborah's arm firm. She had to skip to catch up . . . and because of her reticence, he didn't quite escape as quickly as he might have alone.

His path met the general's. Both men faced each other, and Deborah realized from what stories Tony had told her, these two had never met before.

The world seemed to spin to a stop.

Deborah looked from one man to the other — and the resemblance was uncanny. Tony was the taller but both had broad shoulders, long backs, square jaws. They even shared dark brows and thin, sensual lips.

Sir Richard's gaze took in every line, every plane of Tony's face. He did not speak or move. However, Tony's reaction was swift and strong. The corners of his mouth turned down as he deliberately gave the man his back, a direct cut.

"Come, Deborah." His tone was hard, but she sensed he was devastated — for here was ample proof of who his true father was.

This was confirmation of his deepest fears, the ones played out in his dream. With a flash of insight, Deborah realized why he'd dreamed he'd been the one holding the gun. And, he'd known. He might have always known, and for that reason he had avoided the man . . . until today.

Deborah felt like a traitor for having given Sophia *any* consideration at all. Certainly, as his mother, she had to have understood Tony's unwillingness to be anywhere around this man. Tucking her hand in Tony's arm, she followed him toward the house.

The servants suddenly started moving. The butler hurried after Tony.

But they'd only taken two steps before his mother boldly called out, "We're not leaving. Not until we've had a moment in private."

Slowly, Tony faced her. "Then you will be here a very long time," he promised. Taking Deborah's hand, he led her through the front entry.

The butler started apologizing. "I'm so sorry, my lord. She arrived yesterday, and the whole village is in an uproar. We didn't know what you wished us to do."

Tony cut the air with his free hand. "You had no control, Gibbons."

Inside, the house was wood paneling, stone tile floors, and cool darkness. Portraits of members of the Aldercy family lined this main hall.

A huge chandelier made of iron and copper hung from the high ceiling. Two long wings branched off from the hall, one to the left, one to the right. A set of cantilevered stairs led to the first floor.

More servants hovered off the main hall as if wishing to greet their lord, and yet held back. Deborah assumed they had witnessed the meeting between mother and son and knew better than to bother Tony at that particular moment.

He didn't linger but guided her toward the stairs. "See to our luggage, Gibbons," he tossed over his shoulder. "We don't have much." Abruptly, he stopped, one foot on the higher step, the other on the floor. He addressed the servants. "Mrs. Percival is a special friend of mine. She will be accorded every respect."

Sophia and Sir Richard had come to the door to hear the last of his words. For a second, Deborah was overwhelmed with conflicting emotions. She shouldn't be there, and she had no desire to be a player in the drama between Tony and his parents — for she knew without a doubt Sir Richard was Tony's father.

However, she could feel the tension radiating from him and knew he needed her support. He counted on it, and, God help her, she could not turn away. Not now.

Tony started up the stairs, and she followed.

"I want Mrs. Percival placed in the south room," Tony instructed Gibbons. "Have Mrs.

Carter send up hot water, towels, and soaps."

"Yes, my lord." The butler dropped back.

They reached the top of the stairs, and he started down the hall, his long stride forcing her to hurry to catch up. He opened the door of the second room on the right. The bedroom was handsomely furnished in shades of blue with white accents. The rug of blue, yellow, and red flowers was so thick, her feet sank into it.

"You have a view of the gardens from here," Tony said, shutting the door. He began prowling the room, ostensibly to make her feel welcome by checking the wardrobe drawers and opening the window. She did not join him but stayed by the closed door, cautious.

"The stables are on the other side of the house," he said. "They were built some two hundred years ago. We usually exercise the horses twice a day." He stopped and turned to her as if struck by a new thought. "I never asked, do you ride?"

"Farm horses."

He nodded, his mind obviously preoccupied on something other than the question he'd asked.

She waited.

He leaned against the windowsill, his back to her. There was a long moment of silence and then he said, "Sometimes I think I hate her."

His admission made her blood cold.

"Then other times, I . . ." He let his voice trail off, his feelings unspoken. He brought his focus around to Deborah. "I'm glad you are here," he said fiercely. "I know you don't feel right, but your presence is very important now."

She nodded. Then, with a courage she didn't know she had, asked, "Perhaps you should talk to her?"

"No."

"Why not?"

"I can't." He marched over to the carved stone fireplace. "You're not blind, Deb. *Didn't you see?*"

"That you look very much like Sir Richard?"

His eyes narrowed, his jaw tightened. "They are the reason my father killed himself."

And in his mind, they were the reason for the dramatic changes in his life. Rightly or wrongly. They'd created the nightmares and his own certainty that his father had killed himself over Tony's parentage.

He couldn't struggle against his father, but he could against them.

Deborah moved into the room and took off her bonnet. She set it on the bed. He watched her warily, as if he no longer quite trusted her either.

Trust. How often had he said he trusted her? With a woman's intuition, Deborah realized trust was even more important than love in his mind.

She did not want to betray him . . . and yet, she knew he was going to have to face the truth.

"Perhaps you should ask them why they are here?"

His reaction was swift and predictable. "I don't want them here. I want them gone."

Taking her heart in her hand, Deborah said, "Then you must talk to them, for they won't leave until they've had their say."

His fist clenched. He hit the stone on the mantel, his gaze hardening.

She stood, fearful that in this tangle of duplicities, she might lose something very precious to her.

Time seemed to stand still.

Then he turned away, withdrawing. The same reaction he had given to his mother.

She wanted to cross to him, to throw her arms around him and cling with everything she was worth. But she didn't. She knew he would not accept her. Not then.

"I believe I will go for a ride," he said carefully. "I need to clear my mind."

"Yes, that is a good idea."

He started for the door. When he reached for the handle, she could contain herself no longer. "I love you."

He swung his gaze to meet hers. "I know. I'll see you at dinner." He left the room.

For a long, long time, Deborah stood where she was, filled with regrets.

Tony changed and left the house, feeling much alone. Deborah saw too much, and he feared her verdict. He needed space and a chance to clear his head.

In the stables, he greeted the lads by name. They were bringing the horses in from their evening exercise. He took a moment longer to talk to his head groomsman, Alfred, before saddling a spirited six-year-old gelding named Charger, a horse who lived up to his name. For the next hour, Tony had his hands full. He put Charger through his paces, but the horse was equally hard on him.

Alfred and several of the lads stood along the fence offering joking advice whenever the horse got the better of him. When Tony finally started to cool Charger down, Alfred commented, "Life in the city is making you soft, my lord."

The others, grinning, seconded his opinion with replies of their own. There was nothing to do for it but challenge them all to a race, one Tony won.

However, they were right. When he dismounted, his leg tightened. He waited until he was alone with Alfred to rub a muscle in the back of his thigh. "I'll be feeling this tomorrow."

"Aye," Alfred said around the pipe in his mouth, "but you showed your mettle. 'Tis good to have you back, my lord."

Tony stared out at the rolling moors beyond the stables and said, "It's good to be here." If he had his way, he'd never leave. He and Deb would stay forever, and he'd be happy.

Perhaps never returning to London would solve his problems. He imagined Lady Amelia cared as much about his absence as he cared about what she was doing just then.

Standing out in the yard, he curried Charger in the fading light of day, enjoying the moment alone with the horse. He was much later than he'd planned. The stableboys had finished the feeding and were either seeing to chores or off to their own homes. He put Charger in his stall and started up the path toward the house when the light gleaming off a set of windows caught his attention.

He froze.

The setting sun highlighted the library windows.

Too clearly, he remembered the sight of his father's body. Rage at his father's wasted life roiled though him.

He directed his anger to a living source — his mother. How dare she bring her lover here? Her faithlessness with Sir Richard had killed his father with more speed than the bullet.

And no matter what anyone said, his features were nothing like Adamson's. *Nothing.* He saw no resemblance.

He strode up to the house, using a side entrance that led to the butler's pantry. As he had anticipated, he found Gibbons overseeing the arrangements for dinner.

Tony nodded him over. "Has Lady Adamson left?" he asked.

"No, my lord." Gibbons had been with him since childhood; the butler had been the first to answer Tony's shouts over discovering his father's body. Marmy had been the second. His mother had been in London.

So, why was she there now, so many years later? And why did she remain — against his demand that she never see him again?

"I suppose Sir Richard is still here also?"

"Yes, my lord." He lowered his voice. "He instructed me to set a place for himself and your mother at the table. I've held off doing anything until I heard from you."

Tony swore softly. Sir Richard might rule his mother, but he did not rule this house. He would have countermanded Sir Richard's order until he was struck by the thought that here was the perfect opportunity to demonstrate his absolute disdain for the two of them. Let them have a taste of the Turkish treatment he'd received from society. Let them know how it felt to be standing in a room and ignored by everyone.

On one level, he saw his own churlishness. The past was the past, and he'd risen above all the rubbish. Still, was he wrong to want a little of his own back?

"Set the two extra places," he told Gibbons briskly. "We shall have a *family* dinner."

He left to warn Deb about the circumstances she would soon find herself in. He knew she would not be pleased . . . but that was only because she didn't fully understand. However, when he reached her room, he discovered she'd already been called down.

"Lady Adamson came and fetched her," the upstairs maid said.

Irritation flashed through Tony. What right did his mother have taking care of *his* guest?

He grunted a dismissal to the maid, who hurried away as if scolded. His mother was playing a game. He sensed it. This was a chess match between them. She'd just claimed his queen. Deb was insurance that he would put in an appearance at the dining table. Perhaps they were downstairs flattering her in an attempt to portray themselves as the injured parties.

With long strides, he marched to his room to change.

The time had come to show them he was no powerless adversary.

Deborah was decidedly uncomfortable. When Lady Adamson had knocked on her door asking if she could escort her down, she had not known how best to respond. The offer appeared to have been made out of consideration for a guest. Since the dinner hour was close, and there was no sign of Tony, Deborah did not feel she could refuse.

She sat in a cozy octagonal room decorated in reds and greens, with paneled walls and a gilded ceiling. She wore the cream-on-white figured muslin trimmed in lace that

Tony had had made for her. Lady Adamson wore a blue silk that set her silver hair and dark eyes off to perfection. Sir Richard had changed to a black coat with white breeches and tall black boots. He wore it as if wearing a uniform.

Lady Adamson insisted she be called Sophia, and the general would be Richard. Deborah wondered at such informalities and the pains Lady Adamson was taking to make her husband's mistress feel comfortable. This was not how Dame Alodia and the Matrons would have played the scene.

Sophia was obviously nervous. She rattled on about the history of Alder House, while the general sat silent beside his wife on the striped settee, his eye on the door, his ear on the clock chimes. He waited for Tony. Dinner had been delayed twice.

The chimes struck the half hour. The general's gaze met his wife's.

"He'll be down momentarily," she insisted in answer to his unspoken question.

He grunted his response — a reaction so like Tony's, Deborah stared, then remembered herself and looked away . . . but she was too late. He'd already caught her regard.

"Your wineglass is empty, Mrs. Percival. Please let me refill it."

"Oh, no," Deborah said quickly. "I'm fine."

"No, you are not," he contradicted. His keen gaze honed in on her to the point she felt like a field mouse in the sights of a hawk. He saw everything.

"She doesn't wish another drink —" Sophia started, but her husband cut her off by placing his hand over his wife's.

Gently, he said, "I was not talking about the wine."

Sophia looked from one to the other. She fell silent.

Lacing his fingers with his wife's, he said to Deborah, "You strike me as a sensible woman, Mrs. Percival. One accustomed to direct speaking."

Deborah murmured a response although he hadn't anticipated one because he continued, "Our reasons for being here are of utmost importance to us. I don't know how much Lord Burnell has revealed to you about the family background — ?"

"Please, I do not wish to intrude on a private matter," Deborah responded, and could have added, *because Tony would be livid.*

"We don't ask much," Sir Richard said. "Just a few moments of Lord Burnell's undivided attention."

Tony's voice came from the doorway. "For what reason?" They all turned. He was dressed all in black save for the snowy white neckcloth tied in the height of style. He'd taken time, while they'd been cooling their heels waiting for him, to bathe and shave.

He walked into the room, aware all eyes were on him.

Sophia stood, a naked longing of a mother's love in her eyes. "You have grown very handsome."

Tony's mouth curled cynically. He looked to Sir Richard. "You wish my undivided attention? You have it."

The general stood, obviously wanting to be at eye level, but Sophia stepped between them. "Please, let us have a pleasant dinner. Right, Mrs. Percival?" she asked, soliciting Deborah's help. "We can discuss those *other* matters later."

"Yes, later," Tony agreed pleasantly as if she'd just suggested they go on some lark . . . and Deborah didn't trust this new mood of his.

At that moment, he turned to her, the haughty expression leaving his face. "You are beautiful," he said, holding out his hand.

His public praise brought heat up to her cheeks. There was an air of tension around Tony. Of anticipation. And she feared it did not bode well for any of them. However, she couldn't snub him either. She placed her hand in his, and he grandly escorted her out of the room, blatantly ignoring his mother.

The dining hall was in the opposite wing. An oval table was set for four. The burning candles and gold linen tablecloth gave the room a warm, intimate air. Two footmen under the butler's watchful eye stood ready to serve.

Tony started to seat Deborah at the foot of

the table, the place usually reserved for the mistress of the house. Deborah hesitated, but Sophia did not take insult. She moved to the next place over. Tony even took his own seat before his mother sat down. Again, she did not take offense.

However, Sir Richard was not pleased. Deborah braced herself, expecting him to say something and was surprised when he held his tongue. He seated his wife, then took the chair opposite hers at the table. However, there was a decided hostility in the air between the two men.

Ill at ease, Deborah concentrated on the cream soup placed before her. Sophia cast an anxious glance toward her, but Deborah had nothing to offer. Small talk seemed out of place — or an opportunity for Tony to commit further insult.

One footman removed the soup bowls while another offered braised hare for the next course. Deborah's appetite had deserted her. Obviously, Sophia was having the same problem, while the gentlemen appeared to take great delight in their food.

Or were they using food as another form of rivalry of sorts?

Then, bravely, Sophia put down her fork and made the opening salvo, "I suppose you are wondering, my son, why we have come for a visit?"

Tony's eyes reflected the glitter of the candle

flames. "Does a mother coming to visit her son need a reason?" he asked. His sarcasm was not lost on Sir Richard. He paused in the act of raising his fork to his lips.

Tony smiled, apparently satisfied to have gotten the first rise.

If the two men had had swords in their hands, Deborah had no doubt they would have gleefully hacked away at each other. She placed her hands in her lap. She'd sat in on too many family arguments not to sense what was coming.

Sophia sent a desperate look to her husband, one Deborah interpreted as a silent entreaty for him to keep his temper. "This one does," she admitted, addressing Tony.

"Then what is your reason?" he replied, his voice like silk — and Deborah knew he was toying with her.

His mother took a moment to straighten her shoulders before saying in a clear, decisive voice, "I want to return to London with your blessing."

His answer was succinct. "No."

The word reverberated in the room. Sophia clenched her fists on the table.

Realizing they had an unintended audience, Tony motioned to the butler to remove himself and the servants. The door had barely closed before Sophia said, "You have no reason to keep me away."

"I have the best reason in the world," Tony

replied, his tone deceptively mild. "You drove my father to suicide."

By her expression, if he had cut her with a knife, he could not have hurt her more.

Sir Richard brought his fist down on the table so hard the dinnerware bounced. "You have no right to judge her," he demanded. "Not with your own doxy sitting here at the table."

Chapter Seventeen

Steel-cold anger shot through Tony.

No one criticized his Deb or his love for her. He came to his feet. "You'll meet me for those words."

"So, you're finally brave enough to look me in the eye," Sir Richard said before adding with a sneer, "And what did I do? Save call her what you've called your own mother for years?"

His words struck a blow. Tony replied, "I spoke the truth."

"And so did I."

Tony lunged at him, but his mother stood and reached across the table, placing herself between the two men. "Anthony, Richard, please. No."

Sir Richard came to his feet. "I'm tired of biting my tongue, Sophia. For years, I've done it for your sake, but the time has arrived for this pup to learn to mind his elders."

"I'm no pup, old man," Tony shot back. "Sword or pistols?"

"Tony!" Deb said, rising. "Please —"

Sir Richard cut her off, facing Tony. "I'll not fight you."

"Ah, so my mother's *honor* isn't worth defending?" The words left his lips in reckless anger. However, the moment they were spoken, he realized he'd crossed a boundary he should have avoided. He might have spoken harshly in private, but never to her face.

His mother paled, swaying slightly as if her legs could not support her. Deb moved to her side.

But Adamson did not flinch. "No. I will not fight you because I'd not spill the blood *of my only child.*"

His soft-spoken words resonated in the room. If he had plunged a dagger in Tony's heart, the impact could not have been different. Tony took a step back.

"Richard, please," his mother begged. "This isn't the time."

"It's never the time! Sophia, I've spent years denying he was mine, years apart from him. He's a man now, and he can take the truth like a man."

"*I am not your son,*" Tony said, placing every fiber of his being behind the denial.

His father smiled with chilling certainty. "Yes, you are."

And Tony knew he was right.

For the first time, he let himself admit the truth. The one everyone had already accepted save himself.

Its impact was shattering.

"Then it would have been better if I'd not been born," Tony answered.

His mother cried out and would have col-lapsed except for Deb putting her arm around her, giving her support.

Calmly, Adamson turned to Deb. "Mrs. Percival, would you be so kind as to take Sophia into the sitting room? I believe she could do with a glass of wine. Burnell and I have much to discuss."

"Richard, I beg of you —"

"Sophia, you've trusted me on so many other matters, give me your trust on this."

She stared into his eyes as if wishing it could be another way. Then, slowly, she nodded.

"I'm sorry," Sir Richard whispered.

Her smile was bittersweet. "No, *I'm* sorry."

Tony hated not being the one in control. "Neither of you will tell me anything. There is *nothing* you have to say I am interested in hearing. Come, Deb, let us leave."

But she did not step forward. Instead, she answered, "I believe, my lord, you and Sir Richard have much to discuss. Your mother and I will retire to the other room." She took his mother's arm.

"No, this isn't wise," his mother protested, but Deb was showing her iron resolve.

"We must," she murmured, and steered his mother out of the dining hall, shutting the door firmly behind them, and Tony knew she was not pleased. He'd disappointed her, but Deb had a great capacity to forgive.

He did not.

"Mrs. Percival is a wise woman," Sir Richard said. "I can see why you admire her."

"I don't give a damn what your opinion is," Tony shot back and, suddenly, he almost couldn't breathe in the same room with this man, he started for the door.

"Running, Burnell?"

Tony pulled up short. He turned. "I never run. However, I can't stand your presence."

Sir Richard laughed. "Good. I'd not have a son of mine who was a coward. Although I'm not proud of your boorish behavior."

Doubling his fists, Tony stepped forward. "I am not your son."

A triumphant gleam flashed in Sir Richard's eyes. "And whose son do you believe you are? Welborne Aldercy's? You know better."

Tony looked him straight in the eye. "I am Welborne's son. Or perhaps I came by way of another of my mother's lovers."

Sir Richard refused to be baited. "After I met your mother, there were no others, and we met well before you were born." He walked around the table. Tony resisted an urge to move away from him.

"Let us look at the evidence, shall we?" Sir Richard said. "Welborne was of average height."

"My mother's tall."

"And you have her eyes."

"Do you expect me to thank you for the compliment?"

"No, I'm not expecting any quarter from you, and I'm glad of it. Welborne was a weakling. He had the disease in his blood for drinking and gambling. You have not."

"How do you know?" Tony challenged.

The older man turned very serious. "There is little I don't know about you. I was denied the right to be in your life, but that doesn't mean I accepted it gracefully. I know you could ride before you could walk. I knew what your first words were. That you hated porridge for breakfast, had the pox when you were three, and feared going upstairs alone. You named your first dog Dart and taught him to lie down on command. The two of you went hunting together on a Monday morning and he ran under your pony's hooves and died from his injuries. You wouldn't eat for a week and have refused to own another dog since."

"How could you know?" Tony demanded. No one knew those things about him. His own parents had been busy with their own lives in London.

"Miss Chalmers is my cousin. She served as my surrogate."

Tony felt as if the wind had been knocked out of him. Marmy had been the one person he'd trusted. The one person who had always been present for him.

Slowly, he sat down in the chair Sir Richard — no, his *father* had been sitting in. His father.

Sir Richard was right. Tony had had very little in common with Welborne Aldercy . . . and as Tony had grown older, he'd developed outright disdain for him. He'd hated the emotionalism, the dramatics, the selfishness. Had he not stamped out these human flaws in himself?

"Why did no one tell me?" Tony barely recognized the ragged, raw voice as his own.

His father pulled out the chair his wife had vacated so he could sit facing Tony. "I wanted to, especially after Aldercy's death and before I married Sophia."

Tony couldn't meet his gaze. "It's like a jest, isn't it? Everyone was in on it but me. And I? I'm not even who I thought I was."

"You are Lord Burnell."

"Oh, no." Tony did not hide the disillusionment in his tone. "I'm an impostor. A poseur you put in the place of the real Lord Burnell."

Adamson leaned forward. "There is *no* real Lord Burnell. Welborne was incapable of having children. He was often too drunk, and he had black moods that would send him hiding in his rooms for days."

Something niggled the back of Tony's memory . . . of him being very young and his father arriving at Alder House unannounced. But he hadn't come to see Tony. Instead, he'd stayed to his room. One night, he'd come out and wandered around the house, knocking over things. The sounds had woken Tony. Marmy and Gibbons had quickly directed his father back to his room. That same night, Tony had listened to his father weeping behind the closed door of his bedroom. Deep, heartfelt sobs that had frightened Tony. The next day, his mother had appeared in the day and whisked his father away in a black-lacquered coach.

"Welborne wanted an heir," Adamson continued. "He had several wild schemes he pursued. There's a quack out there who will sell anything. Your mother was very young and quite naïve. Your parents' marriage had been arranged the year Sophia came out of the schoolroom. She didn't know how to handle the husband she had."

"And turned to other men," Tony surmised brutally.

"She was confused."

"How do you know I'm yours?" At that point, Tony wasn't going to save himself any pain.

"You're *mine*." Sir Richard leaned forward, his good arm resting on the table. "Your mother was not adrift for long. The hell of her marriage might have broken other women, but not her. I met her at a garden party in Sussex. I can remember every detail of that meeting. I had returned to England for new orders. I hated the politics of London and wanted to return to the fighting immediately. However, I had to petition Roger Petry for uniforms and supplies for my men. He was a tightfisted bastard, and I hated the idea of dancing attendance on him at his country estate. And then I met Sophia. She was there with friends, and

311

from the moment I laid eyes on her, I fell in love."

His keen-eyed gaze softened. "Can you understand what I'm saying, Burnell? How one minute you are complete and whole unto yourself and in the next, like a clap of thunder, you need this other human as you've needed no other? That what you'd thought was whole was really empty?"

Tony understood too well. Did he not feel that way about Deb? His attraction to her had been powerful and instantaneous.

"My life has not been the same since," Sir Richard confessed. "I would rather have lost my heart to a woman who was free. I didn't." For a moment, he sat as if looking back into time.

He roused himself. "Welborne knew of our affair and that this one was different than the others. Of course, long absences are part of the nature of my profession. Until I resigned my commission, Sophia and I had so few moments together." He looked at Tony. "I wanted a son. When she became pregnant with my child, I asked her to separate from Welborne . . . and she wouldn't."

"Why not?"

"She was thinking of you. What if Welborne pressed for a divorce? What your life would be like? Also, Welborne wanted to claim you. His vanity needed an heir, the estate was falling down around his ears, and the money was gone. Claiming my child was his one chance of rebuilding the Burnell title from a direct descendant of himself." Sir Richard frowned. "He was an amazing man. He could be practically insane one minute and stone-cold calculating the next. Sophia agreed because she thought it was best for you. I was out of the country, or I would have demanded she refuse."

"My life would have been very different if you had."

"Yes," Sir Richard agreed. "I would have taken a post out of England. Both our lives would have been different." He drummed one finger on the table, one of Tony's own gestures. "Of course the irony is here Sophia was attempting to spare you from scandal, and Welborne had to disgrace all of us by blowing his brains out. Here, of all places . . . where you would find him. He ensured you were tainted for life. Not that you haven't been your own worst enemy, Burnell. You've been far too proud and unyielding."

"Qualities I may have inherited from my father," he replied tightly, and earned a ghost of a smile from Sir Richard.

"As you say."

However, something was not right. Skeptical, Tony said, "You wish to paint a different portrait of my mother than the one I see. She was no devoted parent."

Adamson leaned forward. "Good God, man, you don't understand how erratic Welborne could be. From the moment you were born, Sophia worried he would harm you. Her sole mission in life became keeping him as far away from you as possible. You became another excuse for his capricious whims, and he was capable of murder, don't doubt me on that. When he went into his black moods, he could do anything."

"But it was his *own* life he took."

Sir Richard retreated back in his chair. "Yes, and thank God."

Tony couldn't share the sentiment. His own life had fallen apart after the suicide. "Why did you not tell me this tale sooner?"

His father sat quiet. He rubbed his thumb against the side of his hand. Tony waited, silent. His father's gaze met his own.

"We depended upon cousin Beth for guidance. After the suicide, Sophia and I both wanted to let the truth out, but Welborne had left the estate completely bankrupt and everything was under intense scrutiny because of the gossip. Nor were you ready to hear what we had to say. So we waited and, over the years, you and your mother have grown more and more distant. We've wanted to be a part of your life. And your mother has suffered greatly for the role she played. She wants your forgiveness. She wants her son returned to her. However, you are a hard man, Burnell."

"No, a proud one."

His father conceded his point with a smile.

"It's a family trait."

Tony didn't know how to respond. Instead, he said, "So, why are you telling me all this now? Why could we not have continued on as we had?"

"Because your mother and I want to be more a part of your life. We want to be present in our grandchildren's lives. Beth wrote to us of your meeting Mrs. Percival. She thought, having met someone you truly care about, you might now understand our story."

Marmy had thought that?

Rising from his chair, Tony had to take several steps away so he could think. Marmy had been right. Deb had managed to carve a chink in the wall he'd built around himself. A month earlier, he would not have stayed in a room with his father long enough to hear even the beginnings of the tale.

"I know I've given you almost too much to swallow so suddenly," his father said. "I've tried to think of an easy way to break the news and obviously, failed. Sometimes, bluntness is best."

Tony nodded, his mind still reeling from the lifetime of intrigues and machinations. "What happens now?" he asked at last. "Where do we go from here?"

His father stood. "I believe it best we keep your parentage between us. I am prepared to be your stepfather, and the world doesn't need to know differently."

Here was the unkindest twist of all, and Tony came face-to-face with his deepest fear. "I am a fraud. The title is not mine."

"Yes, it is. Welborne and Parliament deemed it so."

"Parliament was not a party to the deception."

His father made an impatient sound. "You want to know the truth? Well, the truth is you saved this title and the estate. You have more right to it than Welborne did."

"I'm not his blood."

"No one will challenge you." His father took a step forward. "Your ownership of the title is an established fact. Besides, you've made your mark on the world. You've earned respect. The agriculture bill before the House of Lords could never have been written without you. And everyone knows you bartered the agreement in the Commons. No one else could have accomplished the feat. You are respected. If you weren't, Longest wouldn't have chosen you for his daughter."

Tony smiled grimly. "Is there anything you don't know?"

"About you? Little." His father reached out and carefully laid his hand on Tony's shoulder. Tony's first response was to jerk away, the reaction of his past.

He forced himself to stand still . . . and slowly, the hand on his shoulder was not oppressive, but welcoming.

"You are my son," his father said. "I could not be more proud."

"But this must remain our secret."

The lines of his father's face tightened. "Yes. However, I don't care what the world believes as long as *you* know you are mine."

Tony didn't know who moved first, his father or himself, but suddenly their arms were around each other, and they embraced as men. "How do we go about this?" he asked the world in general.

"The way we've done everything," his father replied. "One cautious step at a time. And it will work, now that the chasm has been crossed."

Gibbons helped Deborah guide Sophia to the private sitting room they'd been in earlier. He summoned Sophia's lady's maid, an older woman with a competent air. Taking one look at Sophia's white face, she sat her lady on the settee and prepared a brandy and rum.

She looked to Deborah. "Would you care for one, too, Mrs. Percival? 'Tis my own remedy for steadying the nerves. I've been prepared for this moment. We've all known the time would come."

Deborah was about to refuse the offer, but Sophia interrupted, "Yes, Alice, make one for her, too. I believe we shall both need fortification." She added in explanation to Deborah, "I don't know how the night will end."

Alice handed the honey-laced cordial to Deborah, who did find it fortifying. She glanced at Sophia. The color was returning to the older woman's face. However, she did not appear more relaxed.

"Thank you, Alice, Gibbons, that will be all," Sophia said, her voice wan.

The servants bowed out, shutting the door and leaving the two women alone.

Sophia raised her cordial glass. "I rarely drink these. However, Alice is right. Tonight I did need one."

Deborah took another sip. The drink was potent but not unwelcome.

"Please, sit beside me?" Sophia asked, patting a spot on the settee.

With a quick glance at the door, Deborah decided she had no choice but to stay. She prayed Tony would not be long because she feared any more courtesy she gave his mother would be interpreted by him as aiding the enemy.

When she was seated, Sophia said hesitantly, "I must offer an apology. I don't know what came over Richard this evening. When he saw you earlier, he was impressed. He felt you were a woman of good sense. His insult at the dinner table was uncalled for." She managed a tight smile. "He and I have no right to cast stones."

Deborah remained quiet. The man had merely spoken the truth. Shame was a humbling emotion.

Caught up in her own problem, Sophia said,

half to herself, "I didn't make a mistake in coming. I didn't. Everything will be fine."

She drained the glass and set it on a side table. "Tell me about yourself, Mrs. Percival."

Now it was Deborah who needed the fortification. She stared down into the cordial as if it held answers.

"Oh, come now," Sophia said. "We are both sophisticated women. You love my son," she hazarded.

"Yes." Deborah was embarrassed her voice was barely a sound and a far cry from how a "sophisticated" woman would respond.

Sophia seemed amused. "You are from the country?"

"Um, yes, the Peak District, close to Ilam." Deborah finished her drink but held the glass as if it were a talisman to protect her.

"I don't bite, Mrs. Percival," Sophia said firmly, taking the empty glass from Deborah and placing it on the table next to her own. "What is your given name?"

"Deborah."

"A lovely name. It is biblical, no? Deborah was a prophetess. Tell me, can you see what the future holds for us?"

"My lady, if I had known the future, I would never have left Ilam."

Her candidness startled a laugh from Sophia, and Deborah found herself smiling, the ice between them broken.

Sophia leaned forward, the deep blue eyes

that were so much like her son's alert and sensitive, she said, "Do you love my son?"

"Yes." There, she'd admitted to another — and the sky hadn't fallen. "Yes, I do," she repeated with more force. "And more's the pity because he is promised to someone else."

"Ah, yes, Longest's daughter."

"You know?" Deborah asked with surprise.

"Of course." Sophia relaxed against the back of the settee. "Beth, whom you know as Miss Chalmers, is Richard's cousin. She is the only person Tony trusts. It used to break my heart to know he would turn to her before he'd ever ask anything of me. Of course, he would have gone to half of England before me." Her expressive eyes saddened. "I have many regrets," she admitted softly, and proceeded to tell Deborah the story of her affair with the famous general.

"Why are you telling me this?" Deborah asked when she was finished. "This is a private family matter. Why include me?"

"Because you love my son and he has needed someone to love him for so long." She took Deborah's hand in hers. Her skin was smooth, her nails manicured. Deborah's hands were rough and callused in comparison.

Sophia said, "I have always listened to Beth's instincts. She believes you are good for Anthony. But tell me, what is it you want?"

Her question caught Deborah off guard. What did she want? A month ago, she'd left

Ilam wishing nothing more than to escape the expectations of others. Now, she realized, she still was, in a sense, running.

Searching deep within her, Deborah confessed, "All my life, I dreamed about falling in love. My parents were a love match, and I just knew if you fell in love with someone who loved you, there would be no worries, no fears, no daily insecurities. Now, I have more doubts than ever before . . . because my world is larger. It includes Tony and an uncertain future."

Sophia leaned close. "Love is not always easy."

"It isn't, is it?" Deborah said.

"No," Sophia said, "but I'd not have it any other way." She gave Deborah's hand a squeeze. "My son is promised to this other woman. Where do matters stand between the two of you?"

"He offered *carte blanche*. It's all he is free to give."

His mother made a soft sound of distress, and Deborah remembered this had been the way she'd lived her life. "What is your answer?"

Deborah pulled her hand away. "That's where I am the most confused." And in her confusion was the fear she would make the wrong decision.

"Talk to me," Sophia urged.

"I don't know where to start."

"Then tell me what you want most."

"I want marriage." There. She'd said what

was in her heart.

Nor did Sophia laugh. Instead, she said shrewdly, "Beth says he barely knows the girl, who is little more than a chit out of the schoolroom. I cannot see my son with a child."

"Oh, my lady, she is no child. I've seen her. She is beautiful, and her father is very powerful. Furthermore, Tony is committed to seeing the marriage through. It's a matter of honor. Meanwhile, I have one sister who would be scandalized at the idea of my being kept as his mistress and another who prays I will take his offer so her husband can keep his position in Tony's employ."

"And which way will you choose?"

She looked at the elegant lady beside her, and said, "I still don't know. However, I do have one question for you."

"Yes?"

"Is giving up everything worth the sacrifice?"

Chapter Eighteen

Tony and his father left the dining hall having come to terms. They were willing to let their relationship grow gradually.

Out in the foyer, Gibbons informed them Lady Adamson waited in the sitting room; Mrs. Percival had gone up to bed.

His father asked, "You will come see your mother? I'm certain she is anxious to hear what happened between us."

"You can tell her."

His father frowned.

Tony shook his head. "I'm not certain how I feel toward her at this moment, and I'm not ready to deal with her." Old resentments ran deep. "She could have trusted me with the truth instead of leaving it to gossip and innuendo."

"Would you have listened if she had?"

"I don't know."

"Then perhaps she made the right decision."

Tony didn't have an answer. But he did need to find Deb.

He needed her wisdom, her understanding. Only she could help him make sense of the strange twists his life had taken.

"Good night, sir," Tony said, and left, taking the steps up to his floor two at a time. A lantern

323

provided light in the hall. He didn't go to his room but Deb's. One light rap on the door, and he turned the handle.

She was sitting up, waiting by the fire. She still wore the dress she'd had on at dinner but she'd pulled the pins from her hair. It hung down over her shoulders, its shine red-gold in the firelight. She stood.

He closed the door quietly and leaned his back against it. "Were you told?" he asked.

Deb nodded. "Some."

"At least I wasn't the only one in the house not to know," he said.

"Quite a turn of events. Are you angry?"

He made a noncommittal sound. "I'm still too stunned for anger. And in some ways, I'm relieved."

"What do you mean?"

Tony pushed away from the door. "For years, I feared fathering children because of the Aldercy madness. And I used to wait, fearing signs of it in myself."

She actually smiled. "I've never feared you being mad. Headstrong, perhaps. Arrogant, definitely. But never mad."

Her words loosened the tension resting on his shoulders, and he found himself smiling, too. "Ah, Deb, life has no meaning without you." He opened his arms but she did not coming running to him.

"What's wrong?" he asked warily. "What did *she* say to you?"

Deb didn't pretend to not understand whom he meant. "Nothing I didn't ask from her myself." Her gaze dropped to the flames in the fire as she gathered courage. "Tony, I do not want the life of a mistress."

"I don't want it for you," he responded. "If we could do it any other way . . ." Couldn't she understand? This was not his choice, not any longer.

She took a step away from the chair. She looked so young, so beautiful. "You are not free to marry. And perhaps, our destiny was *not* to be together."

"Don't say that."

"Perhaps," she continued as if he hadn't spoken, "we were fated to meet at this time and give each other strength to face our futures."

Her suggestion that they were predestined to part infuriated him. "What have I given you?" he demanded cynically. "I seem to take and take. What have you gotten from me?"

"Everything," she whispered. "Before you, I was like a flower that had never fully opened. Leaving the Valley was my first act of rebellion. Granted, it was a mild one, but I would not have come so far without you. Now, I understand a woman's desires and a woman's needs. I've gained the courage to choose my own course in life."

She clasped her hands together, looking so beautiful he longed to touch her. "This is my decision, Tony. I want to grow old with the man I'm with. I want his shoes under my table in the mornings and under my bed at night. I want him to watch my children grow. I can't share. I won't."

Tony rocked back. He hurt . . . all over. "I can't give you up."

Deb crossed to him. He leaned back, uncertain. She placed her arms around his neck, her breasts against his chest. "I would rather cut my own skin with a knife than cause you pain."

He put his arm around her waist, holding her close, burying his face in the fragrance of her hair. "Then don't leave me."

"We have no choice." She hugged him tight. "Would you cry off from your betrothal to Longest's daughter?"

"I can't. My honor —" he started but could not finish, his words blocked by the hard ache in his throat.

"I know," she agreed sadly. "You won't commit to me and me alone."

"I would if I were free."

"Truly, Tony?" She pressed her hand against the side of his face. "Or is there some other fear holding you back?"

She kissed him . . . and this kiss was a far cry from the hesitant ones of their first meeting. They knew what each other wanted.

Tony lifted her up, her legs coming around his hips, and he carried her to the bed. They undressed each other with swift, sure hands.

He leaned her back onto the mattress. Her

skin was golden in the firelight. He kissed her neck, her chin, her lips, and her ears. He worshiped her with his kisses — and if he could change her mind, he would.

Please, God, he would.

She opened to him, and he entered in one deep, fluid stroke. She arched her back in pleasure, her sharp intake of breath released on a satisfied sigh. Her hand followed the line of his back, her nails tickling his skin. "This is good, so good," she whispered.

He moved then. He knew what she liked and the way she liked it. Her needs and desires had woven into the fabric of his life. He didn't know how he would exist without her.

And then, conscious thought left. He lost himself in the give and take of their lovemaking. She always pleased him. Always. It would be so easy to forget himself in her, to fill her.

But he didn't — because he could not be like Sir Richard. When he had a child, he wanted to be present in his life. He wanted to guide and direct him, to listen to his stories, and to always be there for protection.

She tightened around him, her body lifting off the bed, taking him deeper. He gave her the satisfaction of release, taking joy in her cry of pleasure. Sweet, wonderful Deb.

He pulled out, protecting her, and rolled over on his side. Dear God! He didn't know how he would go on without her.

They lay still, each lost in completion. Then, her arms came around him. "Thank you."

He didn't answer.

She cupped his body with her own. Her breasts pressed his back, her sex cradled his buttocks. She smoothed the line of his hip, her legs rubbing against his.

"Tony —" she started.

"Don't say anything. Let us pretend that we have a hundred nights like this ahead of us. Just us."

She nodded, and tightened her hold around him. With soft sigh, she nuzzled his back and fell asleep.

Tony listened to her breathing. She was wrong when she said he couldn't commit to her. His hands were tied. He was honor-bound to marry Lady Amelia. Sleep for him was a long time in coming and when it did, it was filled with wild dreams born out of his disappointment.

Some of the dreams were real, memories he'd forgotten. He was a child and afraid of his father. Servants always lurked close by, and Marmy was ever-present, ever watchful. Now he understood they had not trusted his father with him.

Trust.

The word was whispered over and over in his dream, and there was Deb. Trust.

She waited for him in the library, in the very spot where he used to dream his father's body had been. She was there for him now and when he lifted his arm, there was no gun, but a sword in his hand.

She opened her arms as if to embrace him — and he woke, startled by the image.

Deb, the one of flesh and blood, leaned over him, shaking his shoulder. "Tony, you were having your nightmare."

It took him a moment to establish dream from reality. He shook his head. "No, it was different."

He glanced around the room. The gray light of dawn gave it a sense of being in another world.

"How was it different?" she asked.

Tony thought of the sword . . . and understood its meaning. He felt no fear or pain, just an indescribable sadness and an acceptance.

Rolling over onto his stomach, his body stretched out beside her, he said, "I'm to let you go — if that is what you wish."

The expression in her dark eyes turned sad. She nodded.

"When do you want to leave?" he asked, his heart breaking.

"Perhaps today would be best. The longer we are together, the harder it will be."

He grunted, acknowledging the truth. "I'll go to my room to dress. I'll wait for you downstairs." He started to rise but her hand on his arm stopped him.

"I love you."

Bending his head, he kissed the back of her fingers. "I know, and I love you. But then, that's the devil of it, isn't it? We love each other too much not to give everything we have."

Before she could answer, he climbed out of bed, pulled on his breeches, and left the room without looking back.

He didn't linger over his toilette. His valet was waiting and shaved him, but Tony didn't want any more fuss than that. He dressed in brown leather breeches and a brown wool jacket — clothes he would be comfortable in for travel.

Deb was still dressing, and she had to pack, although that would not take her long. He went downstairs. Breakfast was being served on a sideboard in the dining hall; however, his appetite had deserted him.

Instead, he decided to give Alfred the word to prepare his traveling coach himself.

Clipped conifers bordered the path to the stables. They were interspersed with billowing silver foliage and the blooms of spring bulbs. Tony went around a bend and came face-to-face with his mother. She'd been bent over examining a flower bed and seemed as surprised to see him as he was her.

For a second, they stood as strangers.

Her anxious smile of greeting did not quite meet her eyes. "I planted these beds, years ago. I wanted to see how they were doing."

He nodded. "I remember. I helped you." His

smile brittle, he started to pass her on his way.

However, she stepped in front of him, and hurriedly said, "I never meant for harm to come to you."

Tony shifted his weight from one foot to another before deciding to stand his ground. They had to come to terms sooner or later. And a bit of the grace that came so naturally to Deb rubbed off on him. For the first time, he attempted to view his mother without arrogance or bitterness.

Here was not the hard-hearted harpy of his childhood imagination, but a woman who had attempted to protect her son.

She misinterpreted his silence. Tears pooled in her eyes. "Well, I must go in. Richard will be down for breakfast shortly. We're leaving today. We do not wish to overstay our welcome."

She ducked her head and would have brushed by him — but Tony could not let them part. Not like this.

He hooked his hand in her arm and turned her around. "I'm sorry." The words flowed from his lips, surprising him at how easy they were to say. "I've been an idiot."

Her tears overflowed her eyes then and ran down her cheeks, but she was smiling. "I'm so glad to hear you say those words."

Her candor startled a laugh from him and before he could think twice, he enveloped her in his arms. Funny, but she'd always seemed larger than life. The woman he held now was a petite, fragile thing. She was bone, muscle, and sinew . . . and time for both of them was passing too quickly.

She seemed to sense his thoughts and hugged him tighter. "I prayed for a moment like this. Oh, my son."

They stood for a moment longer and then she started to step back, having to wipe the tears from her eyes. "I have a confession. You aren't going to be happy. Mrs. Percival and I had a talk last night —"

"Yes, she told me."

His mother raised her gaze to his. "You aren't angry?"

"I'm not pleased. However, she has her own life, her own mind."

"She's a remarkable woman," his mother said. "An honest one. Far from what I had imagined you would choose."

Now here was the crux of the problem. "Well, I believe Lady Amelia will exactly fit what you had anticipated my choice would be for a bride."

"Yes, I hear her breeding is impeccable." Her dry rejoinder made him wince. Then, seeing her words had found their mark, she said quietly, "You shouldn't let Mrs. Percival go."

"No, I shouldn't," he agreed. "But what can I offer her? Neither one of us wants to live on the fringes of society."

"Tony, I'm sorry. I know what it is like to live without the one you love. I pray you find a resolution like your father and I have."

He raised his mother's hand to his lips. "I pray the same. But then, sometimes love is not enough."

"Love is everything," she vowed.

How naïve she sounded. But then, she'd always flouted the rules.

She didn't move. "You won't change your mind, will you?" she said at his silence.

"No, Deborah and I are the sort who always do the right thing." What had once been a source of pride, now sounded like a curse. "Well, please excuse me, Mother, I need to send word to Alfred to have the coach sent round."

She nodded, her expression softening at his use of the word "Mother." Her reaction tore at his conscience . . . and he understood why Deborah refused to accept anything less than what she deserved.

He left to order the coach.

Deborah tried not to think beyond the moment.

If she did, she knew she'd turn weepy and might even change her mind. And she would have no peace in life if that happened.

Sophia and Richard joined them for breakfast — although neither she nor Tony had an appetite. His parents decided that instead of leaving that day, they would wait for Tony's return. To Deborah, that was good. The ghosts were being laid to rest.

Tony insisted on taking her all the way to Ilam. The trip would be a day and a half, even in one of his well-sprung coaches. He tied a horse to the coach to ride on the way back. They'd packed some books and spent the first day snuggled against each other reading.

The books served to provide a diversion. Conversation between them was sparse and mundane. After all, in the past, they'd discussed hopes and dreams. What was there to say now?

They spent the night in an out-of-the-way inn. Deborah debated asking Tony to procure separate rooms . . . and couldn't. The bond between them would be broken soon enough.

They made love over and over. And when they weren't making love, he held her in his arms, and she listened to the steady, strong beat of his heart. She would miss the excitement of their lovemaking, but this human closeness was what she valued most. To be touched, to be stroked, to feel the heat of another body beside hers in the bed.

She knew his scent as intimately as her own. Her fingers had traced every line, every plane of his skin. She knew his flaws and his weaknesses.

She also knew she'd never again fall in love with anyone the way she was with him.

They arrived in Derby late the next morning. Tony suggested they spend the night at Miss

Chalmers's, but Deborah didn't believe it would be wise. She had too many memories . . . nor was she up to his former nanny's keen-eyed gaze.

The coach started on the road along the Dove. The river still flowed fast, a reminder of all the rain they'd had over the past month. The Valley was green with spring.

Deborah sat back against the seat, staring thoughtfully out the window at the passing scenery. Mr. Stanley and his horse Howie would be on their way home from Derby on their mail run. Had anything changed while she was gone?

Tony laced his fingers with hers. She squeezed his hand hard, needing his strength. The landmarks along the road became more familiar. They neared Ilam. The road was busy today and belatedly she remembered this was Market Day.

She waited until she knew they could not go closer without creating comment. "Please have the coach stop here," she said.

He hesitated. His glance fell to their joined hands. She wanted to reach over and touch his hair, to let her fingers feel the smooth roughness of his whiskers. Instead, she said, "It's time. I want to walk rest of the way. It'll be better."

Raising his gaze to hers, he nodded. He knew she didn't want to cause comment . . . and there was nothing left to say.

Tony knocked on the roof, a signal to his driver to pull over. While his driver retrieved her new portmanteau, Tony opened the door and hopped down, unfolding the step for her. He offered his hand.

Deborah was tempted to hang back . . . and yet, she had no choice. They'd made their decision — the honorable one.

When she stepped down, she said, "My sister's house is off across that pasture there, but I believe I will walk into town. Mrs. Luton runs a shop that sells a little of everything. Sometimes, she has fresh bread, and my brother-in-law is partial to her baking. I'll bring a loaf as a homecoming present."

Tony asked, "How far to the village?"

"Oh, it's around the bend." She tied the ribbons of her bonnet. "I'm returning to Ilam more finely dressed than when I left. Everyone will be impressed."

He had no answer. They stood silent a moment. Then he reached into his pocket and offered a small leather purse of coins.

"I don't need it," she said.

"Take the money anyway," he answered. "There's not that much in the purse, and it's important to me that you have a bit of coin about you . . . in case you need it. One never knows what twists life has waiting for us."

"No, one doesn't," she agreed sadly. Had they not learned that lesson firsthand? She accepted the pouch.

"And here," he continued, offering one of his cards from between his fingers. "If you ever need me . . ."

"I know." She tucked the card in her reticule.

For a second, he appeared ready to kiss her but could not. They were not alone. A farmer driving his cart passed them by. He studied the coach with blatant curiosity. And on the hill above the road, several children had caught sight of the coach and ran to tell others.

"You must go," she said in a low voice.

Their gazes met. "Good-bye, my love," he said softly.

She opened her mouth to answer, but her throat closed, choking words back. The tears did spill now. There was nothing left to say. He brushed one tear away with a gloved fingertip, then turned and climbed into the coach.

Deborah stepped out of the way. The driver tipped his hat. "Mrs. Percival." She nodded and stepped well out of the way for the turning vehicle, Tony's horse tied to the back. She could see Tony. He sat forward, his elbows on his knees, his hands forming a steeple where he rested his chin. He did not look left or right. She waited until the coach drove out of sight.

The beauty of the day was at odds with the pain in her heart.

She dried her tears and started walking toward the village. Her decision to buy bread would give her much-needed time to regain her composure before seeing Henry and Rachel again.

The road at Ilam's outskirts was very busy. Even at this late hour in the afternoon, there were still a good number of people out and about. She might not be able to buy her loaf of Mrs. Luton's bread because the woman often sold out on Market Day.

Deborah made her way to the village center. She'd lived in Ilam all her life and yet, today, she felt a stranger. She no longer belonged here. Her path crossed those of people she knew, and yet their faces seemed foreign to her.

She told herself she was being fanciful. She hadn't been gone off to London that long . . . of course, in that time, her whole life had changed. She'd left an untried girl, carried this way and that by the decisions of others. She returned a woman.

The door to Mrs. Luton's corner shop was open, which was a good sign. She might still have a loaf of bread. Deborah entered. The store was empty save for the lace-caped Mrs. Luton wiping her counter clean. Her gray eyebrows came up in surprise. "Why, Mrs. Percival, thou have come home. How was thou's sister in London?"

Deborah smiled at the woman's knowledge of her affairs. Such a tight world she lived in, one outlined by rules and expectations of nosy neighbors. "My sister is most excellent. Thank you for asking. Her precious baby made the trip worthwhile."

"Oh, yes, I like the wee ones."

"Do you have a loaf of your bread? I don't see any on the counter."

Mrs. Luton smiled proudly. "I sold out less than half an hour ago. Sorry."

Deborah started to groan her disappointment, but Mrs. Luton looked beyond her, as someone else entered the store. Deborah started to turn when she heard a hissing noise, like a gaggle of geese had wandered into the cozy shop.

In a way, a gaggle had arrived.

Dame Alodia stood in the threshold, wearing one of her majestic purple turbans. Her companion, Mrs. Hemmings, held her pug, and they were accompanied by a crowd of three other haughty Matrons.

Dame Alodia hissed again, before adding, "Sweep your skirts aside, ladies. There is riff-raff about."

Deborah frowned. She saw no reason for this treatment, although her cheeks burned out of guilt. "Good afternoon, Dame Alodia, Mrs. Hemmings." She nodded to the others, one the squire's wife; the other two wives of wealthy farmers.

"Humph," the dame snorted, pointing her nose in the air, a gesture copied by Mrs. Hemmings and, seemingly, even the dog. The other women blatantly stared. Behind her counter, Mrs. Luton's eyebrows were in danger of climbing all the way to her hairline.

The time had come to leave. "If you'll excuse me," Deborah said, picking up her portmanteau. "I've only just arrived from London and must return home."

But the women didn't move out of her way. "How dare you return," Dame Alodia said in round tones. "Did you not believe we would hear of your running off with a man who was *obviously* not a relative and *obviously* without a suitable chaperone? You have been gone for days. What have you to say for yourself?"

Deborah could think of nothing. Her mind went blank on anything but the truth.

"That's what I suspected," Dame Alodia crowed as if she'd spoken. "I can tell by the expression on your face that your behavior was shameful."

"Shameful, shameful," Mrs. Hemmings echoed.

Now, Deborah's face blazed with heat. How could they know — ?

Dame Alodia smiled, a false expression if ever there was one. "Parson Ames's cousin was on the Derby mail when you willingly took off with a strange gentleman. See, Mrs. Percival? All our deeds, good and bad, always come back to roost."

"Yes, roost," Mrs. Hemmings echoed, while the other women appeared equally appalled by Deborah's behavior. Women whom she'd known all her life, who should have given her the benefit of the doubt.

Deborah shifted the weight of her portmanteau from one hand to the other. She wasn't about to explain herself. Not there. And she would have told them so, too, if she hadn't been blocked inside the small shop.

A small crowd of curiosity seekers were gathering behind them. The village children eyed the commotion while a mother or two lingered to hear what was being said. Worse, the men were taking an interest. Kevin the cooper craned his neck to see inside the shop.

Then, her troubles were tripled. Through the panes of glass in the front window, she saw her brother-in-law Henry cross the main road, determinedly making his way toward Mrs. Luton's door. Her sister Rachel skipped to keep up with him.

The scowl on his face did not bode well.

"Well," Dame Alodia said, raising her voice for their audience, "haven't you anything to say?"

And, setting her portmanteau on the floor, Deborah replied with the first word that came into her head. Tony's word. A child's sound for scaring away bad spirits. She said, "Boo."

Chapter Nineteen

Dame Alodia blinked. "What did you say?"

"Boo," Deborah replied.

The grande dame grimaced her confusion to the Matrons, who shook their heads. They, too, were mystified. Dame Alodia raised her chin. "Why did you boo me?" she demanded.

"Because I finally see you as you *really* are," Deborah said bravely. "You are no benefactress. You are a petty tyrant."

Her statement threw Dame Alodia into a sputtering fit of indignation. She confronted her friends. "She called me a tyrant."

"No, I called you a *petty* tyrant," Deborah clarified, and felt a surge of power. She was not afraid. She'd spoken her mind, and the sky hadn't caved in. Tony would be proud.

At the same moment, Henry pushed his way into the shop. The Matrons happily scooted outside to make more room for him.

Before Henry could say a word, Dame Alodia launched into her tirade. "I'm glad you are here, nephew. She's returned and *pretending* as if nothing had happened."

"I haven't said a word," Deborah answered in her defense. Rachel had entered the shop. They were all crowded together . . . and in spite of her new sense of assurance, Deborah couldn't meet her sister's eye.

"Ah, yes, well the prodigal returns expecting the fatted calf to be killed, but I assure you, Mrs. Percival, such will not be the case! My nephew's generosity is not boundless," Dame Alodia announced before ordering Mrs. Hemmings to take Milton outside. "He does not like tight spaces or the sort of people he is being forced to consort with." She shot a meaningful look at Deborah.

The villagers crowded around the door parted to create a path for the companion to carry the dog out of the shop. Mrs. Luton appeared delighted. The gossips in the Valley would beat a path to her shop door for weeks to come.

Deborah would have followed Mrs. Hemmings if she could. However, Dame Alodia placed herself squarely in front of her, and demanded, "So, what do you have to say for yourself?"

"She doesn't have to say anything," a brave voice said. Everyone turned with surprise as Rachel moved to place herself directly between Dame Alodia and Deborah. She was frightened. One didn't defy the Valley's Social Arbiter without dire consequences — and yet, she had, for her sister.

Deborah was so proud of her.

The dame was not. She looked down her nose as if Rachel were a disagreeable bug. "My dear, we all understand you must give Mrs.

Percival your support. She is your sister, after all." Her words dripped with sarcastic pity. "However, my nephew is the head of your house, and *he* will have something *different* to say. Won't you, Henry?"

All eyes turned on the burly farmer. Henry looked to Deborah, and she knew he was not happy. He rented his lands from his aunt. He depended on her for his prosperity. And not once in his and Rachel's three years of marriage had Deborah ever heard her sister disobey him.

This was not good for Rachel . . . and Deborah was sorry for publicly humiliating Henry, too. Yes, he was overbearing but far more honest than Edmond. Her presence was jeopardizing everything he'd worked hard for.

"There is nothing for him to say," Deborah countered, pleased her voice was cool and steady. "I do not plan to stay in Ilam."

"Which is good," Dame Alodia predicted. "We cannot have your kind in the Valley."

Hot anger shot through Deborah but it was her sister who spoke. "How dare you brand her so? And all the rest of you standing here gawking!" Rachel said to those swarming around the door.

The villagers had the good grace to appear embarrassed. Kevin the cooper actually moved on.

Rachel faced her husband's aunt. "Deborah is the best soul in the world, and I'd not turn her out of my house."

"*Your* house?" Dame Alodia questioned. "Your *husband's* house."

The Matrons nodded from the doorway, seconding her opinion.

Rachel's face flushed with embarrassment, and Deborah wished she'd not come back. Not for the world would she have put Rachel in such a difficult position by pitting her against her husband and his aunt.

Then Henry spoke, "My wife's sister is welcome in my house."

Dame Alodia's mouth dropped open, although Deborah was equally surprised . . . as was Rachel. Neither of them expected his support.

He placed his hands on Rachel's shoulders, the gesture protective and loving . . . so much like something Tony would have done. "I will not judge my sister-in-law until I've heard her story," Henry said. "And I am not pleased to have anyone in my family made a public mockery."

"She disgraces us all," Dame Alodia said. "As a Society leader, it is my responsibility to see standards are kept." She fixed her hard glare on Henry. "Mrs. Percival ran off with a man and was not heard from again until this day. What excuse would you give her?"

Deborah held her breath. She would not lie. If the question was put to her, she'd tell the truth.

But Henry didn't ask. Instead, he said to his

aunt, "She is part of my family now. This is a private matter."

There was a beat of flabbergasted silence, then several people began applauding. Even Mrs. Luton nodded her approval. The Matrons backing Dame Alodia did not appear so smug anymore. Even the dame's haughty air came down a notch.

"Well," she huffed, "then, your house is your responsibility. I hold you accountable, Henry, and we shall discuss this later, much later."

She turned on her heel and started to leave. Unfortunately, her grand exit was blocked by gawking onlookers. She sniffed, and they shuffled out of her way. She left the shop. Mrs. Hemmings, carrying the pug, fell into place behind her . . . but the Matrons didn't follow. Instead, they hung back as if pretending they'd not been part of the earlier accusations.

Everyone watched Dame Alodia's sullen march to her carriage and horses. Then, after her conveyance took her out of town, one gentleman said, "There will be hell to pay, Henry."

"Oh, no there won't," Rachel declared. She faced her husband. "I don't care what she says. We have our life and oh, Henry, I am so proud of you. It's about time someone stood up to her. You were magnificent."

Her words were punctuated by another round of applause. Several of the men offered him a drink at the pub if he'd come by. They all moved outside.

Henry grinned, enjoying the acclaim. Deborah had not noticed before how he'd been kept separate by the other men. "If I'd known this would make me famous," he admitted, "I would have talked back to her years ago."

"Not famous," the miller said, "but less a puppet and more a man."

Rachel met her husband's eye. "I told you."

Something passed between the young couple, a bond. Deborah felt a stab of jealousy.

Henry took Deborah's arm and said in a voice for her ears alone, "Although I will expect an explanation for your actions."

"And you will have one," she promised, although she wasn't certain how much of the truth she would share.

Any further comment was interrupted by calls from one of Parson Ames's children, who came running down the street in excitement. Before he could articulate what he'd seen, a horseman charged into the village. It was Tony.

He pulled up as he saw the small crowd, and for a moment all any of them could do was gape at the sight. His horse was prime flesh, its eyes fiery with spirit, its breeding in every graceful line.

And Tony was a fine figure in the saddle. He was hatless, but every inch the aristocrat and looking more devilishly handsome than any man had a right to.

His gaze went unerringly to Deborah. "I can't live without you." He confessed his love

— right there, in the middle of Ilam, in front her family and friends, neighbors and acquaintances. "Come with me, Deb," he said. *"Marry me."*

Rachel's eyes were open so wide they appeared ready to pop out of her head and more than one woman fanned herself with her hands. Even the men appeared impressed.

Save for Henry. He stepped forward. "And who are you, sir, to ask my sister-in-law to run off with you?"

"I'm the earl of Burnell," Tony said, pride ringing in his voice.

One of the Matrons choked out, "An earl?" She almost swooned, while the others started bowing and scraping.

Henry, God bless his soul, had the presence of mind to say, "What makes you think she would go with you?"

"Are you saying she can't?" Tony demanded, arrogance in his tone.

"I'm saying it is her choice, my lord."

Tony's gaze met Deborah's. "What do you want, my love? I'm offering all I have."

Still, Deborah hung back. "What of that other matter between us, my lord?" *What of Lady Amelia?*

"I made a discovery halfway to Derby, Mrs. Percival," he said. "Something I'd never believed until the moment I'd actually lost you."

"And that was?" she prodded.

"*Love is everything.* Deb, I don't know how

I'll untangle the mess, but I will — with you at my side."

Rachel sighed. She grabbed Deborah's arm. "Go! Don't be a fool. He loves you."

Deborah turned to her brother-in-law. "Henry, is it all right if I go?"

"And make me the brother-in-law to an earl? You need ask?" Then, humor aside, he said, "You have our blessing." He punctuated his feelings with a quick, awkward, brotherly hug. "This will really put my aunt's nose out of joint."

They both laughed.

Deborah turned back to the villagers witnessing this scene. "I'll never forget this moment. Not ever!"

"Go on!" Mrs. Luton yelled, and her encouragement was echoed by the others.

No longer worrying about what was right, what was wrong, Deborah followed her heart.

She ran to Tony.

His horse pranced, anxious to be off. She held up her hand. He captured her by the wrist and lifted her up into the saddle in front of him as if she weighed less than a feather.

It felt like heaven to be back in his arms. To be where she belonged.

"Wait!" Henry said. "What are your plans? Earl or no, I'll not take kindly to you not making an honest woman of her."

"In three days' time, she'll be my countess," Tony answered. Then, heels to horse, he took off. Glancing back, Deborah saw Rachel and Henry standing together, arm in arm, watching them leave.

The rest of their audience was already running off to share the new gossip.

Deborah rested back against his chest. "We've become a new scandal," she said.

"No, love," he corrected her. "We've become a legend."

Tony's coach waited several miles down the road where he'd left it. The driver tipped his hat to her. "Glad to see you back, Mrs. Percival."

"Thank you. I'm happy to be here," Deborah admitted.

Tony hurried her into the coach. "Gretna, Davis, and don't stop until you reach there."

"Yes, my lord."

The second the door was shut, Davis snapped the whip, and the horses were off.

Tony gathered Deborah in his arms. "You're mine now."

She nodded. She tried not to think of Lady Amelia or the scandal.

But he read her mind. "I'm crying off, Deb. I'll take full blame and do everything in my power to see Lady Amelia is not injured in any way." He gave her hand a kiss. "We must risk this."

And she was selfish enough not to argue.

They made good progress. The horses and

drivers were changed along the way. They drove without stopping for the night, sleeping in the coach. If the thought had struck one of them that they didn't need to travel so swiftly, neither said anything. He held her in his arms, promising that the next time they made love, they'd be man and wife.

By luncheon of the next day, they hit the border.

The tales she'd heard of Gretna, the Scottish village where English couples could wed without the legalities, were far more romantic than the reality. There were no marriages going on in the streets, and the people she saw all appeared good and God-fearing.

Their driver guided the horses into the yard of a moss-covered brick inn called, appropriately, the Parson's Knot.

"Well," Tony said, "it has the right name. Are you ready, love?"

Yes, she was ready. However, she had to voice the concern one last time, "I can't help but worry about Lady Amelia. I don't want her to be hurt."

"I'll offer whatever restitution Longest demands save giving you up," he said. "And," he continued, putting his arm around her, "I might point out that while you are feeling guilty, if the tables were turned, she'd not give two shakes about your feelings."

"She's young," Deborah answered. "Guilt grows with age."

He laughed. "Well said. Come, I want to make you a bride." Climbing out of the coach, he offered his hand. She followed him out, and together they made their way into the inn, entering what appeared to be a huge taproom. Their footsteps echoed on the wood floors, which had been recently washed and swept clean. At the far corner of the room was a serving maid and innkeeper, who watched a fashionable couple exchange vows in front of an officious-looking gentleman. He held a black prayer book in his hand and a tankard of ale in the other. The bride's bonnet hid her face, and the groom's back was to them.

The innkeeper, a short fellow with a head full of red hair, approached. "Reid's the name," he said in greeting. "We're having a marrying."

"We'd like to be married, too," Tony answered. "And a dinner and room for the night."

"You are in luck," Mr. Reid said. "I've only one room left." He reached for a sheaf of papers on the bar, marriage certificates. "Here now, let us fill this out, and we'll have you wed in no time."

Deborah's attention was on the couple marrying. The bride was shaking so hard, she had trouble repeating her vows. Wondering if the young woman wasn't in danger of fainting from her fear, Deborah marveled she had the courage to go through with the ceremony at all. Her groom appeared most solicitous but also insistent.

The gentleman performing the ceremony wasn't really a man of the cloth. In Scotland, vows could be exchanged before "witnesses" without any clergy involved and still be considered legal. The witnesses were often referred to as "blacksmiths," a reference to the Roman god Vulcan, who along with being a blacksmith fashioning thunderbolts for the heavens was also the celestial priest of marriage. This blacksmith appeared to be giving his best shot at the Anglican rite, taproom trappings and all. The couple were saying their final "I do's."

Mr. Reid claimed her attention with a few questions. "Your name, miss?"

"Deborah Somerset Percival."

"Are you single?"

"Yes, I am," Deborah said, casting a frown toward Tony.

Mr. Reid caught the exchange and explained, " 'Tis the law. We must ask these questions. So, are you here of your own free will, miss?"

"I am."

He turned to Tony. "Your name, sir?"

"Anthony Aldercy, fifth earl of Burnell."

The words had no sooner left his lips than the bride whirled around, gasping in surprise.

"Burnell?" she squeaked out — and swooned.

Her spanking-new husband caught her before she hit the floor, but he was no less surprised. Holding the young woman in his arms, he practically snarled at Tony like a dog protecting a bone. "Stay back, Burnell. You can't have her. I'll kill you before I let you touch her!"

Everyone in the room stared at Tony, who appeared nonplussed by the threat.

In fact, he acted rather pleased.

"Deborah, have I introduced you to Colonel Phillip Bord? We were schoolmates."

The woman in the colonel's arms started to rouse. Her bonnet had fallen back, revealing glorious blond hair the color of the summer sun. She was beautiful, and Deborah realized they'd met before. "Lady Amelia?"

Tony nodded. "And if I am not mistaken, my friend Bord is about to marry her."

"We *are* married," Bord responded.

"Well, I have the pronouncement," the blacksmith corrected. "You know, what God has joined together and so forth."

"Then get on with it, man," Bord said between clenched teeth. "He's come to stop the marriage!"

"No, I haven't —" Tony started amicably.

However, before more could be said, a thunderous voice announced from the back of the room, "But I have! I'm here to stop this marriage!"

All heads turned to the door, where a thin, hawk-nosed gentleman in elegant clothing stood. He was backed by three hulking henchmen, who blocked the exit. "I've caught up with you, Bord, and when I'm finished, you'll wish you'd never been born."

Lady Amelia gasped, "Papa!" and swooned again, this time for real, her weight taking both her and her intended to the floor. Reid, the blacksmith, and the barmaid scattered around the room, searching for hiding spots.

Tony tucked Deborah's hand in the crook of his arm and introduced the newcomer by saying, "And this, my love, is the famous Lord Longest."

Chapter Twenty

Lord Longest glared out from beneath bushy eyebrows at the person who had interrupted him — and then recognized Tony. His frown grew more alarmed. "Damn but I'd hoped you wouldn't have caught wind of this nonsense, Burnell. Bord deserves to be horsewhipped for stealing my daughter! Don't have a worry. I shall have her back right and tight in London in no time. No damage done."

"I don't care what you say," Bord replied valiantly. He attempted to lift his Lady Amelia from the floor, however, deadweight was hard to move. He settled on letting her lie at his feet. He stood to face Longest. "I love her."

His declaration rang in the air, but had little impact on the man who would be his father-in-law. "Love her?" Longest repeated as if the words were foreign. "Love her all you want, but she's contracted to marry Burnell." His face changed as an idea struck him. "In fact, we could have the ceremony here, Burnell. You're here. My damn daughter's here."

"And grooms are interchangeable," Tony agreed mildly, happy to note that Deb had caught on to the humor of the scene. She almost choked on a bubble of laughter.

"Damn right," Longest agreed, not truly

paying heed to Tony's words.

"I'll die before I let anyone touch her," Bord responded.

Tony leaned close to Deb with a weary sigh. "He's a cavalryman. They are prone to superlatives."

Of course, his words carried. Already livid with rage and frustration, Bord announced, "You will meet me for that, Burnell."

He sounded pompous — and in a blinding moment of recognition, Tony heard himself all those times he had taken slight and demanded a duel. He had been such an idiot. But Deb had saved him. He was a better man now, a man who had his priorities about life straight.

"Phillip, don't be ridiculous," he replied ruthlessly. "The only way I will meet you is if you are asking me for dinner. Otherwise, you can duel with yourself."

"I want satisfaction!"

"You want to marry Amelia," Tony corrected.

His directness let some of the wind out of Bord's sails. "Yes."

"But he won't!" Longest declared. "These bullyboys will make sure he doesn't. Get him, lads," he said to his henchmen, who would have marched forward save for Tony's stepping in their path. He was taller than two of them and more muscular than all. They pulled up short.

"I don't want to marry your daughter," Tony said bluntly.

"Eh?" Longest cocked his head as if uncertain of his hearing.

"I'm not marrying your daughter," Tony reiterated.

"Why not?" Bord challenged, sniffing some new affront even as Longest's manner changed from bluster to conciliation.

"You're upset, Burnell, and I don't blame you. However, I'm certain he has not touched her. I regret you have been a party to this family squabble, but I promise you, my daughter will be ready to be married in three weeks' time, and a more amenable bride you could never hope to find."

"I'm not looking for an *amenable* bride," Tony answered, noting out of the corner of his eye that Deb was enjoying herself and taking mock exception to his words.

"Then she'll be full of spit, fire, and vinegar," Longest replied. "Now, pack her up, boys, and we'll be on our way to London."

Bord stepped in front of his unconscious love and would have taken on all three of them, probably much to his detriment, when Tony put an end to it all by saying for the third time, "I will not marry your daughter. You can wrap her up like a mummy, starve her on bread and water, or cover her with every jewel in the Realm. I'm not marrying her."

"You're upset —" Longest started.

"I'm not upset."

"Your pride —"

"Is intact."

His lordship frowned, stumped. He looked to Bord and back to Tony. Then, in a plaintive cry, he asked, "Then what is it? What must I do to make this right?"

"Let her marry Bord."

Tony didn't know who was more surprised by his words, Longest or the young colonel. "But our contract?" His Lordship protested.

"Should be torn up. We'll write a new one, one that lets Bord marry your daughter and allows me to marry the woman I love." He held out his hand for Deb.

On the floor, Amelia groaned, beginning to come to her senses. Always levelheaded, Deb said, "Here, let me see to Lady Amelia while you gentlemen work on the details."

"Who is she?" Longest asked, as if he'd just registered Deb's presence.

"The woman *I* eloped with," Tony answered easily. "Here now, Mr. Reid. Do you have a gold band I can put on my lady love's finger?"

"We have a box full, my lord."

"Good. We'll have a double ceremony."

Of course, Bord had to comment. He wasn't the sort who liked being left out of plans. "We don't need a double ceremony. Ours is almost finished. I'm not going through the whole rigmarole again."

"You aren't marrying her at all," Longest flashed back. He looked to his bullyboys. "Go on, teach him a lesson."

"Come on. I'll take them on," Bord announced, but Tony wasn't having any of it. Nor did the henchmen seem all that enthusiastic.

"Gentlemen," Tony addressed Longest's bullies, "whatever Lord Longest is paying you, I'll double, *not* to fight. Why don't you help yourself to the ale keg? It'll be on my tab."

The men weren't fools. They turned on their heels and walked straight to the bar, where Mr. Reid was already pouring the first tankard.

"Does your offer for a dram or two extend to the witnesses?" the blacksmith asked.

"After the ceremony," Tony agreed. "I want you to have a clear head while you are marrying me."

The man laughed. "I can manage a ceremony foxed out of my wits."

"I don't want it to come to that," Tony answered dryly.

Mr. Reid carried a handful of rings over to Tony for his perusal. Deb had Amelia alert and, with the help of a serving girl, had moved her to a chair.

Only Bord and Longest stood like two salt pillars.

"I won't give up the marriage contract," Longest declared, starting to find his bluster again.

"You have no choice," Bord countered. "Amelia is mine."

"No, she's Burnell's," Longest argued.

Decisively, Tony said, "I'm marrying Deb

360

Percival. As for your daughter, Longest, I'm willing to honor my end of the contract provided you don't insist I marry her."

"You'd pay me to not marry her — ?" His Lordship said, uncertain.

"Yes, I'll pay you. The settlement will be my wedding gift to Bord."

Phillip was stunned speechless by the offer.

Longest couldn't grasp the generosity. "I won't be out anything?" he repeated, suspicious.

"Well, you'll have a different son-in-law," Tony responded.

"I like him better anyway," His Lordship replied candidly.

Tony laughed, not taking offense. "Good, then the matter is done. Now if you will excuse me, gentlemen, I'm about to be married."

"Wait," Bord said pompously. "Amelia and I must finish our ceremony."

"By all means," Tony replied. Now, he walked toward Deb, *his* Deb. She was attempting to explain to Amelia the turn of events. The young woman was not grasping very much of what she said at all. The gold band in his hand felt good. He'd chosen the heaviest one.

She smiled at him, and he felt his world was complete.

The blacksmith noticed her smile. He said, "You are a lucky man, my lord."

"I'm a lucky man, too," Bord said crossly. "Except I'm not married yet."

His curt tone of voice did not sit well with the blacksmith. "I can finish your vows now, Colonel." Without further ado and no input from the younger couple, he said, "What God has joined together let not man put asunder. You are married. Next!"

Taking Deb's arm, Tony led her forward.

Longest was asking Bord, "Is that all? The deed is done?"

"The deed is done," came the terse reply. "Do you really prefer me over Burnell?"

"As long as Burnell is paying to cry off," Longest answered flatly.

Both Tony and Deb had to stifle their laughter at this exchange. She placed her hand in his. "I believe I'm getting the best end of this bargain."

"I know I am," he whispered, so Lady Amelia and her overbearing father did not overhear.

The blacksmith cleared his voice to let them know he was ready. He opened his book.

"Do you Anthony Aldercy, fifth earl of Burnell, take Deborah Somerset Percival for your wife?"

Tony squeezed Deb's hand. "I do."

"Will you love, honor, and cherish her?"

"Forever." Her fingers laced with his. Her eyes were shiny with unshed tears.

"Well, now," the blacksmith said, "I was going to say 'until death do you part' but 'forever' takes care of the matter, don't it now?" He smiled to Deb and read her name from the marriage certificate Reid had completed. "Deborah Somerset Percival, do you take Anthony Aldercy, fifth earl of Burnell, for your husband?"

"I do."

"And will you love, honor, cherish, and obey him."

"I will."

"You may place the ring on the bride's finger, my lord."

Deb's hands were shaking — or were his own? Tony slid the gold band over her ring finger, where it fit perfectly. As he did so, the blacksmith held his hands over their hands and intoned in a solemn voice, "What God has joined together let not man put asunder. I pronounce you man and wife."

There it was. He was married to the woman he loved. Better yet, he trusted her love.

Longest's bullyboys raised their cups and shouted out three cheers, which echoed around the empty taproom. Tony swept Deb up into his arms. "Where's our room?" he asked Reid.

"Wait, my lord," the innkeeper answered, laughing, "you've yet to sign your names to the marriage certificate."

"Well, I'm not about to put her down. Bring it over here."

The certificate was handed to Deb to sign, and then to Tony, who managed a passable signature even while holding his wife in his arms. Bord and his young wife watched, bemused.

Amelia appeared a touch befuddled by the swift exchange of grooms, but Longest and Bord seemed in perfect accord.

"Our room?" Tony prompted Reid.

"This way, my lord."

Deb put her arms around his neck as, amid good-natured catcalls and hoots of encouragement, he carried her out of the taproom.

Their room was simply furnished. All he cared about was the bed, and the sheets looked clean.

The moment Reid shut the door, Tony dropped Deb on the bed and pretended to pounce right on top of her. Laughing she rolled over, the pins falling from her hair.

On his side, he looked up at her. "You're the most beautiful woman in the world." He lightly touched her cheek, her lower lip, her chin. This vibrant woman was his.

"Tony, I love you."

He lowered his head to rest in the crook of her neck. For a long moment, he drank in her scent, reveled in her warmth . . . and felt such joy, tears stung his eyes. Lifting his lips to her ear, he whispered, "You gave me life."

They made love then, and this time Tony held nothing back. He had no need to. They would have children, herds and herds of healthy, bright-eyed children. And he knew that no matter which direction Fate took them in the future, they would be safe — because they would be well loved.

Epilogue

Of course, there was some scandal. The *ton* would not be who and what they were without gossip.

There had been a great deal of speculation about the Burnell-Longest match. So everyone's eyebrows were raised when the ravishing Lady Amelia returned to town not married to Burnell but to a handsome cavalry colonel named Bord. To make matters more interesting, Longest — whom everyone had heard was done up in debt — appeared quite solvent, and even flashed a bit of new wealth.

So the gossips shifted their conjecture and focused on "Poor Burnell," who they assumed had been jilted for a wealthier suitor. Everyone knew his arrogant pride, and gleefully anticipated fireworks when he returned to Town.

However, when he did arrive, he was escorting a lovely new wife. People were taken with the new countess of Burnell. They admired her dark, exotic looks — rumors were her mother had been an *émigrée*.

But what they soon came to admire most of all was her originality. She was a woman who thought for herself — but, of course! She had French blood.

However, the air of confidence around the

countess of Burnell ran deeper than blood could provide. She was a woman who understood herself and wasn't afraid to speak on behalf of her beliefs.

The *ton* were charmed.

So then the talk changed, with people fawning all over the new countess while feeling superior pity for Amelia Bord, the former reigning belle of the Season . . . except that the countess and the colonel's wife appeared very close friends. And when word leaked out that they had been married to their husbands in a double ceremony after *both couples* eloped to Gretna, well, the story was enough to make the romantic sigh.

Gossip without a victim dies quickly.

Even the old hearsay about Burnell being estranged from his mother turned out to be untrue. She and her second husband, the heroic General Sir Adamson, returned to London for a visit and stayed right there under Burnell's roof. They were even present for the christening of the earl's first child, a son, born almost a year to the date after his marriage.

Some wag observed that Adamson and Burnell bore a remarkable resemblance . . . but no one else noticed. To some, the men's features were as different as night and day — especially to those who claimed to remember Lord Burnell's father, the one who shot himself, poor man.

What everyone did know is that Burnell himself had never seemed happier. And where at one time he'd been stubborn and taciturn, he was now considered the soul of generosity.

In truth, Tony and Deborah were so happy, they were oblivious to the rumors. Especially after Andrew was born.

Henry and Rachel braved the spring rain to come to London to stand as Andrew's godparents. Edmond's nose was a bit out of joint that he'd not been asked. However, Tony tactfully pointed out that Rachel was the older sister of the two — and gave the ambitious man a position overseeing his shipping office in Amsterdam for good measure.

The real surprise of Christening Day came when Henry presented to the earl and countess a gift from — of all people — his aunt, Dame Alodia.

It was a silver baby rattle with a card attached from the grande dame herself. She gushed on with toad-eating enthusiasm for the new baby, and then added a hasty postscript saying she hoped all "misunderstandings" could be forgiven.

They were.

That night in bed, Tony took Deborah in his arms and asked, "So, how would you feel about visiting Italy in the fall?"

She raised her head to see if he was teasing. He wasn't. "Oh, but what about the baby? We can't leave my baby."

"We'll take him with us."

Deborah liked the idea. Dreamily, she laid her head back on her husband's shoulder. This was where she wanted to be. Theirs was a marriage of equals and like minds. "Italy in the fall," she whispered, imagining . . . while her errant hand ran down the line of his body.

His hands slid down to her waist. "Provided you aren't pregnant again," he added.

Her response was to laugh and pull the covers up over their heads. After all, when someone was as in love as she was, who needed Italy in the fall?

As for Tony, he never dreamed of his father's death again . . . but he had everything he'd ever dreamed of.